A Trick of the Shade
Stephanie Caye

1

"No DECENT PARTY STARTS before eleven," I declared, descending from the bus.

"I see you're truly embracing the Montreal lifestyle." My co-worker Chris took a hit off his vape pen and exhaled into the frigid October air.

Well, former co-worker—I'd just gotten fired thirty minutes ago. I should have been getting a head-start on my hangover in some dark, cozy bar, not taking Chris up on a last-minute pity invite to his grad school friends' Halloween bash. But he was cute.

We rounded the corner and faced a brick apartment building that pulsed with bass as if to say, *challenge accepted.* It could have had three separate parties going, easy.

"See, Jude?" Chris chided. "Early can be fun too."

I shot him a teasing look. "I'm withholding judgment 'til we get up there."

"Well, keep in mind that some of us have to hit the library early tomorrow."

"That's not the flex you think it is." I laughed, but it only served to remind me that while Chris was in his mid-twenties too, he was a grad-school student working part-time to finance his education, whereas I was racking up final paycheques from minimum wage jobs in the quest of absolutely nothing.

One thing I wasn't exactly racking up was friends, and he *was* cute—in a laid-back, wouldn't stay over kind of way—so I gave in and followed him up to an apartment on the second floor. It was crammed full of people holding black paper cups. Open bottles of wine littered the cheap coffee table in the centre of the room. Someone had made a haphazard attempt at late October festivity by draping orange and black crepe paper around.

"Can I get you a drink?" Chris asked.

"Wine's not really my thing."

"Somebody was bringing jello shots, I think." He stepped away, greeting another person briefly before adding to me, "Be right back."

I bit back a smile and waved him off. Jello shots and wine. Jesus Chris. Hadn't realized I'd be so young when I got 'too old for this shit.' The room full of eager grad students bubbly with plans and ideas and life goals felt too daunting without some liquid—or gelatin—courage in my hand. I did a quick lap and then peeked out onto the apartment's front balcony.

It looked empty, somewhere dark and quiet to forget my so far shitty night and get to know Chris better. I slipped outside. The chill of the Montreal autumn made my skin prickle under my thin jacket.

To my left, a chair scraped.

"Hey, sorry," I said, taking a step back to keep from interrupting a private moment already in progress.

A sharper set of goosebumps danced through the hairs on my arms. They were deeper than a simple reaction to the fall night's chill—the alarm bell of my early-warning system for magic.

My hesitation gave my eyes time to adjust to the dark. A woman got to her feet. She'd been crouched beside someone else in a chair. The sitting person's head had slumped to the side and I caught a sparkle of dark liquid on the limp arm that dropped over the armrest.

The woman adjusted a knit tuque over her dark hair. She snapped something in French.

"What?" I stammered, immediately correcting, "Quoi?" Not my best.

"Are you fresh from the portal or what?" She spoke in accented English, but not like a Francophone. More like a full-blood Faerie.

Then she cocked her head like a dog who'd caught a scent. Her expression settled into a glower.

"Ah. Une clébarde."

Switching to French didn't make that less offensive. If she hadn't wanted me to understand her calling me a 'mutt,' she'd have used the sing-song Faerie language.

Redcaps weren't known for their decorum, though. From the stories I'd heard working for the Consilium, they were known for their ferocity.

"Aren't you supposed to dye that hat with blood won in *battle*?" I asked, nodding to the unconscious kid in the chair behind her.

"Blood is blood." Disdain flashed in her eyes. She touched the crimson tuque. "But I'm game if you want a battle." She put an arm back over her shoulder and pulled a narrow sword from a glamoured sheath, simultaneously drawing a shorter dagger from the darkness around her hip with her other hand.

Damn it, I really needed to start being more attuned to glamour.

I vaulted over the balcony rail, falling for only an instant before shifting gravity around myself. I aimed my personal 'down' toward the side of the building. It let me land safely on the wall like Spider-Man without any of the messy webbing. Getting to my feet put me horizontal to the ground, and I darted up under the shadow of the balcony floor as the redcap jumped over the rail herself.

She landed on the grass three stories down like a graceful cat. She spun in a circle with her sword extended, searching for me in the courtyard. Then she twitched and looked up.

I thought I'd stayed hidden underneath the wooden balcony, but she could clearly sense me the way I could sense her.

I tapped into my own Faerie power to let the world spin around me again as I moved out from underneath the balcony. I climbed casually back over the railing. Then I leaned out and waved to her. "Why don't you go find another party?"

The redcap bared her teeth, sword flashing in the courtyard lights. She didn't scale the building to get back to me, though. Instead, she sheathed the sword on her back and spun on her heel in one fluid motion. Not that interested in a battle, I guess.

I should have gone after her, stopped her from replenishing her cap with more human blood. But I wasn't Consilium anymore—the Consilium no longer existed, in fact—and it wasn't my job to hunt down predatory Faeries. It wasn't even a hobby.

Someone moaned beside me on the cold balcony: the redcap's victim. The human woman had come to, or halfway at least. She blinked in the darkness and struggled to get out of the chair on wobbly legs.

"Oh, shit, you cut yourself," I said, too loudly.

She didn't notice my unconvincing tone as I helped her to her feet. She mumbled something about wine, paying no attention to the gash on her arm. Glamour was a hell of a drug.

Two people rushed to us when I hauled her inside—her friends, apparently. In the indoor light, the cut on her arm didn't look too bad. It hadn't hit any major veins, just deep enough to give the redcap's hat a little sip of blood and her powers a boost.

"Always at the centre of the action." Chris appeared beside me, two jello shots in each hand.

"It's a curse." My sigh made him grin, and he held out his boozy spoils.

"You want red or purple?"

"Definitely red."

2

AN HOUR OF AWKWARD small talk at the now *almost* Faerie-free party was enough to kill my buzz. Chris was in his element, though, always a charming extrovert. When I'd had enough of strangers and made my exit, he came along to the bus stop. He clung to his excuse about having some kind of class group project to work on tomorrow at the library.

"At least you don't have to be up at the crack of dawn," he complained.

"You're right," I agreed. "I've got all night. Guess getting canned has its bright sides."

"All night, huh? Can't have you spending it alone." He cast me a sidelong glance that made me smile. I'd already made up my mind to bring him back to my place.

"Takes you a while to catch on, Professor."

Freezing drizzle sprinkled lazily down from the clouds, blowing across the back of my neck and making me bunch up the collar of my corduroy jacket. Should have worn a hoodie underneath. Half-frozen drops covered the grass beside the sidewalk, ready to start accumulating as snow.

"God, I love Halloween." Chris took a breath of the cold air. "You got any spooky plans tomorrow?"

"Helping tipsy people destroy plywood with dangerous weapons from five to ten." Even though I'd gotten fired from the thrift store where he and I had worked together, at least I still had my job at the axe-throwing place. One tiny paycheque was better than nothing.

He snorted. "That sucks."

"It's fine. I don't really like Halloween anyway." I never had, not even as a kid. Trick-or-treating in the trailer park hadn't been a good time. My mom had always refused to drive me to the more lucrative candy-giving neighbourhoods. Cherry bombs in trash cans and egging houses with my friends as a teenager had been fun enough at the time, but it had never held any mystery to engage me.

Dressing up like a sexy monster was nothing special when you were only half-human every day. My Faerie father's genes had won out over my human mother's to give me less iron in my blood and the supernatural ability to alter my gravity and walk up walls. Neither of those were things I could use outright on *any* day in the human world, even the celebration of the weird and freakish.

But they still came in handy.

Electricity exploded across my skin. Something flew at us out of the shadows. I shoved Chris away from the redcap who'd launched herself at me. I barely avoided the swipe of her sword.

Hitting the pavement on my hip, I threw up a hand and snapped, "I don't want to fight!"

"Shouldn't have maligned me!" the redcap snarled back. Her long and short blades flashed under the street-lights.

Faeries and their goddamn drama.

I scrambled to my feet, snatching the squirrel-proof metal lid of a trashcan at the mouth of the alley I'd stumbled into.

The redcap took that as an offensive move. She brought her sword down on my makeshift shield with a force that almost drove me to my knees. The clash of metal echoed off the buildings around us.

I tilted the lid to the side to block the thrust she made with her dagger. I didn't give her time to recover her balance, shifting gravity to turn *forward* into *down*, so that I fell straight at her. The trashcan lid slammed into her shoulder, knocking her over. I swiped the tuque from her head as she fell.

Yuck. Still wet with blood.

The redcap shrieked, one hand going to her head too late. Her sword clattered to the ground. She glared at me through eyes that had become too large and too dark to be human. Under the harsh streetlight, the full curves of her body were now sharp angles, and her stylish clothing hung off of her in a decidedly inhuman way.

"This affects your glamour, huh?" I dangled the knit hat. "Seems lazy." Most Faeries who came into the human world could alter their appearance without needing a prop.

She hissed, flashing her dagger, so I edged the sword closer to me with the toe of my boot. It was a thin blade with a fancy handle, surprisingly light in my hand when I stooped to pick it up. The edge gleamed wickedly.

"Let's call it a draw," I said, tossing her the hat. Pretty magnanimous, given I'd won the fight.

She tugged the tuque on over her bobbed hair and returned in a blink to the pretty, human-shaped woman she'd been on the balcony. Her hand holding the dagger twitched like she might attack again. The short blade was dull and beige coloured, the edges stained brownish. Seemed like what she'd use to cut her sleeping victims in lieu of a regular sword battle to provide a river of blood.

Casting a longing look toward the weapon in my hand, she bared her teeth again and then stepped back into the shadow of the alley. She merged with the darkness there, gone in an instant, leaving me adrenaline-high and hungry.

And facing Chris's wide-eyed, terrified face. He'd pressed himself against the far wall of the alley. He gaped at me like he didn't recognize me.

"Hey," I started, lifting my free hand as my mind raced for a good explanation.

Before I could come up with one, Chris turned and fled, feet pounding down the alley toward the next street over. He rounded the corner in a matter of seconds, disappearing almost as quickly as the redcap had, but less magically.

So much for that hookup. I could text him tomorrow, when the fight was more distant and easily explained as a product of too many jello shots. It wouldn't do much to save tonight, though.

I turned the sword in my hand to examine the fancy, metal handle. I didn't know how to use the weapon—the redcap's dagger would have been more my speed, but I wasn't going to argue with a free sword. Did Faeries have a magical connection to their precious possessions? While not every fairy tale I'd ever heard was real, I didn't want to bring the sword home and have the redcap follow. Maybe I could hock it, though.

Thanks to the impending holiday, only one guy gave me a second look when I climbed onto the bus with it ten minutes later.

"What're you supposed to be?" he asked, as I settled into an empty seat across from him.

"Faerie princess," I returned.

He scoffed and went back to his phone, not impressed with that answer.

You and the Faerie Court both, buddy.

3

"I THOUGHT WE'D GO look at that dog this afternoon."

Gracie nearly choked on her coffee. Her husband was using the code they'd devised years ago: *Home isn't safe.* She managed to swallow and set the paper cup aside on the park bench, straightening the phone against her ear.

"Got time to meet me?" Ted finished.

"Which one?" she asked. *Is this serious?* Was he testing her? He'd done that a few times when they'd first come up with the codes—in order to memorize them—but there was no reason for it now.

"The black Lab."

Not a test. He'd have said 'golden retriever' if he were giving her a false alarm. His voice was still light and cheerful, but Gracie picked up a grave note underneath.

"Okay," she managed.

"Text me the address and I'll meet you." That was the signal that she could speak freely. Ted thought someone on his end might overhear him.

"Where are you?" she demanded, fighting her dread. As far as she knew, he'd just taken the morning off work and slept in.

"At home. I'll meet you there."

"In town?"

"Yeah." He knew where she meant without further information.

Gracie checked her watch. Almost noon. "I've got the car," she said. "Two?" She glanced toward their black station wagon hybrid, parked just beyond the playground.

"Don't worry about it." Ted didn't agree to her time and didn't mention how he would get into the city, but he was nothing if not resourceful.

"Grab the lock-box?"

"Already got it. Kiss Rye for me. Love you."

"I love you, too." Gracie lowered her phone once Ted had disconnected the call. She let out a slow breath to calm her still-racing heart, but the initial panic had eased.

They had originally come up with the idea that the warning concerned picking up a dog because, at the time, they'd both agreed they couldn't keep a pet. Their lives in the Consilium were too chaotic and unpredictable—evinced by the fact that they needed a secret mode of communication in case of emergency.

Ironic, considering that now they had a child.

Gracie retrieved her coffee from the bench, slung her purse over her shoulder and stood up, calling, "Riley!"

From underneath the slide on the playground across the sidewalk, a small head of curly, dark hair poked out. Her son picked himself up and toddled over.

Gracie met him halfway, sweeping him into her arms. "We've got to go meet Daddy."

"Where?" The three-year-old was in what Ted had dubbed his 'professor phase.'

"Did you leave any toys?" Gracie craned her neck to peer under the slide, where another little boy still played in the sand. She couldn't remember now if they'd brought anything with them.

Riley shook his head, putting two fingers in his mouth.

"Wanna stay," he said.

"I know, kiddo, but we can't." Gracie wiped a sudden sheen of perspiration from her forehead despite the chilly day and glanced quickly around the playground. She didn't know what she was looking *for*.

They were only three kilometres from home. She yearned to drive to the apartment, peer around the corner and see what she could make out going on at their building. What was happening there?

Instead, she focused on her immediate next steps to quiet the fluttering of her heart, putting one foot in front of the other and carrying Riley to the car.

He chattered in her arms about the slide but her mind raced ahead to the jumble of decisions facing her. Should she drive into the city or ditch the car and take public transit? She didn't have much cash—she'd have to stop by an ATM, out here in the suburbs so it was harder to trace their whereabouts. And she barely had any of Riley's things. All she'd brought along to the park was a plastic cup of orange juice with a lid and a straw and a wooden toy train engine he wouldn't go anywhere without. He had his jacket, mittens and boots against the October cold, and the railroad engineer's hat that was supposed to be part of his Halloween costume, though he'd worn it since September and seemed to have no plans to stop.

The sharp honk of a car horn froze her in place, throat tight. She blinked and realized she'd walked right into the parking lot without checking for traffic.

"Oops," Riley said.

"Yep, oops," she murmured, forcing a smile and wave at the driver who'd braked for her. Once the car was past, she checked both directions twice for more traffic and pressed on toward her escape.

She set her coffee cup on the roof of the car to buckle Riley into his car seat. She always felt better with a plan, which was why she hadn't called Ted's idea of the dog codes ludicrous when he'd suggested it. This type of situation hadn't been beyond thinking back then.

She wanted to believe she'd never expected to have use for any of those precautions after their break from their old lives five months ago, but of course she had. Even though the Consilium itself was officially defunct and she and Ted had new jobs and what passed for a normal life, the past never seemed to let go that easily.

"Where?" Riley asked again.

"To meet Daddy," Gracie repeated, flexing her hand to banish the trembling and making sure he was buckled in tight.

"Where?"

"Madame Thomson?" An unfamiliar voice from behind made Gracie's shoulders stiffen.

She turned, closing the car door to put a barrier between the stranger and her son.

The man stood less than a metre away, dressed in a generic suit and dark coat. A briefcase, which would have completed the stereotypical look, was missing. His shoes were wrong too. Dark to match the suit, but obviously cushioned, and with laces. Made for running, though less conspicuous than tennis shoes. Either way, an odd figure at a suburban playground in the middle of the day.

"'Scusez, j'suis en retard." Gracie yanked the driver's side door open, snatching the coffee cup from the top of the car.

The stranger seized on what he thought was her moment of hesitation and lunged forward.

Gracie popped the lid off the coffee cup with her thumb, tossing the contents at him. It wasn't hot, but it took him a moment to realize that as he cursed and fell back, giving her enough time to jump into the car and slam the door. She engaged the automatic locks and pressed the ignition button. Throwing it in reverse, she nearly hit the man.

He stumbled out of the way and she sped off, slowing only briefly to check for oncoming traffic as she tore out of the parking lot.

"Mama?" Riley whimpered from the backseat.

"It's fine, sweetie." Gracie's eyes darted to the rearview mirror. No tails, either on foot or by automobile. Yet. "It's okay."

4

I DIDN'T SLEEP WELL. I'd been having nightmares I couldn't quite remember, ones that woke me suddenly in a cold sweat. The only sensation that remained after I blinked awake was falling—heavy, fast, flailing, with no way to stop myself, no way to shift gravity. I could have been forever plummeting off Aubrie's balcony in Toronto last March, or over the edge of Niagara Falls like I almost had in June.

It was ridiculous. I, of all people, didn't need to be afraid of falling. Today I needed to be afraid of running down my bank account with only one part-time job. I'd have to ask for more hours at Bûcheron Urbain. The axe-throwing gym was a better job for me than sorting donations at the thrift store—my Faerie powers didn't really give me any advantage to throwing weapons, but it definitely felt more badass.

Speaking of badass . . . I leaned over the side of my bed to reach underneath where I'd stashed the redcap's sword. It shone, pristine and silver in the daylight.

The apartment beyond my bedroom door was quiet, which meant that my roommate was either snoozing off a coke crash or hadn't made it home yet. I dressed and grabbed my hoodie and jacket from the hook by the front door, then headed to the dépanneur at the end of the street for a cup of coffee. After the caffeine hit, I'd retrieve the sword and check the nearest pawn shops.

Hopefully it was fancy enough to net me a little spending money, and also not made of some Faerie-only material humans wouldn't recognize.

In line for the caisse at the dep with my coffee, my eyes roved over the daily newspapers. A familiar face in grey-scale made my shoulders go rigid. I stepped out of line, my heart beginning to thud against my ribs, and picked up the last copy of the Gazette, the only daily in English.

Body of Missing Montreal Man Found

And here I'd thought JM had just ghosted me. Was it sick that it made me feel a little better to know he hadn't been avoiding me, he'd just been dead? I swallowed a laugh that made my stomach shift uneasily.

The smiling picture of the man I'd known gazed out at me from the page: wind-swept blond hair—grainy grey in print—and that chiselled jaw and thick neck of a former rugby player. He'd been working his way through night school, aspiring to dentistry, and despite that he'd been a lot of fun for a week or so before up and vanishing.

> *The body of 26-year-old Ahuntsic resident Jean-Michel Marburgh was found Tuesday evening. Attempts were made to resuscitate him, but Marburgh was declared dead at the scene. He had been reported missing two days ago after failing to return home from work. Alexandre Proulx, SPVM spokesperson, said the body bore "marks of violence" which makes this Montreal's thirty-sixth homicide of the year. Investigators [see **Missing**, A9]*

I rifled through the pages with enough disregard for the unpaid-for paper to make the guy behind the register glare at me. I ignored him, because a second, smaller head shot on page A9 with the rest of the article made my heart drop into my shoes. This one wasn't JM.

> **Missing** [cont. from A1] *from major crime are asking anyone with information to please come forward.*
>
> *Two days prior, the body of another Montreal man, 27-year-old Trevor Gale, was discovered in a Pointe-aux-Trembles marina. Proulx has confirmed that both men's bodies had "similar marks." The homicides are being investigated as related, though initial information indicates the two were not acquainted.*

"Hey!"

I snapped the paper down in favour of the scowling face behind the register as the cashier added something else in French. Familiar enough now with working off context and facial cues, I dug some coins out of my pocket, slapped them down on the counter and left without my coffee.

The best thing about my neighbourhood was the dark, grimy sports bar two blocks away. They must have bought a panini press just to qualify as a restaurant so they could start serving booze at noon. I was the only woman there, and the only person under 60, as usual, but none of the early-drinking, grizzled Quebecois men paid attention to me.

Alone at one end of the bar with a shot of whisky, I read the article twice more, trying to draw further meaning from the words.

I stared at the printed photo of JM. He'd introduced himself by the nickname, those two letters. It'd sounded like a really affected version of "Jim" to an Anglophone like me, but I hadn't asked what it stood for, even in two dates. *Jean-Michel.*

And Trevor had seemed like a nice-enough guy for the hour or so that I'd known him on a dance floor. I'd been planning to let him take me home after he settled our tab at the bar, but then he'd disappeared. Maybe I was overcompensating in my memories because he'd been dredged up in boat ropes. If I hadn't read the article, I wouldn't have even remembered his name. I'd met JM two nights later. Now they were both dead.

"You've seen that." Somebody settled on the stool beside me—somebody who spoke English with a Wyoming-accented drawl in a Francophone bar.

I turned with a sigh as Abe tipped his cowboy hat back on his forehead with one finger. His weathered face was troubled. "How'd you find it?" he asked.

"I didn't have some tingly Faerie feeling, if that's what you mean. I went out with them." I kept my voice low but tapped JM's picture on the front page.

"Both of them?" Abe straightened up, interest piqued in a way that made me want to squirm.

"Guess you were right about her." A kid with messy blond hair settled himself on a stool beside Abe.

"What *about* me?" I included Abe in that sharp question since the newcomer had addressed the comment to him.

"That you'd be helpful." The freckled adolescent didn't make the word a compliment. He looked about fourteen, dwarfed by an oversized black puffer coat, but he held himself like somebody a lot older.

"I don't think you're allowed to be in here," I said.

"I'm hardly a human child."

"This is Gordon," Abe said, before I could argue with the kid's self-assessment. "He's a mage from the palace. Mab sent him over."

That introduction along with the flat note in the cowboy's voice put me on high-alert. Mages, as far as I knew, were Faeries who'd studied and cultivated stronger magic powers than the ones they'd originally been born with. Faerie magicians, and usually political elites.

"I'm not sleeping with him," I said.

Gordon snorted. "Don't flatter yourself."

"This isn't about progeny." Abe didn't crack a smile, voice still tense. "We ought to go somewhere more private."

I gestured to the empty stools around us. Two of the bar's elderly clientele were playing the lotto machines on the other side of the room and the others sat at the far end of the bar. The bartender had glanced over when Abe had joined me but hadn't seemed to notice Gordon's youthful face. Teen Mage probably had some glamour to make people overlook him.

"We're fine here," I said, preferring to stay within eye-line of bystanders who might jump in to help a damsel in distress if our conversation turned ugly. Abe and a palace mage might not be too happy with my running out on Miranda last summer, or my stealing a bunch of cash when I went.

I tapped the newspaper. "What's this got to do with you guys?"

"Both men were killed in such a specific way that the police think they were victims of a serial killer," the cowboy said, keeping his voice low. "It's something from the Faerie realm."

No wonder he'd wanted to go somewhere private.

"A *Faerie* serial killer? Are you *serious*?" I winced, realizing I'd raised my voice and gotten the bartender's attention.

"Ça va bien," Abe told him, raising a hand.

I couldn't even bring myself to make fun of the halting clash the cowboy's flat American accent made taking on the simple assurance in French. It seemed to assuage the bartender, or maybe Abe did that with some magic. He'd never explained how a good ole boy, part-human Faerie healer from Wyoming had gotten mixed up with my aunt's retinue anyway.

"How were they killed?" I asked.

"Their hearts were cut out." This from Gordon, short and matter-of-fact, as if somehow I should have already known that horrifying detail.

I gaped at him, unable to think of anything except the euphemistic quote the police spokesperson had given the Gazette: '*marks of violence*.'

Yeah, a missing heart probably qualified.

I managed to signal the bartender for another shot as a bitter exhaustion settled on my shoulders. Why couldn't the Faeries just keep their shit in their own backyard?

Abe reached up to take hold of the top of his hat, then plopped it down on the bar between us. He ran his hand over the smooth, bald scalp that contrasted with his craggy face and made his age difficult to discern.

"Heard of the Harbinger of the Host?" he asked. "The Shadowed Mab?"

We both paused as a fresh whisky was delivered into my hand, the bartender retreating without noticing Gordon.

"No. There's another Mab?" I balked. "Why's she over here cutting out hearts?"

"*She's* not." Gordon scoffed. "Shades aren't corporeal. As such, they can't hold a knife, much less cross through a portal to get here."

I opened my mouth to ask one of ten questions that queued in my brain, but Abe explained first.

"A shade is a Faerie cursed to live forever as a . . . well, it's something like a ghost. It was a common curse back

. . ." He waved a hand to convey *a long time ago*, "but it's been outlawed for a while."

"Faerie ghosts? For real?" Faerie immortality was a common myth that had been dispelled when I'd joined the Consilium.

"Shades aren't ghosts," Gordon broke in peevishly. "That comparison is vulgar. The curse doesn't kill them. It transforms their bodies into a non-material state and disperses the bulk of their magic into the collective. They don't require any mortal sustenance like food or drink and they cease to age, but they're not *dead*."

He paused to take a breath and cast Abe a sidelong glance. "Are you *sure* she worked for the Consilium?"

"I didn't hang out in the library," I snapped. "I hit people. You want a demo?" When he neither backed down nor manned up, I challenged, "If these shades lose their magic when they're cursed, how's she getting her hearts?"

"The Shadowed Mab's a different story on the magic front," Abe started.

"Yes," Gordon took over, a little ruffled. "I referred to shades in general. The Shadowed Mab is . . . well, she's ancient. She's built up a considerable amount of magic and power in the time she's been cursed."

"And a cult," Abe finished.

"Great. I was hoping for 'cult' on my Faerie bingo card," I muttered. Gordon's first remark hit me again in an uncomfortable way. "Why *did* you come to me?"

"You were here." Abe used a folksy, amiable tone, but it only highlighted his real meaning: *You're here and so are these murders. You've followed shitty, cult-leader-type people before.*

And I already had a murder on my rap sheet. I hadn't cut out Alan Cain's heart, but I'd stabbed him pretty close to it. Abe was empathic and could supposedly see my feelings play across my face. There was no use trying to hide my discomfort from him.

"Needed new friends." The excuse had seemed innocuous enough before the words passed my lips, but dread twisted in my stomach as Chris flashed through my mind.

I slid off my bar stool, but as I reached for my wallet, Abe had his out first.

"I got it," he said. "You think of something?"

"No, I just . . . I gotta go." I nodded a quick thanks to the cowboy for paying for my drinks, then headed out, leaving the newspaper behind. I didn't want the Faeries knowing Chris's name, whether or not he was involved. And he wasn't, he couldn't be.

Neither Abe nor Gordon stirred from their stools and it didn't appear that they were following me. They couldn't have possibly bought my lie, so maybe they had other leads to check out.

I retrieved my phone from the back pocket of my jeans and texted Chris: *Hey, how r u?* After a moment's hesitation, I added, *Thanks for the invite—not a bad party, even early.* I straightened my shoulders and took a deep breath. My heart had started slamming itself against my ribs like that would help the situation.

After giving it a good thirty seconds, I checked my phone again, even though it hadn't buzzed. Chris normally answered texts fast, like the phone was an extension of his hand. He'd probably just gone to a friend's place last night, drunk and scared, and by now he didn't even remember what weird Halloween costume had freaked him out so badly. Maybe he wouldn't even remember me fighting somebody.

Or maybe he did remember and he was afraid of me. That would make sense why he wouldn't answer like normal.

I let my fingers tap anxiously against the phone but didn't send another message. I didn't know his friends. Didn't know much about him at all. We'd gotten along on a few shitty work shifts at the thrift store. He'd taught me some Quebecois profanity. We'd texted a bunch. He'd invited me to a party. That was it.

Not quite. I actually had his address somewhere. I scrolled up in our text thread, thumb slashing across the screen until I got a couple of weeks back.

He'd texted me in the middle of my shift, thinking he'd left his ID badge in his locker at work. He'd asked me to look for it on my break, then sent me his address, wheedling me into bringing it over after work if I found it with the promise of beer.

I'd gotten into an argument on that shift with my boss Ty. It had left me fuming, tired and aimed toward my local sports bar to blitz everything away. Chris had found his badge two hours later, apparently stuck in one of his textbooks as a bookmark.

Bookmark. The library! Chris was studying there with a group today. *Crack of dawn.* That had to be why he hadn't answered my texts: he was busy studying. Or maybe he was regaling his group with the terrifying tale of my fight with the redcap.

But definitely not missing a heart somewhere.

5

I HOOFED IT TO the bus and, searching Chris's university's website on my cracked phone screen as we crawled through the city, discovered that there were in fact seven libraries there. One was closed on Fridays, and two others seemed too small and niche to host a project meeting, so that narrowed it down a little.

Was this crazy, hunting him down at his study session? He had to be there, just not answering his phone, because there was no way that some Faerie Ghost Queen I'd never even heard of was going after guys I knew. JM and Trevor must have had something else in common.

I started with the largest library, which seemed to be the main one. It was louder than I'd anticipated, at least in the room full of long tables where groups of students sat in clusters. The noise put me on edge. I scanned their faces for my former co-worker as I moved through, thinking of what to say when I found him.

Wanted to make sure you were okay after that sword fight last night. Fucking weird, right?

Hey, I swear I'm not usually a psycho stalker, but there's this Faerie cult . . .

I headed through quieter stacks of books and wandered the aisles in the sparsely populated computer lab, refusing to let the tension in my muscles push me into a trot. My weak excuses didn't matter anyway. He wasn't here.

Finally, I had no choice but to plaster a smile on my face and approach each study group in turn to ask after him.

On my third try, I got the usual head shake but a different response.

"He didn't show."

"Oh. Okay." My mind raced for a good reason to press further. Should have planned this conversation too. "He told me to meet him here so he could give me a book. Is he just running late?"

"Got me." The guy shrugged. "Haven't heard from him today."

"If he shows up, could you just tell him to text Jude?" My stomach churned with frustration but I kept my tight smile. I thanked them and hightailed it out. Undercover wasn't my strong suit.

This didn't mean Chris had been snatched by a supernatural serial killer. Maybe he'd just gone to the cops about the sword-fight.

Working through increasingly less believable explanations for his absence, I reached the front lobby. A familiar face in the entryway froze me in my tracks. My heart wrenched itself further off-beat.

Daniel stopped at the same moment, gaze fixed on something beyond me.

Flustered, I glanced over my shoulder. Nobody there except a Black guy in a navy pea-coat who'd just pulled out his phone a couple metres back. When I spun back around, it was just in time to see the library door closing as my ex made a hasty exit.

"You've gotta be kidding me," I said to no one in particular.

Moving at a jog, I caught up to Daniel half a block down. He hadn't broken into a run, just a brisk walk, but he pulled up short when I swung around him demanding: "What the hell was that?"

"Jude?" He looked startled.

"You see me and bolt and you think I'm not going to follow?"

"What? At the library?" Daniel glanced back toward the building.

His question had enough honest surprise to annoy me. Libraries weren't my preferred hangout, but it wasn't like I'd never set foot in one. Still, a second glance over his shoulder made it seem like maybe it wasn't me Daniel had been fleeing.

"Who are you looking for?" I asked.

My voice made him flinch, but it won me eye contact again. He looked much more pulled together than the last time I'd seen him five months ago—clean-shaven now, dark hair trimmed short, clothing not covered in blood.

And not immediately pointing a weapon at me. That was a promising sign. Since last summer—more likely since last March, when I'd nearly killed him—he tended to carry iron. It functioned as Faerie kryptonite in the human world, strong enough to ward off even a hybrid like me.

"What are you doing here?" He met my question with a question, stepping around me at a polite distance like he was avoiding a puddle on the sidewalk. Or staying just out of my arm's reach.

My throat tightened. There was no easy answer to that question that didn't include Aubrie's name. I'd tried going back to Toronto—I *had*—but the city didn't fit anymore, like a sweater I'd stretched out of shape with my bad choices. Actually more like a sweater I'd hacked apart with sharp scissors and left in tiny ribbons because a guy told me to. Not just any guy—Spencer Aubrie, friend, mentor, destroyer of the Consilium, would-be king of the combined human and Faerie worlds. I'd blown up my life for him.

That had left me with so many different neighbourhoods to avoid back in Toronto, so many bars and bus stops that flashed me back to what I'd been thinking, feeling, the last time I'd been in those spots. When Aubrie and I had been plotting, last fall. When Daniel and I had been sleeping together, last winter. Or when I'd murdered Danny's father and then nearly beaten him to death in service to Aubrie.

I swallowed my unease. Despite feeling it claw bloody trails all the way back down my throat, I managed a cool and steady reply. "I'm learning French."

"Ouais, c'est ça?" Sarcasm leached into Daniel's voice. He followed the three words I understood with something much faster and more complicated. Because of course my ex spoke French fluently, along with English, Faerie, and who knew what else. Never sleep with a translator if you don't want to be made to feel inferior for only speaking one measly language.

Once Daniel had finished his French test, I returned my Stubborn 101 response:

"Ça va bien."

I could have blinked and missed the brief smile that crossed his face, but at least his voice warmed a degree or two.

"Weren't you headed for a beach?"

He remembered. I hadn't expected that.

"Didn't get my passport." That had been one prize my aunt the Mab had promised me last summer in return for turning over Daniel and the spell he'd memorized. I'd given it up to protect him instead. A tiny dent in the debt I owed him.

"You know you don't actually need magic for a passport, right?" he asked.

"No, but you need either money and time or *lots* of money," I returned. "Not a problem *you'd* ever have, I guess." He'd inherited a good sum from his father, and if I remembered correctly, his mother had been pretty well-off too. I didn't know exactly how much, but he didn't have a day job that I knew of and didn't seem to charge for championing humankind against Faeries.

"The Mab's not bankrolling you anymore? Tiara didn't fit, I guess?"

"Getting knocked up with a royal baby didn't fit."

It was so rare I could leave Daniel speechless. I revelled in the win, then seized on it to challenge, "Why are *you* still in Montreal?"

He recovered with an awkward shrug. "Why wouldn't I be?"

"Well, last time I saw you, you were stealing a spellbook and leaving me to cover for you." I hadn't meant to piss him off, still aiming for friendly banter, but he tensed.

"I didn't ask you to cover for me."

I put my hands up in surrender, regretting the misstep. Daniel tended to be up on supernatural threats. Ever since the Consilium had fallen, he'd been freelancing, using whatever was left of the Consilium resources for investigating and countering Faerie activity. So maybe he knew about this dead Faerie queen harbinger thing. Couldn't hurt to check.

"Let's catch up." I nodded to the illustration of a steaming cup of coffee in the window behind him. "Or do you think you can outrun me?"

For a second, he seemed to consider the latter challenge, eyes flickering over my shoulder across the street. Then he turned with a sigh and pushed open the door to the cafe.

The place was busy enough that neither of us bothered going up to the counter to buy anything. I snagged a little round table in the back and slouched down in the chair that faced the windows and door, so that I could see the whole store.

Daniel sat with his back against the wall, resting one arm on the back of the chair. He asked again, "What are you really doing here?" As if thinking better of the question, he specified, "In Montreal," so I couldn't easily wriggle out with a vague answer.

I tried anyway:

"Toronto was boring. And my old roommate's wife's brother was driving here so I just came along and then . . . stayed." The words came out in a stammer I hadn't expected. I shed my jacket over the back of the chair, rubbing my hands to warm up and avoid his eyes.

My spur-of-the-moment move to a province where I barely spoke the official language hadn't been the soundest decision I'd ever made, but at the time I'd been up for a challenge. I'd felt lost here in Montreal, in the best way possible. Five short-lived jobs later and now hunting what was apparently a Faerie serial killer, I felt lost in the bad way.

But we weren't here to rehash my shitty decisions.

"Have you heard of the Shadow Mab?" I asked. "Apparently she cuts out hearts. Or her cult does. Do you have, like, books on it? Maybe in particular something about where she'd hide?"

Daniel eyed me with a dubious uncertainty, like he wanted to refuse, but he couldn't seem to help considering my information.

"It's familiar." A note of interest crept into his voice. "Cult of the Unfading or . . . the Undying? It's kind of a thorny difference." He switched to the low, thoughtful tone that meant he was pretty much talking to himself now. It stirred an uneasy swell of affection in me.

At least I could still count on Danny to be into this bullshit.

"Abe called her the *harbinger* of something," I added, "and that seems like it ought to be—"

"The Harbinger of the Host." Daniel snapped to attention. It wasn't a question.

"Yeah, that's it." I didn't love his reaction. "What is that?"

At the sound of the bells above the cafe's door jangling, he glanced over his shoulder and shifted suddenly in his chair. He put his back to the door before standing up.

"Get up," he said. "Take your coat."

The urgency in his tone cut off my first snide remark, but I still stood more slowly. I tugged my coat on while trying to peer over his shoulder and see who'd spooked him. Some guy in jeans and a navy pea-coat had just stepped into the cafe.

The guy did give me a sense of déjà vu. Ah, right—he'd been in the library lobby on his phone behind me when Daniel had turned tail and run.

Okay, so it hadn't been me Danny was dodging.

I walked to the back of the store, turned left and ducked into the back hallway, which led to bathrooms and an alley entrance.

Daniel followed, careful not to turn toward the man who'd come through the door.

"Who is that?" I asked, poking my head back out to check.

"They're interested in the Consilium. They've been looking up all of the surviving agents."

"Who's *they*? And why not just let them find you and see what they want?" I peeked out once more. "Obviously you're curious if you're hiding back here, not—" Behind me, the door to the alley clicked and I spun to see Daniel disappearing through it. "—running."

I cast one more glance out into the shop. The guy from the library was headed right for me. Rushing to catch the door before it fell shut, I emerged just in time to hear a grunt from the alley.

A second man—this one a white guy with a brown ponytail—had Daniel pressed against the brick wall, arms pinned behind his back.

"Whoa!" I exclaimed, holding up my hands and taking a step back.

The guy from the store nearly crashed into me from behind. Whether or not he thought I was an innocent bystander, he tried to grab me and I dodged.

On instinct, I shifted gravity to swing myself up above the doorway. I spun and glared down at them from my hands and knees on the brick wall, tense to attack. No tingle of Faerie magic—these guys were human.

"Rogers!" the white guy shouted, startled.

Daniel used my distraction to shove himself off the wall, pushing the guy back.

I leapt straight for the Black guy, Rogers. My boots slammed into his chest and the two of us tumbled to the cement. With a gasp like somebody coming up from the ocean, he clung to my legs, trying to get the upper hand and straddle me. Should have made myself heavier when I'd pushed off the wall, broken a few of his ribs. That would have kept him down.

We rolled to the side, through a rank puddle that smelled like liquid garbage. I managed to kick and scratch my way free of his weight.

I staggered to my feet and collided with somebody else. When I turned to check who I'd hit, I saw Daniel—and his former captor brandishing what looked like a heavy, black taser at us.

Rogers got to his feet with a huff, one hand to his side. Maybe I *had* cracked his rib. He stepped forward to separate us and I fought to keep a grin from breaking over my face. Me and Danny, back-to-back, surrounded by bad guys.

I'd had worse days.

"On your knees," Not-Rogers barked, knuckles white around the taser's handle.

I reached back and linked both my arms with Daniel's.

"Flip me!" I hissed, then pushed off without giving him time to argue.

He fell into an awkward crouch to let me spin gravity and somersault over his back. I kicked both legs out straight to meet Rogers' chest first and knock him backwards, then smashed into the second man as I swung over.

Daniel darted forward, grabbing my elbow as I stuck the landing, and hauled me toward the street at the end of the alley. We raced down the sidewalk and around another corner.

Several people jerked out of our way and one called after us, but nobody chased us.

"Where do you come up with these things?" Daniel demanded, as we slowed to a walk. He put a hand to his left shoulder, flexing it with a wince like my escape plan had hurt him, before casting another glance back for pursuers.

"My roommate's got HBO." I shucked off my corduroy jacket. It had taken the brunt of the foul alley puddle. The zip-up hoodie underneath was damp on one sleeve, but the miasma of trash bag water hung less heavily on it. I patted my head and my messy bun, checking to see if my hair was damp.

We stopped at a traffic light and I wiped my hands on a dry section of my jacket before brushing my knuckles across my cheeks to clean them.

"Do I have garbage on my face?" I asked.

Daniel glanced over automatically. His expression seemed to soften as he studied my face, but when he met my eyes, his gaze snapped back to the orange warning hand in the pedestrian signal across the street.

"Above your right eyebrow," he said.

"Thanks." My cheeks burned. I sucked in a deep breath to still the butterflies that had hatched instantly in my stomach when he'd looked at me. *Just the iron he's undoubtedly carrying. Probably just the iron.* "How'd you find out about these guys?" I asked, rubbing the clean sleeve of my jacket against my forehead. "Is there a social media account I'm not subscribed to?"

"Ted. Gracie's husband."

"He's doing the social media outreach?"

"He's been keeping tabs on everyone left from the Consilium." Daniel ignored my quip. "This new group accosted an ex-Consilium archivist at the university library. She was the sixteenth they've taken into custody, but the first we heard about."

The light changed and we crossed the street.

"That's why you were at the library, investigating her disappearance?" I asked.

"Walking into a trap."

"Good thing I chased you down." I couldn't help rubbing it in a little. Yeah, I owed him—I'd probably never stop owing him—but I wasn't above pointing out when I did come through, even accidentally. "You're welcome, by the way."

He cast me a begrudging look but didn't actually thank me. I was pushing my luck at this point. Plus, I'd cornered him into the cafe to get information about the ghost serial killer, not to get a new problem dumped on me.

"So, the Shadow Mab," I said. "The Host. You know what that is? Talk."

"I don't have time." He checked his phone.

"A Faerie's running around Montreal cutting out hearts and you *don't have time* for it?" That was so out of character I'd have suspected some kind of shapeshifter had taken Daniel's place, except my skin wasn't tingling.

Plus, the annoyed look he gave me seemed too on-brand.

"I have to meet—" He stopped, expression changing as something occurred to him. "Gracie."

He hesitated again, then admitted, "Who actually specialized in the Host."

He eyed me suspiciously, as if this wild coincidence were my fault.

I'd take it.

"Then let's go," I said.

6

Daniel wished he could be more surprised to find himself sitting on a city bus beside Jude. He wasn't optimistic enough to say he hadn't expected to see her again, but finding her in Montreal was strange and running into her at a university library seemed even more bizarre.

Somehow, 'bizarre' felt more intriguing than bad.

His left shoulder throbbed from the stunt she'd pulled him into to get away from the agents. Despite surgery and physical therapy, the permanent damage from a griffin's claws in Niagara Falls had left those muscles too tight to stretch as they normally would. He'd never been especially adept in a fight, but the reminder of his new limits still vexed him.

As usual, Jude had no such restrictions. It had been almost comical to see the shock on the two agents' faces when she'd flipped up onto a wall with the grace of a dancer, then held herself there with her hair and clothing obeying her singular gravity, rather than the regular one to which they were subject. She was a force to be reckoned with. She'd been that since before he'd met her.

If it hadn't been for the agents' genuine surprise, Jude's appearance at the library in tandem with theirs would have been suspicious. Taking orders from another mysterious organization didn't really fit her now, though. She'd learned better.

They both had.

So Daniel only *half*-regretted telling her about Gracie's arrival. He wanted to be immune to the gnawing, persistent interest her questions had triggered, but mastering his curiosity had never been his strong suit. Jude had pieces of a new puzzle, and Gracie might have the others. The fact that it wasn't necessarily a puzzle he should be trying to solve didn't stop him from wanting to.

Whether Gracie would agree remained to be seen.

Jude didn't speak much as they travelled to the public outdoor square where Daniel had arranged to meet his sister. He studied her unobtrusively on the bus as she stared out the window. She didn't seem to be looking for anyone. Her thick brown hair picked up the sun through the dirty window, burnishing it with sparks of gold. She'd let it grow out since her coma—since she'd been poised on top of him in his apartment in March, slamming a fist into his face.

A low scratching in his head had persisted since she'd grabbed his hands back in the alley twenty minutes ago. Now it resolved into a dull headache, mingling with the ache that radiated up from his shoulder. He reached into the pocket of his jeans to touch the three iron nails he carried. The tips were dull and he'd had to clean rust off them when he'd found the cache at the bottom of the box with his mother's books. The cool metal eased his anxiety and blunted the headache, but not as much as it used to.

"They spoke English," Jude said, intruding into his thoughts as she turned to face him. "Those guys in the alley. No accent. And 'Rogers' isn't what I'd call a French name. You think they came from Toronto? How do they know about the Consilium anyway?"

"I told you, we haven't found much out yet." Daniel kept his voice low, though everyone else he could see on the bus was wearing headphones. "As far as we can figure, they've collected twenty-three former agents."

"Twenty-three in the whole world? Weren't there, like, a few hundred before?" Jude winced, as if expecting him to point out that she, by collaborating with Spencer Aubrie, had been indirectly responsible for most of those deaths.

He couldn't bring himself to bother, even now.

"In Canada," he corrected, keeping his tone neutral. "We don't really have any contacts overseas anymore."

"Nobody's come after me," she said.

"Maybe the Consilium scrubbed you from their records." It felt like an excuse and Daniel regretted it. There hadn't been time for any kind of informational purges between Alan's death and the attack that Aubrie had orchestrated with the Faerie Court to decimate the Consilium offices. Still, the men in the alley *had* seemed shocked to see Jude's power.

"I'm not that lucky." She snorted at the suggestion, then added a quiet, reluctant, "Sorry."

"For what?" Daniel bristled despite himself.

"I don't know."

That about summed up things between them. Her supposed remorse about their past had served him so far but he couldn't let himself fully trust her. Yet here he was, taking her to meet his sister and nephew.

When they reached the broad, public square downtown, Daniel scanned for Gracie and found her sitting on a metal bench shaped like music notes on a scale.

She had her arms tight to her chest like she was cold, her petite form dwarfed by the giant brown leather shoulder bag she carried everywhere. With one leg crossed over the other, her foot bounced slightly in an uncharacteristic nervous tic.

Riley played on the ground beside the bench, assembling a line of pebbles.

Gracie tilted her chin up as she saw Daniel but her eyes narrowed when she spotted Jude. She remained still, like she might not get up to greet them.

Jude recognized her, though, and made a beeline toward her before Daniel could.

"Hi, Grace," she said. "Out for a visit with the kid?"

"You could say that." Gracie looked to Daniel, as if wondering what the other woman already knew, then asked Jude in the same bright, terse tone: "What the hell are you doing here?"

"We met a couple of agents just now, like the one you saw this morning. Jude surprised them by bouncing off the walls," Daniel said, to assuage the same immediate suspicions he'd had about her associations.

"Lucky," Gracie returned, her frosty tone belying the word. She got to her feet with a wary reluctance and brushed away a long strand of her dark hair that the wind had sent into her eyes. "How'd you two run into each other?"

"University library," Jude said, as Daniel answered, "Accidentally." The dull ache in his head made him snap the word more sharply than he'd meant to.

Riley seemed to notice them then, slipping behind his mother's legs. He peeked shyly around her knee.

Daniel caught his nephew's eye and gave a small wave. Riley lifted a chubby hand and rotated it back and forth in an imitation before his eyes darted to Jude.

"This is Riley," Gracie told her, reluctant but compelled by some ingrained politeness, as if she had to set a good example for her kid.

"Hey, I'm Jude."

"Hi." Riley's response came out in a brief bark, quick enough to make even Gracie crack a smile despite herself.

"Nice hat," Jude added.

"I drive the train," Riley agreed, replacing the 'r's in the words with 'w's. He touched the brim of his floppy, old-time engineer's hat with reverence. "Hal'ween."

"You like trains?"

"I like trains!" Riley shouted, jumping up and down with one hand still clutching his mother's jeans, as if the word had loosed some pent-up excitement.

"He hasn't really napped today," Gracie said. She sounded annoyed, like Jude's very presence had triggered this fit of train love. She scanned the area around them, eyes roving without turning her head. The tension in her jaw triggered Daniel's own, notching up the intensity of the rasp in his skull.

"Jude has questions about the Host," he said, in a probably-futile attempt to move their awkward encounter along.

"The Shadow Mab, actually." Jude jumped in. "Specifically anywhere that she might want to hide and cut out people's hearts."

Gracie's eyes widened and she made a covert gesture toward Riley. It was too late, though. They had the toddler's full attention.

"Of paper," Jude stammered. "Cut-out paper hearts. I'm going to be Valentine's Day for Halloween."

To her credit, she kept smiling brightly at Riley and ignored the amazed stares she got from both Daniel and Gracie.

The three-year-old looked impressed. Apparently Jude had pulled that hasty lie off with him.

Gracie seemed considerably less placated. After giving Daniel another warning look, she rattled off a quick summary as if that might somehow get rid of Jude.

"The Shadow*ed* Mab," she corrected, "used to be a Mab a long time ago. Now she's a shade. If shades exist, anyway. There's—there's a whole debate about that. I can give you a reading list if you want." An ironic twist in her tone spoke to her expectation of being taken up on the offer. "Supposedly, she had a cult of followers sworn to—"

"Has," Jude interrupted.

"What?"

"She *has* a cult. They're, you know—" Jude's eyes flickered to Riley, "—with the hearts."

"Seven men?" Gracie blinked, startled. The annoyance melted from her expression. "There's a ritual to make her corporeal again. Bring her back to life."

Another flash of pain went through Daniel's head, and he clutched the warm iron nails in his pocket. Neither the women nor Riley noticed, too focused on each other.

"It's happening here? In Montreal?" Gracie finally sounded intrigued. "Why?"

"I don't know why," Jude said. "I just need to know more about this second Mab and her cult and if there's somewhere they'd hide or stash their victims or—"

"Rituals have rules," Gracie said, "a sacred location for sacrifice." She considered for a moment, eyes roving the area again. Her attention now seemed fully split between spotting potential pursuers and digesting Jude's information. "Did the victims have anything in common?" she asked. "Other than being men?"

"I knew both of them." Jude hesitated. "Not well, but, uh." She chewed on her lower lip. "And the guy who might be missing now, I know him."

"Someone's missing now?" Gracie's eyebrows shot up and Daniel glanced to Jude in surprise. Her urgency made more sense but why hadn't she mentioned that sooner?

Nausea crashed over him as the throbbing swelled in his skull. He'd placed himself a good metre from Jude in the open square but the distance wasn't helping anymore. Neither were the iron nails in his pocket.

"We shouldn't stay out here," he managed, fighting to keep any sign of the panic off of his face.

"What do you suggest?" Gracie's tone sharpened, daring him to invite Jude back to their safe haven.

The adage about the cat—and, for that matter, Pandora—skipped through Daniel's mind, but he couldn't stand being outside any longer. He needed the familiar respite of passing through his front door. No matter what he brought home.

7

THE FACT THAT DANIEL had willingly invited me back to his apartment felt like a step in the right direction—one where he didn't despise me. I'd wrangled his address five months ago thanks to Miranda and then again by virtue of holding a magical artifact he'd needed, but even before that, before I'd betrayed him, it had still been me inviting myself over with a bottle of tequila.

I followed him and Grace and her kid up to the third floor of a brick six-plex that, from the unbalanced front door and peeling paint on the stairs, had seen better days.

Waiting while Daniel unlocked the door, I cocked an eyebrow at the giant crack in the plaster beside the door frame and remarked,

"Classy digs."

He ignored me, letting Grace and Riley in first, then following and holding the door open to me like an after-thought.

"She's not wrong." Grace seemed to agree with my sarcastic assessment as she entered.

I didn't have time to enjoy the moment of judgmental camaraderie. As I stepped across the threshold, pain pierced the back of my neck, sizzling down my spine. I gasped and spun around, half-expecting to see somebody with a giant needle or an ice pick.

Instead, a tiny, transparent human-ish figure with wings shimmered in the air just outside the apartment door, then disappeared.

"What?" Grace had turned to stare at me.

I'd been standing with one hand against the back of my neck, staring out the door for a few seconds, and now I had everybody's attention. I opened my mouth to demand an explanation, but stopped. Standing closest to the door with me, Grace hadn't seen the little sparkly winged thing.

Maybe I'd imagined it. A sylph. I remembered the word from when Abe had used it months ago. I'd never seen one, but it was some kind of Faerie spy bug.

I checked my hand for blood as I lowered it from my neck, but didn't really expect any. Sylphs were bound to people—humans, typically, but apparently they also worked on half-humans like me—with a spell.

Telling Daniel and Grace the truth was only going to make them more suspicious of me, and would no doubt freak Riley out. I already had a pretty good idea who'd pinned the sylph on me and it was a relief to have it gone.

"Sorry," I said, "I—" I trailed off from the lie as my eyes caught on a nail at the top corner of the door. One had been driven into each corner of the wood, wrapped with thin, copper wire that stretched around the whole door frame. A piece even ran along the floor, between two floorboards, creating a neat little rectangle around the door. Some kind of dried flowers had been woven into each side. "What is this?"

"A ward," Daniel said. The word earned him a startled look from Grace.

"What's it for?" I asked.

"Protection."

At least it seemed like I was on the guest list. The sylph, not so much.

"How'd you do it?" I stood on tiptoe to study the even, precise twists of the wire.

"It took a few tries," was Daniel's non-answer.

"What's a few?"

"Fourteen."

"*Fourteen?*" I turned to stare at him. "How the hell did you know when it worked?"

"When it didn't catch on fire." His tone was dry but the smattering of dark, burned spots around the wood at the top of the door indicated he wasn't joking.

Grace muttered something that sounded like profanity under her breath and moved away from us.

"Are you sure we're safe here?" she asked her brother, adding pointedly, "From people who won't be kept out by a magic *ward*?"

"It's not leased under my name, or one I've used before," Daniel said. "I haven't seen anything suspicious since moving in and nobody followed us from the cafe. So for now, yes." He paused. "As safe as anywhere else."

Even if the answer didn't put her fully at ease, Grace shed her jacket and took Riley's off, then produced a pad of paper and a pack of crayons from her shoulder bag for him.

I couldn't erase the memory of a shapeshifter wearing her face opening a door to me at the motel in Ontario five months ago. This Grace eyed me with a wary skepticism, not the blank way the shapeshifter had looked at me. That meant this was probably the real one. I didn't know where we stood. She hadn't been friendly when I'd met her back in June. I couldn't exactly blame her, after I'd put her brother in the hospital and killed her father, but at least then I'd helped save the world.

"There might be something about the Host in the books." Daniel headed past the sofa, running a finger across the spines of books piled haphazardly onto the shelf beside the television. Not finding the one he wanted, he started down the hallway toward the back of the apartment.

I followed, entering a small bedroom. Mismatched cardboard boxes full of books and papers had been shoved against two of the four walls and the end of the bed.

"Should we each take a section?" Grace appeared at my side and stepped toward the nearest box. Her voice had turned brisk and business-like, still shot through with a thread of disparagement, like she couldn't believe she was wasting her time to help *me*. But she was, so that probably meant the Shadow Mab and the Host were a bigger deal than I wanted them to be.

"No." Daniel straightened up, the word sharp. The tone faded at our surprise. "Just . . . I have a system."

I'd never known Daniel to be a neat freak, but he was usually more organized than this. Usually more minimalist, actually, but Abe had told me he had all of the leftover information that hadn't been destroyed when the Consilium went down. Looked like it was all being stored here. The faint whiff of ash told me some of it had been salvaged from burned buildings.

"Those are fine." He gestured to the boxes on the wall with the window.

He didn't want me looking through everything. Couldn't really blame him.

I tried to exchange a look with Grace but she ignored me in favour of pointedly crouching down to go through the box by the door. So she didn't buy this *system* either.

But I was on thin ice here anyway, so I made my way across the little room to the boxes stacked beside a desk under the window. It felt oddly awkward, going through Daniel's things in his bedroom, even if he was a metre away.

I picked gingerly through a box of half-charred hardback books, some that were falling apart and some that already had. I tried to summon up the brief lesson we'd had back in high school about book research, but they

hadn't spent much time on it because the Internet existed.

Too bad the Consilium hadn't gotten that memo. They'd been really into hard copies.

I was supposed to look for an index in the back of the book, but surprise, none of these had one. I didn't have time to skim every page, not with Chris missing. Now that I was close to something that might contain clues to his whereabouts, anxiety I wasn't used to had started to twist my stomach again.

"Here." Daniel held an open book.

I leaned over his left shoulder to read, forcing myself to ignore the familiar scent of his skin and whatever soap he still used rising to meet me at this proximity.

> *Shade, n.: A Fayrie made incorporeal and banished to a far corner of the other world. Achieved through a High Curse, trans. loose-ly as "The Fade." Speculation that the curse is no longer used and the realm cannot be located leads one to dismiss it as myth. See also, Grover's translation of* <u>Treatise on the Fayrie Dead</u>*, incl. "Extraordinary Situation of the Unfaded Mab," and Hanover's chapter "Harbinger of the Host" from* <u>A Thorough Study of the Faerie Host</u>*.*

"Never heard of Grover," Grace said, standing at Daniel's other shoulder. "I know the Hanover manuscript. The Consilium had it." She shook her head and surveyed the boxes around us. "But I gave you everything I had from them when we moved."

"What's the Host?" Everybody seemed to know this shade as the Harbinger but I'd never heard of it.

"It's also called the Wild Hunt," Grace said, pausing to see if that helped me. When it didn't, she went on, "It was an ancient army led by a former Mab and her consort. They pillaged both worlds thousands of years ago, but in battle with the other noble families, her consort was killed and she was cursed to become a shade."

"Why's she 'The Harbinger'?"

"A harbinger is—"

"A warning." When Grace seemed taken-aback, I added, "I know big words."

The corners of her lips turned up at my sarcasm, but her voice remained terse as she explained,

"The shade knows the location of her dead consort. Raising her is supposedly the first step to unleashing the Host again. We've never found confirmation that any of this was true, though. The Wild Hunt is widely assumed to be a myth."

"Two guys missing hearts says 'confirmation' to me," I muttered. I reached for the book Daniel still held open, and he passed it to me. Keeping a finger between the pages he'd found, I closed it to read the cover: *Tales and Laws of the Fayrie Realm as told to Edward Lacey III.* "Who's Lacey?"

"No idea," Daniel said. "Most of these books were written by Consilium members past, but some were perceptive laypeople, or first-hand accounts of . . . Antagonist influence."

The way he hesitated before saying the Consilium word for Faerie made him seem uneasy about it, like he didn't want to use it as a slur. He'd never been uncomfortable saying it before. I didn't love the term personally, given my heritage, but I'd gotten used to it while working for the Consilium.

From the front room, Riley called for his mother.

"Marianne Nguyen might have a copy of Hanover here in Montreal," Grace said, heading for the door.

"Don't know her," I said.

"You wouldn't. She's an academic."

Ouch. She didn't seem to notice my scowl, waving a hand dismissively as she added, "She's a professor now, at . . . somewhere. We weren't really friends." Her cool tone said they'd been more like rivals.

After she'd left the room to check on her son, I flipped the book open again and scanned the measly paragraph a second time. Directions to a new wild goose chase.

"Grace has more stuff, though, right?" I asked.

"Maybe not now," Daniel said.

"What's *now*?"

"She and Ted . . . retired." He said the last word like he wasn't sure he'd chosen it correctly.

I wasn't either. A clandestine organization founded to defend the human world from a Faerie invasion didn't seem like the kind of place that offered a pension at the end of your career. Well, nobody did that. But the Consilium had seemed more inclined to send flowers to somebody's funeral after they either bit it in the line of duty or keeled over from old age in a dusty occult library.

Before Aubrie had burned it all to the ground, anyway.

"Do you have some way of getting in touch with Abe?" Daniel startled me out of those thoughts.

"Not really," I stammered. "He tends to find me. I don't know if he even has a phone, or if it would work in the, uh, house." I narrowly avoided calling it the 'safehouse.' I doubted Daniel would consider the place where he'd been imprisoned and tortured last summer 'safe'.

"Jude." Grace's voice filtered in from the front room, a note of weird urgency in it.

When I reached her in the living room, she stood in front of the TV with the controller in her hand. She'd been changing channels, maybe looking for something kid-friendly, but she'd stopped on the five o'clock news.

"Looks like the news found out about the, uh, heart coincidence." She picked her way around that delicately, probably because her son was still colouring on the floor, lifting his head occasionally to glance at the TV.

I struggled to swallow a lump in my throat but it felt like I was choking instead. The banner under the photo of a familiar man was in French, and I didn't understand the anchorman. The photo wasn't Chris, but another face I knew: Ty, my boss from the thrift store. The guy who'd fired me last night before I went out to the party.

"What's it say?" I managed, as Daniel joined us.

"They identified another victim in Montreal Nord last night," Grace relayed.

"Where, specifically?"

"I missed it. I'm sorry." She paused. "Is that the man you're looking for?"

"No." I could barely appreciate the gentler tone she'd used. My shoulders felt tight. *At least it wasn't Chris.* The terrible thought brought me no relief.

Because that didn't matter. It could still be him next—I was no closer to finding him than I had been this morning at the library. It was a certainty now, a hard knot in my chest, that *I* tied these guys together. The three had nothing else in common. Somebody was trying to get my attention.

Why? The frustration circulating under my skin turned into anger. I wanted to punch the wall, feel my knuckles crack plaster and leave a dent to satisfy my answer to the question no one had asked.

Instead, I strode to the front door and yanked it open.

"Thanks. And sorry," I said over my shoulder, refusing to meet Daniel's eyes. He'd be judging me, no doubt. He understood better than anyone the ends that men I knew came to.

"Wait," he said, stopping me before I could leave. "Give me your number."

"Why?" The request startled me.

"In case I find anything else."

The idea that he was still offering to *help* made me spin around, primed to tell him to fuck off and not bother. There was no riding to the rescue here. It was already too late to solve the mystery. I was too late figuring this out and now three guys were dead, maybe more.

Daniel didn't regard me with the pity or scrutiny I'd expected, though. I managed to bite back my first impulse and recited my number for him to tap into his phone. I waited a beat to see if he'd offer his, but when he didn't, I didn't bother asking. I knew where he lived. For now, anyway.

I pounded down two flights of stairs. Whoever the fuck was doing this was circling closer and closer. Like they'd started out grabbing the first guy they saw me talking to, and then worked their way in. I'd known Trevor for maybe two hours. Long enough to remember his face, at least. JM for a week. Ty for a couple of months, working together.

Had someone been watching me at work? My hand went to the back of my neck as I stopped on the ground floor. Could the sylph have been how these assholes were spying on me?

I had to know for sure who'd put it on me. The only lead I had on Abe was the safehouse. It existed on another plane, somewhere between this world and the Faerie realm, and could appear wherever it was summoned.

I placed myself in front of the door to Daniel's building and slapped a hand against one of the glass panes. I'd watched both Miranda and Abe open a random door to reveal the house before, and neither of them had said a spell aloud, or seemingly taken time to seek out any particular door.

With a growl of annoyance, I closed my eyes and tried to summon . . . something. I never had to *think* about using my power over gravity—never had to plan or navigate shifting the world around my body. My power just happened naturally, unconsciously.

The door grew warm under my fingers and I shoved it open. Instead of the uneven porch and a cold Montreal street, I faced the foyer of the Faerie safehouse.

8

"IF THESE 'ETHERIC TRACES' are as obvious as you think, somebody's tail should've twitched." Abe stood beside the cold, empty fireplace, giving Gordon the full power of his dubious stare.

"That's some sort of regional reference?" The mage sprawled on the rickety sofa, looking and sounding every inch the blasé teenager he appeared to be.

"You know what it means." Abe wasn't in the mood to humour the callow quip or invite more of them.

The mage sighed heavily.

"The Shadowed Mab disappeared from the Bie'lelhii just before the first murder occurred," he said, repeating the information he'd given when he'd first arrived, "and you're right, were she elsewhere in the world, she should have been sensed. It's unprecedented for a shade to leave the boundaries of the territory. Their essences can only adhere in that particular space of the world, as we know from the—" He switched to his native language to recite the name, something that Abe made out to be *Uprising of the Ten in the Blood of the Garden*, then finished, "Are you familiar with that history?"

"Nope." Abe let the short word speak for his interest, but Gordon didn't take the hint.

"It's fascinating. A group of shades conspired and tried to march out of the Bie'lelhii, thinking for some rea-son that the magic in their curse had decayed enough to allow them to leave and overthrow the Mab herself. They, of course, all dissolved into nothing as soon as they crossed out of the realm. We've been unable to determine why. The magic that created both the curse and the realm is ancient and unfortunately, lost to us—"

"Have they sent actual search parties out into the world along with the spells to look for her?" Abe interrupted. There was no substitute for good, old-fashioned checking under every rock.

"It's not really my department."

Repressing the urge to roll his eyes, Abe retrieved his hat from the coffee table. For all the mage's childish quibbles with English idioms, he certainly had a decent handle on them.

Gordon had shown up unexpectedly yesterday with an assignment from the Mab to investigate the murders in Montreal, but hadn't bothered to give his resume. Like the smattering of other Court mages Abe had met over the years, he seemed to think his title adequately conveyed his qualifications.

As Abe turned to leave the room, something stirred in his chest. Occasionally, his empathic abilities lent themselves to more than just seeing emotions placed before him. *Angry company coming*, they warned him.

The front door swung open and Jude stormed in. Abe didn't have to read her emotions with his power. Pain and uncertainty were written across her face as she met his eyes.

"There's three victims now," she said.

Abe rested his hat against his thigh. "I'm so sorry, darlin'. Who?"

"This guy Ty. My boss." Jude shook her head. "I mean ex-boss. Because he fired me last night, not because he's dead. Also that, though." She seemed to notice her own drift from the pertinent information. Her emotions changed as she drew back into herself, forcing away the uncomfortable and bringing back something she felt easier with: anger. "Why the hell did I have a *sylph* on me?"

"Security measure." Abe refused to wilt under her glare. He hadn't had a hand in that business and he wasn't falling on his sword for Miranda this time. "Your aunt insisted. How'd you find out about it?"

"I went to see Daniel and he's got a ward on his door." She waved a hand dismissively as she tried to slip past further explanation. "The sylph was *not* invited in."

"He's—?" Abe stopped, startled. "Hell." He moved toward Jude, trying to usher her into the hallway and away from Gordon. "Have you eaten? I can whip something up."

"Don't fob me off with food!" she snapped.

Abe turned to give her a more meaningful look, out of the mage's eye line.

She frowned at him, catching on. "You'd better be whipping up something really decadent and apologetic like chocolate milkshakes," she said, stalking past him into the sunset-lit kitchen.

The fake backyard visible through the large windows was always the same. Always dusk. Since the house floated in whatever the space was between the human and Faerie worlds, the yard wasn't actually ever there when you told the door the location you wanted to exit and went out, but it looked real from where Abe stepped into the room.

Once he'd joined her, Jude lowered her voice and gestured over his shoulder toward the living room. "Did *he* put the sylph on me?"

"No." Abe shook his head, cutting through her irritation to his point. "Did Daniel see it?"

"The sylph?" Jude balked. "Could he? I barely saw it."

"Exposure to magic tends to make humans more likely to see through glamour." That really wasn't a situation Abe wanted to deal with, not now. "And practice helps. If he made a working ward . . ."

"Well, maybe that's why he wants to see you."

"Me? What for?"

"You'll be shocked to discover that he didn't say." Jude dropped the sarcasm as she paced across the kitchen. "How are they getting the sylph on and off me?"

When she spun to face him and realized that he didn't understand the question, she clarified, "Last June, after you sicced the one on Danny, you had to take it off him before you could see what he'd been up to. How's Miranda pulling that off?" She blanched. "Christ, is she *drugging* me? I *knew* I only drank three beers last weekend—"

"This is a different type," Abe admitted, trying to dispel her disconcerting suspicions about her aunt's interference out of some automatic loyalty for Miranda, though he didn't really know why he bothered. "Tech we didn't have access to before. Connected sylphs—they can channel directly from one to another."

"Faerie tech." Jude's disdainful scoff didn't hide her unease. "Can someone put it back on? Remotely? Magically?"

"I don't know all the tricks, but—"

"Who can see the feed? Just Miranda? Could somebody have used that to see the guys I met up with? Is that how they found JM and Trevor and Ty?"

Her twitchy, anxious anger made more sense. The idea of the sylph as an agent of the Shadowed Mab hadn't occurred to him, but sylphs didn't have enough intelligence to do anything malicious without being controlled by a spell. Plus, Miranda's protections for her heir would be nothing less than airtight, no matter how reluctantly she might make them.

"Can't imagine it's unsecured—" he started.

"Don't think it's escaped my knowledge that you're cutting me out of the conversation." Gordon appeared in the kitchen doorway.

"Wouldn't assume anything could escape your knowledge, son," Abe drawled, stuffing his frustration down hard.

"I'm more than twice your age," Gordon snapped.

"Tell that to your face," Jude muttered.

Gordon ignored her dig, keeping his focus on Abe to demand, "Who's got a ward?"

"None of your business," Jude put in.

"If the function of a royal sylph was disrupted, it is *absolutely* my business." The mage turned on her, drawing himself up to his full height, which was still two inches shorter than her. "As a representative of the Mab, it's my duty to enforce her law and her decisions. And while the Court *has* generally adopted looser regulations when it comes to magic in this world, humans making wards is strictly against the—"

"I didn't want the sylph, and it's gone." Jude's voice sharpened. "That's all you need to know."

Gordon's jaw twitched in annoyance but he didn't press her further. He had to know as well as Abe did that one human seeing through Faerie glamour or constructing a ward wasn't an emergency, especially right now. Still, the mage seemed like the stringent type who'd insist on pursuing it.

Abe wasn't in the mood to follow the rules and make an official report back to Miranda and her Court. Despite Gordon's insistence that 'regulations' were looser, they'd all been extra twitchy about human interference in magic lately. Maybe they'd always been like that—Abe hadn't exactly been an accepted part of the old guard in Faerie.

It was hard to want to do Miranda any favours after she'd saddled him with this obnoxious mage and not even had the manners to tell him the plan to his face. Gordon showing up with orders rather than a face-to-face conversation with his old friend felt like being Mab had gone to Miranda's head. Or maybe Abe was just back to being too human to be trusted.

"*Why* didn't you guys tell me this old Mab was killing guys to bring herself back to life?" Jude turned the conversation with an indignation only she could manage.

"*She's* not," Gordon returned.

"Didn't get that far," Abe answered her question. "You had places to be." He studied her as hints of guilt and fear skittered across her face. He tried not to delve too deep into emotions unless he'd been given permission, but it was impossible not to see flickers, especially in someone who hadn't trained themselves against it.

"How do you *know* it's not her?" Jude asked. "You said she was powerful. Do shades just float around wailing, or what?"

"Their minds function at the same level as ours," Gordon said. "They're conscious and aware, with distinct identities and personalities, but they're supposed to remain in the Bie'lelhii forever with no mortal desires—"

"Land of Shades." Abe translated the word from the tricky Faerie tongue.

"Like, Faerie hell?" Jude asked.

"We don't know what it's like," Gordon said. "Few mortals have ever gone there and fewer returned. But a *shade* can't pass from one world to the other. As I was telling Abe, they can't even pass beyond the confines of their land. It's physically impossible. They disintegrate if—" He hesitated, turning his head slightly to sniff the air. "Why do you smell like a dumpster?"

"Uh, rude." Jude frowned at him.

Abe smelled it too. It had gotten stronger when Jude had shifted the jacket she held from one arm to the other.

"Yeah, okay," she said, gesturing to the jacket. "It's this. I was wearing it when I ended up rolling around in an alley."

Gordon looked from the jacket back to her face. "This is something humans do for fun?"

"Obviously not," Jude told him witheringly. "I was fighting this—" She hesitated, and Abe could see from the brief flashes of changing emotion that she was editing her explanation in real time. "—redcap," she finished. "Last night. I ran into her feeding at a Halloween party. She was feeding, I mean, I was drinking. She attacked me and my—a friend, while we were waiting for the bus. My coat got stained." Without giving them time to jump in, she moved on to: "You don't think she—could she be a cultist?"

"Where was this?" Gordon's expression lightened, latching onto a lead. "I'll check in with the local captains and find her."

"Captains?"

"It's a designation." The mage waved a hand. "It . . . look, it doesn't matter." For once, his interest superseded his love of condescending explanations. "Give me any details about her you remember. I will try to find her."

9

"WHAT HAPPENED TO THE two-bedroom?" Gracie asked, pouring Scotch into two mismatched glasses. "I'd have rented something if I'd known you were hiding in this hovel."

"A one-bedroom apartment is not automatically a hovel." Daniel accepted a glass as she joined him at the bar that separated the kitchenette from the living room.

"Yeah, but this one kind of is."

"When are you expecting Ted?" he asked, to deflect her critique. When she took a hasty sip of Scotch before responding, he wished he'd chosen another subject, but she collected herself almost immediately.

"I haven't heard from him yet," she said, voice calm despite her fingers tightening around the glass. "But hopefully tomorrow."

She forced an ironic lightness into her tone and shot back, "What's new since I've seen you? Other than the sketchy guys chasing us around town, I mean. Weren't you dating somebody? Lily? Fern? Daffodil? It was a flower name."

Of course she'd remember that, even in their current situation. He regretted having mentioned it to her, especially now that he had to wrack his memory to even summon the details. It seemed like a distant dream. After he'd recovered from the worst of his injuries last June, he'd had a brief flirtation with the idea of a life that didn't revolve around the supernatural. Even tried to put it into practice for a few weeks. Before the static in his head had brought him to the conclusion that he couldn't have one.

"Rosanna," he said.

"Close enough." Gracie sipped her drink. "What's she up to?"

"I wouldn't know. That was three months ago."

"Yes and *some* people maintain relationships that last longer than a few nights." His sister sighed again. She stared into her glass a moment before saying, voice terser, "You're acting like Mom, you know. Jumpy, disconnected. Thinking something's after you."

"Something *is* after me," Daniel pointed out, annoyed. "Us."

"Wards won't stop humans. Which, if *Jude* freaked them out, our new friends are." Gracie studied his face, then asked, "How'd you even make those things?"

"Mom's notebooks."

"The ones I flipped through were all incoherent garbage."

"I found one with a few more useful sections."

"Can I see?"

Daniel got up to retrieve the battered, spiral-bound notebook from a shelf near the TV. He should have shown it to his sister weeks ago, or at least told her about the find, but he hadn't expected her to be interested.

Gracie opened the notebook, taking care with the yellowed pages that had turned brittle from being shoved into a cardboard box for almost twenty years. She ran her fingers over their mother's writing. For someone living in constant fear of supernatural surveillance, Maggie Cain hadn't ever varied her straight, legible penmanship in any attempt at subterfuge.

Something seemed to catch Gracie's eye and she read for a moment, then flipped the book closed and handed it back to him. "You know she left Alan to get away from this shit. To get *us* away from it."

Daniel nearly laughed at the rosily nostalgic view of their childhood she couldn't possibly believe.

"Which was clearly successful based on the wards and salt cleansing in every house, not to mention the weekly visits to the gun range," he agreed.

"That doesn't mean it's not worth trying again."

"So you're taking Riley to the range tomorrow?"

"I *should* be taking him out trick-or-treating." Gracie sighed. "It was all planned. He loves his costume."

Daniel couldn't help but feel twinge of sympathy for his nephew, but at least Riley was probably too young to understand that he was missing out on anything. "Next year," he said.

"Right. I can't take my kid out on Halloween because we're too busy hiding from the *real* scary things out there."

"It's also supposed to snow tonight."

"I'm not sure he's going to have a normal life."

"That's dramatic." When he realized the sudden turn was serious, Daniel altered his tone to amend, "He will."

"We didn't."

"We turned out fine."

"You think *Rosanna* would agree?" Gracie snorted a laugh into her Scotch, then set it aside and picked up where he'd dodged her question. "I just think you ought to be focusing on the dangers a little more relevant to us, instead of jumping to Jude's beck and call."

"By doing what? Keeping watch out the window with binoculars for suspicious cars? When there's an Antagonist out there cutting out hearts?"

"Hearts from male bodies that used to be close to your ex. Yeah, keeping watch with binoculars seems like it'd be safer—"

Something rattled in Daniel's head, blotting out the rest of her words. Jarred by the pain, he dug into his pocket to touch the iron nails, but the buzz didn't recede the way he'd expected. His stomach still threatened to bring the Scotch back up.

The feeling drew him to the window and he peered out while his sister's voice continued in the background. Across the street in the lot-sized neighbourhood park, a silhouette in a Stetson reclined on a bench.

"It's trash night," Daniel said, cutting Gracie off. At her startled look, he added, "I just remembered. I'll be back in a minute."

He made a show of yanking the black trash bag out of the kitchen garbage can and tying it up, then took it with him as he pulled on a sweatshirt hanging by the door and hurried out of the apartment.

Leaving the bag on the porch of his building, he crossed the street to approach the park. Once he was close enough that he wouldn't have to shout, he demanded, "How did you do that?"

"Do what?" Abe tipped his hat away from his face. "Oh, you mean poke the magical hornet's nest in your head? Thought it'd get your attention."

The way the cowboy eyed him while he made the statement made Daniel feel like he'd failed a test.

"Jude mentioned you wanted to chat," Abe added.

Wanted was a hell of an exaggeration. How had Jude gotten to him so fast? After the way she'd stormed out of Daniel's apartment earlier, he hadn't expected her to remember his reluctant question about how to get in touch with the Antagonist healer.

He forced himself to sit down on the bench. He didn't trust Abe, but the other man hadn't played him false before, and he didn't have a lot of other choices.

"Back in June you told me the Court had my blood," he said. "That they could find me with it. Do they still have it?"

" 'Course they do." Abe raised an eyebrow. "You thought they'd just pour it out? Nah, son, you were a headache before, and as far as the Mab's concerned, there's a good chance you'll continue to be one. *I'm mighty certain of it.*"

"I haven't made a move against the Mab." Daniel bristled. "She's the one who—"

"You stole a spell. You and I both know you stole more than that, but the Mab knows you took the incantation. It's obsolete now, by the way—wouldn't do anybody any good. They've changed the ciphers on the books." The cowboy sighed. "Still, it makes 'em skittish having it out here. Point of pride, keeping Faerie magic in Faerie."

"I didn't *steal* anything," Daniel snapped.

"You want to say the Consilium appropriated the incantation and you just found it—well, fine, I'll grant you that. But you definitely lifted the grymoire. No way around that one." Abe half-smiled at Daniel's surprise, tapping his own head. "It's hard to lie to me, not that Jude didn't try. She convinced Ilse the book went over into the river and Ilse told the Mab the same."

"And you didn't you tell her otherwise?"

"What's the point? You destroyed it." Abe didn't make it a question, but something in his tone said he didn't quite believe his own statement.

That was probably the best proof he'd get that he could trust the cowboy. Daniel plunged ahead before he could give it second—and third—thoughts.

"I want my blood back," he said. "Everything they're using—anything they *can* use—to track me. In return, I'll give the Mab the incantation back."

The cowboy shifted uneasily. "She's not going to accept a written copy."

"I know." Daniel tried to keep his expression neutral, not to allow any urgency into his voice.

Abe arched an eyebrow as if he'd picked up on it anyway. "That bad, huh?" An edge of sympathy tinged his voice.

Daniel hesitated, reluctant to be candid. But this was why he'd sought the cowboy out, and there was no point lying to an empath.

"I can feel the spell all the time," he said. "It . . . hums and whispers." It wasn't actually a sound, but he couldn't coherently explain the feeling it sent through him. A vibration in his bones, in his being. "I need it out of my head."

The static surged as if the spell had taken offence to the suggestion of eviction. It vibrated in a hiss like dry leaves on concrete and then resolved into a vicious, foreign tongue that Daniel couldn't quite grasp. The ward calmed it when he was at home, and carrying iron kept it from encroaching too heavily on his thoughts when he had to go out, but neither quieted it entirely.

"It wants to be used," Abe said. "Memorizing spells is bad business." His voice held no judgment but Daniel resented the words anyway.

The cowboy added, in a tone that seemed meant to be light but landed like a stone, "Your father'd be using it like one of those evangelicals to cast the Faerie out of all of us."

He was right. Alan would have used it as often as he could.

The thought of exorcising Antagonist blood from strangers like some twisted faith healer tightened the knot in Daniel's stomach.

"Contrary to popular belief," he managed, "we're not the same person."

"Could do a little more to distance yourself from his legacy." Abe glanced skyward as if considering the situation further, then said, "I know a mage who works memory spells. Could probably go in and slice it out clean."

Even though Daniel had expected a suggestion like that, the thought of an Antagonist in his head, sorting through his memories, still made him flinch. The jackhammer of his heart almost drowned out the dull throbbing in his head.

Abe stretched his legs and got to his feet, politely pretending not to notice.

"I'll run your offer up the flagpole," he said. "Be in touch."

The rush in Daniel's head receded as the cowboy moved away down the street. He stayed on the bench until his fingers went numb in the night air.

When he finally returned to the apartment, Gracie sat at the kitchen bar, frowning at her Scotch.

"Where's your dumpster?" she complained. "Three blocks off?"

"Ran into a neighbour."

"You've never spoken to any of your neighbours in your *life*. Mom taught us better."

Daniel shrugged off his sweatshirt, wincing at the twinge in his shoulder. He made sure the door was locked before settling back onto the stool beside her and taking a swig of the Scotch. He ignored her eyes boring into the side of his head, certain she could read the betrayal on him.

That was ridiculous. His sister didn't know that the memorized spell was serenading him at all hours with a purr like a chainsaw. She would never be able to guess that he'd made a Faerie bargain and invited an Antagonist to rifle through his mind.

"I thought you were supposed to wear that sling for another two weeks." Gracie must have seen him wince, eyes on his shoulder. "Are you still doing physical therapy?"

Her casual pestering put him back in more comfortable territory, and he felt easy enough to return dryly, "Did I mention how glad I am that you're here?"

Gracie laughed. "Oh, you don't have to—it's obvious."

IO

I JUST BARELY MADE it to work on time at the axe-throwing gym, Bûcheron Urbain. I stashed my stinky jacket in a locker, hung up my hoodie in the hopes that it might air out, and pulled my shift in my long-sleeved t-shirt.

I was antsy to map my way over to Chris's apartment using the address in our text thread, but I needed the continued paycheque. I'd stolen some money from my aunt last summer, but apparently cash conjured up from a magic Faerie house doesn't last long in the human world—literally. After exactly a week, tens of thousands of dollars had turned into crunchy, dried leaves. I was just lucky I'd remembered to be a responsible adult and stashed a couple thousand in my nearly empty bank account each day that week. A five-figure bank balance sounds like a lot until you're frittering it away on rent, food, transit fares and processing fees as you run from government agency to government agency trying to go legit and rebuild your identity because your wallet and IDs disappeared while you were in a coma.

Maybe I'd made my life too complicated.

Halloween night was pretty quiet in the gym, but we did have a few couples and one group. I spent most of the time, as expected, cleaning and hauling plywood boards. My manager Marco pulled rank and made me tell the customers they couldn't throw axes and knives while in costume, for liability reasons. Taking the brunt of their dirty looks and muttered sacrés didn't bother me like it might have another night, but it didn't make the shift go faster either. The minutes passed like sand dribbling through an hourglass, twisting my nerves tighter with every tick of the clock. I almost forgot I was supposed to ask Marco for extra hours.

I waited until we'd closed and cleaned up, and the two other employees had headed home or to parties.

"I can take some more shifts," I said, as he locked the door.

"I don't think so."

"Why not?" His dismissive tone sparked my annoyance, lighting the fuse on a frustration that had been coiled up waiting inside me all night.

His response was in French, and fast. I got about three words: *parce que, parler, français*. Like a rhyming poem about how I didn't speak the language.

"I'm learning," I said, correcting hastily, "Je suis en train d'apprendre."

"When you can give the safety lecture in French, we'll talk, eh?" The breezy dismissal hadn't left his tone, and to top it off, he threw me a half-hearted salute, as if this was a concession I should be grateful for.

I forced a smile onto my face. Smiling was supposed to make you feel happy, right? Forced happiness might keep me from decking him and losing this job entirely.

"À la prochaine," he said, starting to walk away.

"Bonne soirée." I spat the words like poison. I did not hope he had a good evening but I held off adding, *maudite Halloween, asshole.*

A glance at my phone told me it was just after eleven. I headed the opposite direction to hop a bus, hoping my transit card would hold out.

Chris's garden apartment was dark and quiet when I reached it. I cupped my hands and peered through the glass panes of the front door, but I couldn't make anything out. With the flashlight on my phone I searched the tiny patio area outside the door for a spare key, lifting the mat and running a hand along the top of the door frame. No such luck.

When sirens started somewhere nearby, I seized the opportunity and slammed my elbow backwards into the glass. I used a wisp of my power to give the hit more weight. The glass shattered as the noise swept by one or two streets over and began to fade again. I gingerly knocked more glass inside so I could get my arm through and turn the lock.

Slipping into the apartment, I toed the broken glass out of my path and my boot scraped something gritty. I'd smudged a white line running along the floor just inside the threshold.

Well, that didn't seem good.

I tapped the toe of my boot through the particles, dispersing the line a little more, then crouched down to examine the tiny crystals. No scent. Too grainy to be cocaine or some powdery drug—not that that made sense to run in front of your door.

It looked like salt. Was Chris superstitious enough to use salt like this? Maybe he'd seen me fight the redcap and wanted to protect himself? Salt was a sort of defence against certain magic, if I remembered my Consilium training right, but how would he know that?

"Hey, Chris?" I called, straightening up.

No answer. The dark apartment turned out to be a studio, so there wasn't much to search or anywhere to hide. I checked anyway, then stopped in the open bathroom doorway when something gleamed from inside.

Upright in the free-standing bathtub, it seemed to have the form of a person, but it shone wetly in the dim light that came through the window. I flipped the light switch.

Not Chris.

A massive, hulking. . . *thing* stood in the bathtub. Like a crude person made out of murky, green jello. It was translucent, its form skewing the lines of the bathroom tile behind it. No neck, just a bulb of a head sitting atop broad shoulders. It had no features: no nose, mouth or ears, but there were concave depressions where eyes should be.

It didn't move when I hit the lights, but its eye-indents did seem to twitch. How could the thing see?

"Chris?" I whispered, despite knowing it wasn't him. If he'd been some kind of squishy green Faerie, I'd have felt it when we met and my skin would be electrified again right now. I felt nothing except my heart fluttering in my chest. "What are you?" I asked.

It didn't respond. No mouth. No vocal chords.

But following that logic, there shouldn't have been muscles to move it forward, to let it lift a leg over the lip of the bathtub.

I couldn't help watching as it climbed out, leaving no trace on the porcelain. I'd really expected it to drip, or to squelch messy, green footprints.

Distracted by its clumsy movements, the creature caught me off guard. It lunged forward with more speed than it had used getting out of the tub, a sludgy arm shooting out and almost swiping me.

I leapt back and snatched the first weapon I could find—a brush hanging on the side of the toilet tank.

Brandishing that at the thing, I snapped, "Stop!"

No ears. It oozed toward me.

I stabbed the brush into its chest area. The head of worn nylon fibres slid through the green blob, parting it like liquid, but then the gelatinous flesh closed around it. I tried to yank it out but it stuck, cemented.

The thing almost got a gooey arm around me before I jerked back. I turned gravity and dropped to the ceiling, landing painfully on the spindly antique light fixture and making the bulb flicker. I rolled away from it, propping myself up on my elbows and glaring down at the gunky creature.

It reached up for me, its flesh changing and reforming like liquid to lift it a few inches toward the ceiling.

Panting with exertion, I kicked at it with one leg. My boot struck its arm, but the goop closed around my ankle. I pressed myself down on the ceiling and struggled to yank my foot from the mire.

The creature held fast, the same way it had closed around the toilet brush that still flopped from its chest.

Increasing my gravity again to make myself heavier didn't help. The thing seemed rooted to the floor with the same amount of force I'd used to pin myself to the ceiling. The plaster under me creaked in warning. Rather than fall up into the first-floor apartment, I let myself drop awkwardly back to the tiled floor. I made the landing on one leg, my other still stuck in the thing's arm. At least I pulled Swamp Thing off-balance, but that didn't last long. Holding me partially upright, its arm glop began to inch like mud up toward my knee.

I struggled away, flailing an arm to grab something—anything fixed. My fingers closed around the nearest towel bar and I gripped it with both hands, hauling myself against it. I tapped into my gravity again to help me huddle against the wall.

The thing still didn't let me go, oozing up my leg as it slid across the floor.

Then it stopped. The arm began to bubble with a faint sizzling sound. The goo thinned, melting around my boot and dripping from my leg but disappearing before it hit the tile. The reaction continued up the thing's arm and into its shoulder, liquefying it inch by inch.

My leg came free. The release threw me off balance so that I slammed into the towel bar. I fell, but I scooted back toward the wall without stopping, pulling my legs in tight to my body. My heart raced in my chest. I hadn't realized I was shivering.

The creature continued to melt, quicker now. Whatever had started disintegrating its arm moved through the rest of its body like lightning. It didn't make a sound, though, didn't flail or seem upset—just stood there, disappearing. After a few seconds, the toilet brush came free and clattered to the tile.

Once the creature had vanished, I let out a breath and examined my leg. The thing hadn't left any liquid or stain on the fake leather of my boot, or on the dark navy dye of my jeans. Despite the fabric being dry, the skin beneath on my ankle tingled like it had fallen asleep. I rubbed it to disperse the feeling, turning my leg. Some of the salt from the door had stuck in the treads of my boot. It wasn't much, but apparently it had been enough to disperse the bathtub monster.

I searched the spot where it had disappeared. The tile was, well, not *clean* by any measure, but there was no trace of green ooze.

The lines of the tile blurred. I glanced up to see if the bulb was still flickering from my impact. It shone solidly, though—not the cause of the dark spots creeping onto the edges of my vision. The pins-and-needles feeling swept from my leg up past my knee and then diffused through the rest of my body.

Exhaustion hit, strong and unnatural enough to stir a spike of panic that helped me fight to get to my feet. Even clinging to my gravity like puppet strings to hold myself up, I couldn't make my muscles move. I slumped back onto the floor before passing out.

11

Gracie tossed and turned most of the night, twitching at every noise in the unfamiliar apartment. She fell asleep just before dawn, but Riley woke maybe three hours later, too excited about being in a new place to fall back asleep.

He kicked and squirmed in bed, asking if they could play, have breakfast, draw, watch TV—all while she stubbornly dozed. When he finally went quiet, she had no choice but to prop herself up on an elbow. She found him pulling books from the boxes stacked along one side of the bedroom.

Mindful of the creative and detailed illustrations she'd regularly come across in similar Consilium books, Gracie got upright with more speed than she'd have thought possible.

She let Riley run ahead to the living room and changed from the t-shirt and boxers she'd borrowed from her brother back into her previous day's outfit. She'd need to pick up new clothes, at least a few pairs of socks and underwear for her and Riley. Just until they knew their next move.

"Where's Uncle Danny?" Riley demanded, investigating the empty sofa where her brother had insisted on sleeping.

"He'd better be picking up groceries," Gracie muttered. She'd almost forgotten how empty the kitchen was. It was like looking back in time to her own apartment before

Ted had come into her life. Conditioning. *Don't keep too much around that you'll have to abandon if you need to take off.*

Suppressing a swell of anxiety for her husband, she tapped her phone to wake it up and found a text. Not groceries. No, her brother was out in search of Antagonist books. He'd gone to see Marianne Nguyen. Gracie wanted to be annoyed, but she had to admit that Jude's news about the Shadowed Mab *was* concerning. She'd spent years studying the Host and while it was supposed to be mostly myths and rumour, it wasn't anything she wanted to see come to life.

Aubrie's awful stunt last summer had been bad enough, as close as she ever wanted to come to the end of the world again.

Going through the cupboards in the kitchen, she found a half-empty box of cereal and a bag of ground coffee. The refrigerator greeted her with a carton of eggs and a carton of milk, almost at the expiration date. It passed the sniff test, but she tried an experimental bite of the cereal before presenting it to her son. Then she rifled through the cupboards for a skillet to cook eggs in.

Ted usually handled the cooking. His current radio silence had played a part in her sleepless night. Had he been hauled off somewhere by men like the one at the playground, strange guys in suits and running shoes? No, he was smart and capable. He was laying low, leading their pursuers off, keeping them safe. That had been the plan. She just had to wait.

Once Riley was fed and Gracie had downed two cups of dark, gritty liquid caffeine, she delivered him the computer tablet from her shoulder bag so that she could jump in the shower. She had to stick to a routine to stay sane.

Maybe there was a park nearby with a playground. After she'd re-dressed, Gracie pulled out her phone to check the map, then changed her mind. They shouldn't go out. Sticking to the apartment and showing their faces as little as necessary outside would be safer. Just in case.

Riley put aside the tablet eventually in favour of scribbling on the pad of paper from yesterday. He must have been feeling more comfortable in the new place, because he began asking inane questions every couple of minutes, the way he usually did at home.

"What colour is a moth?"

"Usually brown or grey."

"What's the bird outside?"

"I don't know." Gracie retrieved Lacey's book from the bedroom, left open and face-down on one of the boxes to mark the page about shades. The disregard for the old, cracked spine annoyed the pedant in her. Daniel knew better.

"It's black," Riley announced as she returned to the room.

"Is it big? Maybe it's a crow."

"I think it's a eagle." Riley focused anew on his paper, seemingly intent on drawing whatever he'd seen outside.

Gracie curled up beside him on the sofa and skimmed the book for lack of anything else to do. This one had been her father's. There were passages inked out and editorial notes in his handwriting. Alan hadn't gone so far as to cross out Lacey's every use of the word *Fayrie* and replace it with the Consilium's preferred term, *Antagonist*, but maybe he'd just never gotten the time.

"Mama, draw a hat on it." Riley slapped a piece of paper over the book's pages.

"How do we ask?"

"Please draw a hat." He reconfigured the sentence automatically and jabbed intently at the blob-like figure that could have been a bird.

"What kind of hat?"

"Like mine." He touched the brim of his engineer's cap.

Once Gracie had finished sketching a cap onto the blob, Riley snatched the paper back and began to colour it in, pushing outside of the lines she'd made.

She glanced back down at the book. Nothing relevant but the page her brother had shown them yesterday, the definition of shades and the references upon references that she didn't know how to find. More mysteries she didn't know how to solve.

A sentence caught her attention again. *See also Grover's translation of the* <u>Treatise</u> . . .

She'd told Daniel and Jude yesterday that she'd never heard of Grover, which was true, but seeing the words written out triggered her memory: *Treatise on the Fayrie Dead* was the full title of what she knew more colloquially as Al-Amin's *Treatise*. Edward Lacey III hadn't bothered to add the original author's name to his notes.

Gracie *had* Arthi Al-Amin's *Treatise*. At least, she'd had a photocopy in her old Consilium office years ago. Her assistant had packed it all up and delivered it after she went on maternity leave and someone else took over her office, so she *should* conceivably still have it somewhere. Maybe in a box in her closet, or under the bed.

A soft rap at the front door made her heart leap into her throat.

Riley slid off the sofa, eager to greet whoever it was, but Gracie slipped ahead of him, keeping her steps and posture casual. She peered through the peephole and then brushed her son away from the door so that she could yank it open and throw her arms around the neck of a man bundled into a camel coloured coat.

"Daddy!" Riley copied his mother's example and threw himself at his father's legs.

Ted laughed and disentangled himself from their embraces, helping Gracie to scoot their son inside the door before closing and locking it. His eyes lingered on the iron nail pounded into the top corner of the door, but he didn't remark on it.

"What took you so long?" Gracie complained.

"Grabbed the train to Ottawa," Ted answered. "I used the credit card a few places around town—" He passed her a new, canvas shopping bag with cheap packages of socks and underwear for all three of them, "—then I caught a ride-share back."

"A *ride-share*? What—you and a bunch of students?" Gracie rolled her eyes, but the relief that fused through her left no room for actual derision.

"I'm hip." Ted adopted a cocky attitude. The rich morning sunlight coming through the windows gave his ebony skin a golden cast as he grinned at her. "I tok the tiks and gram the . . . things."

"I tok," Riley echoed, hitting his father's leg for attention.

"Yeah, I've heard that about you," Ted agreed with a laugh. He took off the backpack he wore and passed it to Gracie. "Contents of the lock-box, as requested," he told her. "And the closet—minus one axe. I really couldn't hide that one."

"What's a lock-box?" Riley asked.

"A box with a lock on it," Ted returned, reaching down to pick him up.

The toddler skittered away, hurrying back to the sofa and insisting,

"No, I'm *drawing!*"

"Got it." Ted took it in stride, but stifled a laugh and buried his head in Gracie's shoulder to muffle the sound as his exhaustion gave way. His laughter sent warm, familiar vibrations through her. Waves of relief crashed over her again to have him safely back.

"We missed you," Gracie assured him, as he straightened.

He removed his coat and draped it over one of the stools at the bar that separated them from the kitchenette.

"I don't know how long Ottawa will throw them off for, but better than nothing." He scanned the apartment behind her, thinking to ask: "Where's your brother?"

"Errands." Gracie didn't have the energy yet to get into everything that had happened yesterday. She pulled a sheaf of papers—a mix of birth certificates, leases, deeds and other documents—from the backpack. They had extra copies of all of these important papers in two different safe deposit boxes, but the less running around they needed to do, the better.

The bag was still lumpy and heavy, so she unloaded a small jumble iron tools—a large, heavy wrench, three old railroad spikes and a squared-off iron hammer with a wooden handle, which she'd been told by the flea market dealer was some kind of vintage cobbler's tool.

She should have put her folder of Consilium papers in the lock box with the rest of this, or somewhere safe, but it hadn't occurred to her. The leftovers from her London office had just become an anonymous manila envelope in her belongings. If she'd had more forethought, she'd be able to get to Al-Amin's *Treatise* now.

Of course if she'd *known* there was some shifty new wannabe Consilium popping around with the potential to drive her out of her apartment into hiding, she could have made better plans too.

"Why didn't you tell me about this new group?" she asked, keeping her voice light and even for Riley's benefit. The question had been burning in the back of her mind since Daniel had filled her in on the details yesterday.

"I honestly didn't think it would come to anything." Remorse coloured Ted's voice.

"But you told Daniel about it."

"Well, he's . . . still *involved* with that stuff. We're not. I didn't want to get pulled in if I didn't have to, so I just passed along information because I've still got contacts he doesn't." Ted made a frustrated noise in the back of his throat, but his expression made clear that the annoyance was self-directed. "I'm sorry," he said.

"I know." She did. Her husband wouldn't lie to her on purpose.

If the agents had been at their apartment yesterday, they'd probably taken anything that looked relevant, so she shouldn't go back to the apartment to check for the *Treatise*. Even if Ted had led the enemy off last night, they would still return to the apartment as a base when they turned up no traces of him in Ottawa.

She couldn't walk up to the building, arrive out in the open where she might be spotted. But maybe there was another way.

"Could you find a number for me?" she asked. Despite being alone, with no civilians besides her son to overhear, she switched automatically to blander, less-detailed words. Her ex-security officer husband had gone into cell phone records to pull phone numbers before—it would probably be one of the easier hacks he'd done lately.

"Whose?" Ted asked.

"Jude Waldron's."

Before Ted could question further, Riley shouted, "Jude!" from the couch. When he had both his parents' attention, he added, "She likes my hat."

"Jude was here?" Ted's voice betrayed nothing.

"Daniel ran into her."

"So *he* needs her number?"

It would have been so easy to agree to that, to pin it all on her brother, who wouldn't argue—wouldn't even know, in fact—but Gracie and her husband had made promises to stop hiding things from each other. Even though he'd made an error in judgment, it didn't give her permission to pretend to do the same.

"He's already got it," she admitted. "But I need to talk to her and I don't want him *involved*."

12

I woke to sunlight, lying on a hard, tiled floor with one leg twisted under me. My limbs protested, stiff and cold, as I pulled myself up. With a groan, I stretched my leg out and rubbed it to bring the feeling back. That gesture brought back the memory of the unpleasant tingle sweeping through my body and knocking me out, so I glanced around the bathroom. No more green monsters.

No Chris, either, I found when I double-checked the rest of the apartment. Bringing my phone to life showed that I still had no messages. So he hadn't come home last night. Probably not the night before either.

At this point, he had to be in trouble. I hated the gnawing, anxious feeling starting in my stomach, a sense of running away from something that I couldn't see.

No. I do not run away from things. Things run away from me.

Salt and broken glass still lay scattered in front of the door. Nobody seemed to have noticed it from outside, but I pulled the sleeve of my hoodie over my hand anyway to turn the knob and let myself out.

As I crossed the park a few blocks over, headed for the bus stop, a flock of sparrows swept low overhead in a clacking rush of wings. They turned in one graceful movement to swoop down at me. Startled, I braced to duck, but the brown and white bodies whooshed past me. They converged, then dropped like a giant, feathered stone and melded into a human shape.

Gordon pulled a feather off of his chin, rubbing it between his fingers to let it drift away on the cold wind that blew past us.

I gaped at him, checking over both my shoulders. Had anyone else been close enough to catch that? A group of kids kicked a ball at the far end of the park's field but weren't paying attention to us, and a guy walking his dog on the distant sidewalk was too far away to have seen anything.

"I was glamoured," Gordon said, noting my expression. "Your instincts are decidedly . . . human." Then he surveyed me, wrinkling his nose to remark, "And you haven't showered since last night."

"No, I haven't," I snapped. "I got roofied by some Slime Monster after work and passed out on a bathroom floor."

Gordon opened his mouth, then reconsidered whatever he'd been about to say and snapped it closed. He studied me for another ten seconds before finally asking, "Define 'roofied' and 'Slime Monster'?"

"I need coffee first. And, like, a pastry. Or, god, a breakfast sandwich." My stomach growled in appreciation of that plan and I tightened my shoulders against the chilly wind, looking past him to search for the nearest restaurant.

"I'm sure we could produce an adequate breakfast at the house." The mage beside me wasn't shivering like I was. In fact, he didn't even seem to notice the cold through his open puffer coat.

"Pass."

Gordon looked affronted, taking my casual dismissal more personally than I'd expected.

"You'd rather discuss arcane spells in full view of humans?" he sneered.

"I'd rather not discuss arcane spells at all. Is that what the Slime Monster was?" A spell. It made sense, actually.

I hadn't felt the usual tingle in my skin that Faeries in my close vicinity set off. I wasn't usually triggered by magic itself, at least not that I knew of.

Aiming for the other side of the park, I asked over my shoulder, "How is a *spell* corporeal?"

Gordon hurried to keep up with me.

"It's a Sending," he said. "A spell made flesh. They're popular for hunting. Back home, not here," he added, as if he expected me to be defensive about Faeries hunting in the human world. "They're very versatile. They can change shape, flow around their prey and take its form, transporting it alive. Useful whether you're seeking something large or small."

"Why was it in my co-worker's bathtub?"

"Obviously I don't know." The mage's voice turned frostier. "What was it doing when you encountered it?"

"Just hanging out. Waiting for Chris?" I argued back to myself without giving the mage a chance to weigh in. "But why? And how? I only decided at the last minute to go to that party with him. Who could find his place that quickly and dispatch a spell to snap him up?"

My aunt could have. Since the Shadow Lady had been a Mab at one point, maybe she and her minions still had that kind of reach.

"Clearly, it didn't," Gordon said. When I cast him a puzzled sidelong glance, he added, "*Snap* your friend up. If it was still waiting in his apartment."

The unexpected revelation tried to warm me, like a candle in a freezing warehouse. Yes, maybe Chris was somewhere safe. At a friend's house. Sleeping at the university.

I'd never been an optimist at heart. It was hard to start now.

Teen Mage trailed me into the first cafe I saw. Bells jingled above the door as we entered. He came up with me to the counter and waited while I ordered a coffee and a quiche, then requested an herbal tea. He paid for the meal with a real or Faerie-forged debit card.

My phone buzzed in my pocket. The cracked screen showed *Unknown number*, so I dismissed the call and jammed it back into my pocket. No time for scammers today.

"How'd you find me?" I asked, as we settled at a table near the back of the cafe with our drinks.

"My skills are far superior to yours," he said. "You can sense me when I'm this close to you. I can sense you at a distance."

His condescending tone warred with my appreciation of his buying me breakfast. He was probably right, though. Full-blood Faerie plus mage meant he had more serious power than anything in my casual, half-human arsenal.

"I sought you out because we've found the—" Gordon's voice lilted on a word I didn't know, too sing-song and foreign to be either English or French. The Faerie language had a strange musical quality.

At my blank look, he added, "Saskia."

It took me a moment to realize that was a name, not another word in the foreign tongue.

"The redcap?" At his nod, I pressed, "And did you talk to her? Interrogate her? Is it her?"

"We haven't spoken to her, no. We've made applications to the Archduke."

"You're going to need to go back and explain everything you *assume* I already know."

The mage studied my face as if he thought I might be fucking with him. When he came to the conclusion that I wasn't, he frowned.

"Saskia is the daughter of the Archduke. We can't demand an audience with her without a significant . . . royal investment."

"I'm royal. I say do it."

"Yes, the request has been made on your behalf."

We both paused as one of the cafe employees approached with my warmed quiche on a plate. After he'd retreated behind the counter and presumably out of earshot, I cut into the flaky crust and asked,

"Who's the Archduke?"

The exasperation on Gordon's face primed me for another comment on my lack of esoteric knowledge about the Faerie world. Everybody expected that since half my DNA had come from that foreign world, I somehow knew all the politics. That was particularly stupid because with human blood in my veins, Mab's heir or not, I couldn't even set foot in the place.

The mage settled on a diplomatic answer:

"An influential noble."

"Let me get this straight, I don't get to be a princess, but he gets to call himself an *archduke*?"

"In fact, his title actual is—" Another cascade of tinkling Faerie words flowed out of Gordon's mouth.

"Archduke it is," I concluded. "What's he doing over here?"

"He owns property in this world. A few clubs and hotels. And participates in other ventures." Before I could ask for clarification, Gordon parted his jacket to reveal the t-shirt he wore underneath: black with a faded white logo.

"Broken Brooms," I read, then hesitated, taking a sip of my coffee. "The band?"

"Yes."

"Wait." I studied the t-shirt for another few seconds as the full realization settled on me. "This big, bad Faerie Archduke is a member of a super-famous alternative rock band?"

"Lead guitarist."

"Declan Raj?" I cut off another piece of quiche. The name came to me from too much time spent browsing the tabloid corners of the Internet on my bus commute. I couldn't quite picture him, though. "So much for Faeries keeping a low profile."

"The Mab would agree with you."

"Then, what—this guy knows all the underworld dealings and would be able to tell us gossip about the Shadow Mab? Or do you think he's a cultist? I'll bet working a coup around his tour schedule would be a bitch."

"We should return to the house and await his summons."

"His *summons*? No thanks." I tensed as my phone buzzed again. Still an unknown number. I dismissed it and stuffed it back into my pocket. "I'm going home to take a long shower."

"There's a shower at the house," Gordon said.

And the hot water never ran out in the magical Faerie house either, unlike in my apartment. Still, I came by my mistrust honestly.

"Why do you want me to go to the house so bad?" I eyed him, trying to make sense of that. Taking in the tight set of his shoulders and perpetual frown on his face, I couldn't help asking, "Are you afraid to be out here with humans?"

I fully expected the narrow-eyed, disdainful scoff I got in return.

"Of course not," Gordon said. "It's merely a slow, uncomfortable world. I have no interest in humans. They're all the same."

Before I could argue, he added, "You try so hard to be different from one another and invent categories to separate you, but you *are* all the same. Imagine if even two-thirds of the species in this world were intelligent. Trees, insects, tigers, salmon—all with the power of speech and the same higher brain functions humans lay claim to."

"You have talking salmon in Faerie?" When he frowned to indicate that I hadn't understood his point, I clarified,

"So, you'd rather hang out in the house because you're bored here?"

"The house simply feels more natural. Not exactly like being at home, you know, but—" The mage seemed to realize we were almost bonding and stopped himself.

But I wasn't finished with my breakfast, so I prompted,

"Why'd you decide on 'Gordon'?" As far as I'd been told, Faeries always chose new names when they came into our world, mostly because humans couldn't make the vocal sounds necessary to pronounce their real names.

"I liked the name, so I took it."

"That's how you guys choose human names? Because you *like* them?"

"What'd you expect?" He scowled.

"More cunning, I guess. Did you just *like* being a teenager, too?"

"Appearing human is more complicated than it sounds for most us. This body is the simplest form glamour can create to fit my personal being on your side of the portal. There are, of course, several types of shapeshifters for whom body-glamour is more easily manipulated, but funnily enough, they tend to be less adept at working environmental glamours." Gordon continued to talk, moving into something about the physiology of shapeshifters, and my interest waned.

His voice became background noise as I finished my quiche. I'd go home and get my shower, then what? Wait to be summoned by the Faerie Archduke? I didn't have any other leads for finding Chris.

When the mage paused to take a breath, I dove back in.

"So glamour just chooses your body for you?"

"At a base level." He frowned, annoyed at my simplification. "Do you really know so little about glamour?"

"Never needed it." Nor did I need another lecture on it. I grabbed my to-go cup of coffee before Gordon could assign me homework and shrugged my jacket back on.

The mage got to his feet and followed me out.

"I should stay with you," he said. "For protection. You're no longer under the purview of the Mab's sylph."

Maybe that was why he kept trying to herd me back to the house. The thought wasn't comforting.

"I'm not interested in being under anybody's purview, thanks."

Gordon eyed me uncertainly, but seemed to accept that. He reached into his pocket and extracted something, holding his fist out to me. When I extended a hand, he dropped a small, brown-speckled egg into my palm.

"If you need to contact me, break this," he said.

The egg could have fallen out of a bird's nest around here, if it had been spring instead of fall. The shell was smooth but not as delicate as I'd expected, and my hand hummed with electricity.

It made me feel a little guilty for ordering the quiche.

"Throw it, smash it, stomp it—whatever," Gordon added. "I'll feel it and I'll find you."

"Sure." Not a lot of chance of that, but it didn't hurt having a way to get in touch with the mage, and more importantly, Abe.

Without a goodbye, Gordon burst into a flock of birds and disappeared into the sky.

I glanced around again covertly as I tucked the egg into my hoodie pocket, but nobody cried out or pointed at the mage's magical exit.

Pulling out my phone to text Chris again, I found a waiting voicemail. I expected spam, but I started the message anyway.

Not a robo-call.

"Jude, it's Grace. Look, I'll try you twice more this afternoon from this number. Please answer your phone."

13

DANIEL RAPPED ON THE professor's door for the second time. The office appeared dark inside, and no students had been waiting despite the fact that Marianne Nguyen was supposed to have office hours from eleven to one.

"Are you looking for Professor Nguyen?" A voice from behind startled him. "She hasn't shown up today."

He turned to find a woman wearing an unzipped winter coat, carrying an armload of books and loose papers. Dark-skinned and pretty, she seemed too old to be an undergrad. Maybe another instructor.

"She has office hours again tomorrow morning," she added. "Maybe try back then."

"I will. Thanks."

"No problem." She headed past him, the heels of her boots clicking on the linoleum as she rounded the corner.

He waited until the noise had receded a comfortable distance, then glanced up and down the hall for onlookers or cameras. He tried the knob and it turned in his hand, letting him into a small, messy office. Daylight peeked through the blinds on a window behind the desk, enough that he didn't need to use his phone as a flashlight, which could have drawn attention from outside.

One wall was a bookshelf, filled with rows of books with others stuffed in on top. He put his attention on the desk first, since the bookshelf would take longer. It held a stack of papers, several books and three half-full coffee cups, all ice cold, as well as an empty space for a laptop. The books were all new, with library stickers.

Underneath them, a hand-written receipt caught his attention. It was from a local store, Antiquités Eclairé. He knew the name because Consilium researchers had regularly made a pilgrimage there from Toronto. Supposedly the place sometimes had legitimate books and artifacts. The receipt he held wasn't for a purchase from the store, but a sale to it: *Livres, misc.* $525.00.

Professor Nguyen had sold books to a Consilium-frequented occult store. It seemed like a long shot, but Daniel grabbed the receipt anyway and jammed it into his pocket. Then he turned to the over-stuffed bookcase. He skimmed the titles on the spines—where the books *had* legible titles—and pulled a few off to check them, only to put them back. Nothing he recognized from the Consilium, and nothing that seemed relevant.

Heavy footsteps echoed at a distance, growing steadily closer. Daniel willed them to pass by, but a shadow came into view in the frosted glass window on the door. He crept toward the door, wedging himself behind it when somebody tried the knob.

The door swung open and he held his breath as someone entered. Two people, large and broad-shouldered from what he could see through the frosted glass. Probably not Professor Nguyen.

They came in slowly, as if expecting someone. As soon as they turned, they'd see him.

Daniel slammed the door into the shoulder of the nearest one, darting from behind it at the same time to slip out of the office. The man he hadn't hit swung a fist that cuffed him in the side of the head, knocking him back into the desk.

The two men who'd been at the library and who'd chased him and Jude out of the coffee shop yesterday glowered at him from the doorway. Rogers and partner.

Daniel felt behind him on the desk for anything that could be a weapon. His fingers closed around a pencil, which didn't give him much confidence, but he chanced it anyway and tried to dodge between the two goons.

Rogers caught him by the back of his coat, swinging him into the bookcase beside the door. Hardcovers dug into Daniel's ribs and he released the pencil on the edge of the shelf, bracing his free hand to shove himself backwards.

The bigger man twisted Daniel's left arm to hold him against the bookcase. A sharp spasm burned through his shoulder as his muscles tried to stretch but stiffened instead.

He curled the fingers of his free hand against the shelf, trying to breathe evenly through the pain so he could think.

The second agent shut the door and then went through Daniel's pockets with brisk efficiency, removing his phone. He hovered to the side, messing with the device.

Probably expecting to find a fingerprint or face lock, the agent grunted in annoyance.

"What's the pass-code?" he demanded.

"Fuck you."

"Seems long for a pin," Rogers remarked, shifting the pressure on Daniel's arm to pull his left shoulder further out of shape. At his hiss of pain, Rogers chuckled. "Ah, this is the bad one, huh?"

A flood of shock numbed the burn for an instant. How did Rogers know about his shoulder? That injury had happened *after* the Consilium. There shouldn't be any record of it. Unless these agents had access to hospital records—and to the alias he'd been using for medical treatment at the time.

"What are you doing here?" The second agent asked, glancing around the office as if they'd missed something obvious.

"Looking for Professor Nguyen." Daniel gave them that one. His heart raced but he tried to breathe shallowly to keep from putting further pressure on his shoulder, where something felt ready to tear.

"Lucky you," Rogers said, voice tinging with irony. "We know where she is. Might even be able to get you an appointment with her." He nodded to his partner, who produced Daniel's phone again.

"How about you call your sister," the second man said. "Have her come meet you here. You can both see Nguyen."

Daniel hesitated what he hoped was long enough to be convincing, but not so long that they'd rescind the offer and come up with something worse.

"Fine," he muttered.

The second agent held the phone in front of him on the bookshelf so that he could use his free hand to type in the pin.

As soon as the agent's grip loosened, Daniel slid the phone forward, letting it plunge to the floor. He slammed his heel down on the screen hard enough to render it inoperable.

"Hey!" came a shout from outside, a woman's voice. "I know you're in there and I already called security!"

With both agents momentarily distracted, the pressure on Daniel's left arm relaxed enough to let him move. He snatched the pencil from the bookshelf with his free hand and stabbed it over his shoulder, rewarded when Rogers bellowed in pain and shifted his weight back.

Daniel bucked him off, freeing himself, and swung at the second man. He didn't connect but the other agent stumbled backwards to avoid him, giving him time to swipe the shattered phone from the floor and get the door open. Arm throbbing, he dashed out and swung around the next corner, running blind down the hallway away from the entrance he'd come in.

Someone hissed at him from a cracked door. With the heavy tread of the agents behind him, about to round the corner, Daniel threw himself toward it.

He stumbled into another dark office. A shadowy figure shut the door with enough care to make it silent. The woman he'd met in the hallway pressed her back to the door and locked it. This office was on the inside of the building, without a window. It made the frosted glass in the door opaque to the hallway outside.

They both listened to the hasty footsteps reach their end of the hall and pause. Daniel winced as someone rattled the knob, but the woman didn't move, and the men outside passed onto the next door, then continued away.

Neither he nor the woman spoke until the hallway had been silent for a good minute. Then the woman let out a deep sigh and turned on the lights.

Daniel blinked against the sudden brightness. They were in another office, a similar size to Professor Nguyen's, but sparser. "Are you sure you should—"

"They're gone." The woman waited another moment, then nodded. "Yeah, pretty sure."

"*Pretty* sure?"

"I'm all for hanging out in the dark together if you want, but I've also got a lot to do today." She jerked back, surprised as she focused on him in the overhead lights. "Wait, I know you. How do I know you?"

"We just met—" Daniel gestured to the hallway.

"Obviously. But no, you look like—" She straightened up as it came to her. "You're Grace's brother."

Too startled to answer, Daniel stepped back. His thigh connected with the desk behind him, causing it to creak.

"Darren?" she guessed, then snapped her fingers. "No, Daniel? Right? I'm Theresa Foster."

His expression must have made plain that the name meant nothing to him, so she added, "Tess. I was Grace's assistant on the Mumbai dig. I think you and I actually met once, at her wedding."

Daniel didn't remember her, but his sister's wedding had been five—six?—years ago, and mostly comprised of people he hadn't known. "Sorry, I—"

"No worries. It was a long time ago." She hesitated. "But Grace never mentioned me, huh? Guess she's still pissed I went to work for Marianne."

"Marianne Nguyen?"

"Yeah, I'm her research assistant. She got snatched by those assholes yesterday." Tess ran her hands back over her hair in a gesture of frustration. "I saw them come in. They told the secretary they were cops, but I doubt it." She hesitated, giving Daniel time to fill in any details he knew about the agents, but he didn't have any, so she finished, "I was going to use my lunch break to check out her office. Guess we had the same idea."

"Which Consilium office did you work in?" Daniel asked, still uneasy.

Tess's expression closed, eyes narrowing.

"Vancouver, after I got back from London," she said. "You want my ID number?"

"The Vancouver office got blown up last March, just like Toronto," Daniel pressed.

"It was my day off." Her tone turned defensive, angry—a tone he recognized painfully well. He heard the shame in it. "Where were *you* when Toronto went down?" she challenged.

"In the hospital." Jude's beating had saved him from dying with his colleagues when the Faerie Court had attacked.

"Well, you win." She squared her shoulders, as if pushing her anger back down. "Grace and the hubby were still in London. Marianne was visiting her sick sister. We've all got some jackpot reason we aren't dead."

The self-contempt dripping from the words washed roughly against Daniel, rallying his own guilt.

"I'm sorry," he said.

"No, I get it." Despite the words to the contrary, she still sounded angry. "I probably wouldn't believe me either. I only know you because I vaguely remember you from my boss's wedding." As she spoke, she seemed to slough off her guarded tone.

"Look," she said with a sigh. "I'll give you my number and you can have Grace call me. She'll remember me. She'll vouch for me."

When Daniel didn't move for his phone, she raised her eyebrows expectantly. He fished the shattered device out of his pocket and showed it to her.

She left the door to tear a piece of blank paper from the bottom of a stack on the desk, jotting numbers down on it. Straightening and passing it to him, she repeated, "Have Grace call me. We seriously need to compare notes."

14

GRACIE HUGGED HER COAT around her body as she studied the little trees on the faded wallpaper in the unfamiliar house. She didn't like the feel of this place, whether from some actual instinct or just the knowledge that it belonged to the Court, but it was a necessary evil. She was just glad Jude had answered her third call and agreed to help her use the Antagonist house to condense the distance between her brother's apartment and her own, forbidden one. Even though Jude's first question had been along the lines of, *what's in it for me?*

"Tell the door your address," Jude said, standing beside her at the front entrance. At Gracie's raised eyebrows, a smile eased its way across her features. "Seriously."

Gracie took a deep breath and recited her home address to the front door. Did the thing record that information? Did it matter? Unlikely they'd ever be going back to this apartment again to stay.

Jude opened the door and the outside scene had changed. They walked out into the lobby of Gracie's off-island apartment building fifteen kilometres away from where they'd met, right through the front doors.

"That's so weird," Gracie said, without meaning to.

"You get used to it." Jude shut the door behind them, replacing the foyer with the street scene outside the glass.

Gracie stopped in the tiny lobby, half-expecting to hear the pitter-patter of little enemy agent feet descending on them.

The place was silent and empty, like any afternoon. She led the way and they took the elevator to the fourth floor. The door to the apartment was locked, but the knob seemed to turn easier in Gracie's hand than she remembered. Was that just her imagination or had someone broken in?

She unlocked the door and let it swing gently open. Illuminated by the grey daylight coming through the open curtains, everything in the apartment seemed more or less in order, though she noted a few things that might have been rifled through. It didn't speak to her housekeeping lately that she couldn't immediately pick out the signs of an intruder.

Nothing stirred inside, but Gracie still hesitated, muscles tense for someone to try and grab her. When that didn't happen after a few more seconds, she stepped inside. Still nothing.

Jude followed her in and had the sense to close the door quietly behind them.

"I'll just be a second." Gracie headed for her bedroom. She'd stuffed the folder from her old office into a plastic box that fit under the bed, along with other things important enough to save but not important enough to take up space in the lock-box.

She hauled the box out from under the bed and lifted the top, fingers combing through stacks of papers and folders until she found an old-school manila envelope with a string closure. She extracted it and unwound the string from its paper circle—high tech security, here—then thumbed through the sheaf of papers until she found a set of photocopies: Arthi Al-Amin's *Treatise on the Fayrie Dead*, English translation.

Gracie tucked that under her arm and put the folder and the rest of its contents into a canvas shopping bag from her closet. She grabbed herself two shirts and a pair of jeans, then took the same for Ted. Finally, she made a quick tour of Riley's room, grabbing his two favourite picture books and a threadbare stuffed octopus, along with three changes of clothing, and stuffing them all into the bulky bag. Anything else to grab while she was here? Given it was probably the last time?

She upped that to definitely, since she'd given the address to a magical Antagonist house.

It wasn't the first time she'd walked away from a well-earned life. Usually it hadn't been her choice but her mother's that they move with no warning because the house—or the city, or the province—was compromised. A few, like walking away from her father as an adult, had been her own decision. But *probably*, she concluded grimly as she headed back down the hall to the front room where Jude waited, *this won't be the last.*

"Got it?" Jude eyed the bulging bag hanging from Gracie's shoulder.

"All good." Gracie passed the sheaf of papers from under her arm to the other woman. "Al-Amin's *Treatise*, as promised."

Jude rifled through the papers, frowning, until she found the chapter she wanted. She pressed the extra photocopies back on Gracie, already skimming the pages.

"We can find a copy shop," Gracie said pointedly. She accompanied that with a jerk of her chin toward the door. Before she could argue, Jude had folded the papers into quarters and stuffed that into the back pocket of her jeans.

"Guess you're not fully retired after all, huh?" she remarked.

"Who told you I was retired?" Gracie demurred.

"Daniel."

"How polite. I guess he's upped that from 'quitting.'"

Jude seemed to note the sharpness in her tone, but interpreted it differently than Gracie had intended.

"I really didn't come looking for him yesterday," she said, as if an excuse were required. "It was a coincidence. Wrong place, wrong time."

"If you say so."

"I *was* trying to do the normal life thing too, you know," the younger woman insisted. "I'm just a little low on marketable skills and generational wealth." With a sigh, she turned back to the door, putting her hand on the knob. "You want a copy shop around here or should we go back into town?"

"Let's go back." Gracie wished desperately for this to be over. She shouldn't have called Jude at all.

On the other hand, she'd gotten the papers she wanted and all it had cost was a modicum of embarrassment for being a domineering older sister. She was going to be that no matter what, and why did she care what Jude thought of her, anyway?

Jude summoned up the Court's house, leading Gracie inside. After the door had shut on Gracie's apartment, Jude rested her hand on the wood again, doing whatever magic she did to make the transport work. She pulled the door open a second time and they both stepped out, stopping short.

They stood in the wide, polished lobby of what looked like a hotel.

"Where—?" Gracie started.

Jude hissed in annoyance, turning back toward the door. The hallway of the magic house lingered beyond it, dim and cramped in comparison to the airy atrium with its marble floor and gold accents shining under soft overhead lights.

"Miss Waldron?" A voice from the left made both women turn.

An Asian man in an expensive blue suit had come to greet them at the door. "The Archduke sends his apologies for interrupting your passage, but feels it's imperative that he speak to you."

Gracie cast Jude a covert glance to see if she made sense of this.

Jude's startled expression faded into recognition. "The Archduke, huh?" She turned to Gracie. "Sorry, but I need to talk to him."

"Do *not* leave me here." Gracie wished she'd had the forethought to save her coolness toward the other woman for *after* Jude got her safely home.

Jude seemed too focused to notice or gloat, but she made clear to the man in the suit,

"She's with me."

15

After leaving the university, Daniel took the métro off-island and spent an hour pacing the nearest mall, keeping an eye out for pursuers. He hadn't caught a glimpse of either the agents or Tess Foster on his way out, but he couldn't shake the tension from his muscles. It exacerbated the burning pain that radiated from his shoulder up into his head.

He bought a meal from the food court and filled the paper soda cup with ice, pressing it to the space where his shoulder met his neck as often as he could without being too obvious.

Mindful of the shattered phone in his pocket, he ducked into the first mobile phone store he saw and bought a replacement. The clerk raised an eyebrow when he produced his old, ruined device but helped him extract the SIM card and load it into the new phone.

The card still seemed to be in good shape, because a minute after Daniel turned the new phone on, it pinged with a message.

Still up for 5à7 tonite?

Zeb. Daniel had completely forgotten they were supposed to meet for drinks. He considered cancelling, but it would be the third time that month he'd avoided his friend, and he hadn't yet warned Zeb about their new pursuers. Not that a group hunting down Consilium members should be interested in Zeb, who'd never been part of the defunct organization, but Daniel had promised to keep him in the loop and he wanted to make an effort.

He texted back in the affirmative, then almost used cash to take a cab back into Montreal, but in the end he decided to stick to the anonymity of his transit card and the crowd of a public bus. He arrived at the bar he and Zeb had previously agreed on forty-five minutes early and snagged a table near the back, ordering a shot of whisky and a beer. The whisky he downed immediately, but he left the beer untouched. He passed the time restoring his phone to some semblance of its previous incarnation, turning off every location and tracking ability he remembered and searching for new ones.

The bar got crowded right around five o'clock. Not long after, a wiry, Hispanic man with heavy, silver gauges shining in his earlobes made his way through the crowd.

"How'd you get the only table d'espionnage in the place?" Zeb asked, surprised to find Daniel already there.

"What's a spy table?"

"One where nobody can shoot you in the back." Zeb nodded past him and Daniel realized he'd chosen a chair in the corner of the bar.

"I got here early," he said, as if that were an answer.

"Guess you don't need a refill." The other man slung his jacket over the back of the second chair at the table and nodded toward Daniel's nearly full beer.

"Not yet."

Zeb headed to the bar to get his own drink. When he returned, he settled himself in his chair and ran a hand back through his short hair, seeming relieved to relax.

"How's it going?" he asked, taking a swig of his beer.

"There's some new group hunting down the Consilium survivors. You should keep an eye out."

Zeb considered that. "It's simultaneously refreshing and annoying how we don't do small talk."

"Sorry." Daniel chuckled despite himself. "Je veux dire, ça va? Boost any cars lately? Other crime? Fill me in."

"I said fifty-fifty good and bad." Zeb rolled his eyes. "Why d'you think they'd be interested in me?"

"I don't know. They're aware of things that happened after the Consilium." His shoulder twinged in agreement.

Zeb stiffened. "Like the museum?"

"No. I don't think so." As far as Daniel knew, they'd cut the security cameras and gotten out clean at the O'Meara museum. He'd checked the news for a few weeks after, when he could, and hadn't come across any mention of the theft. If this new group thought he, Zeb and Jude had taken the agate cross from the museum, it could only be a suspicion. "All the same, it's not a bad time to get out of town for a while."

Zeb fixed him with a knowing look. "That what you're doing?"

"Maybe," Daniel conceded. It was what Gracie seemed to want, anyway.

"Très croyable." The ironic tone didn't lift until Zeb sighed, taking another drink of his beer, then ventured: "Maybe I can help."

"It's safer if—"

"—You don't have to worry about me."

"I wasn't going to say that."

"Tu veux dire que tu ne vas pas utiliser ces mots."

"Gracie's here," Daniel said, by way of explaining his reluctance to involve his friend. "In Montreal. At my place. With my nephew. And Ted's probably joined them by now. It's a one-bedroom and . . . it's a lot. So I'm not in this alone but, honestly, man, I don't have room."

"Sounds more like you need a place to crash."

"Then you'd definitely be in the cross-hairs."

"You say that like it's a bad thing."

"Can't wait to get stabbed again?" Daniel wished the words back almost immediately.

"No." Zeb downed the last of his beer, unfazed. "But I don't run from a fight."

"It's not your fight."

"Then why are you warning me about it?" Zeb challenged.

Daniel tapped his fingers on his sweating glass but didn't lift it, prompting his friend to add,

"You know you're really bad at asking for help, right?"

"I don't want your help." He kept the words as neutral as he could manage. "I want you to stay out of it, but you needed to be aware. I don't know what this group is doing with the people they take. I don't know anything about—"

A slow, painful vibration started in his bones, bringing a swell of nausea and stopping him short. His eyes snapped to a cowboy hat moving at a distance through the crowd.

Bolting up from the table, he managed, "Be right back," before he left Zeb and pushed through the crowd to reach the bar. He scanned for the brown Stetson in better light. The spell in his head pushed him toward the narrow hallway to the bathrooms.

Stepping into the hall was like crossing a barrier, moving into another world. The noise of the bar dipped under the increased grinding of the magic in his skull, pointing him toward one of the bathrooms.

Abe and a hulking man who towered even over the cowboy hat waited inside.

"Sorry about the—" Abe tapped the side of his head to indicate triggering the spell. He nodded toward the giant beside him. "This is the pal I told you about," he said. "Can excise the incantation from your memory. Won't view or touch anything else, won't harm you or do any damage. And afterwards, you get your blood back." The cowboy flashed a vial between two fingers.

"Here?" Daniel cast an uncertain eye around the empty bathroom, regretting asking the cowboy for help all over again.

"Rather go back to your place?" Abe returned. "Or the house?"

"No." Sickening dread filled him at the thought of being in that awful Antagonist house with the incantation howling to get out. Leaving with these two to go anywhere else would mean dodging Zeb, and with the spell already going wild, Daniel wasn't sure he had the capacity to explain the situation to his friend. Zeb might assume he was under a thrall and try to intercede.

Abe prompted, "If you change your mind, Mab's orders to our friend here are to kill you. He tries to do that, I'm liable to step in to help you out and then he'll kill us both. I mean, look at him. He could rip both of us in two without breaking a sweat."

The mage cast a sidelong glare at the cowboy as if resenting the sly humour in his voice as much as Daniel did.

"You want that on your conscience at the Pearly Gates?" Abe finished.

"Honestly wouldn't mind right now," Daniel muttered. But he couldn't run. He had no other options. This was what he'd asked for. The spell buzzed like a swarm of hornets, swelling to a crescendo that made him feel faint.

He winced as a new, low voice echoed in his head. The melodic rhythm of the foreign language tugged at his memory as he fought to translate, but the big mage's words came too fast.

"Wait," he snapped. "I can't—temporary what?"

The mage glanced to Abe and the two seemed to have a wordless conversation.

"He says there might be some side effects," the cowboy relayed. "Disorientation, headache in the short term. Temporary memory loss, maybe."

Daniel's stomach shifted but he managed to nod, then returned his eyes to the mage.

"Your word," he reminded him. The giant would be the one performing the extraction. Abe was part-human, his word meant nothing. He had nothing to lose.

The large man extended a hand, as if to shake on the deal. Words echoed in Daniel's mind, in halting, accented English.

"I will take only the spell which have been offered. I will not observe or change another native thought, memory, impulse or desire. This is given my word."

The telepathic voice stirred the spell in his head into a fury, making Daniel dizzy enough to see double. The air around them grew heavier and breathing became a challenge. He had no choice but to brace himself and extend his own hand.

The mage's closed around it like a clammy vice.

16

OUR GUIDE LED US into a mirrored elevator operated by a special key. Grace shifted uneasily beside me as we ascended, so I tried to play it cool, like I knew what was doing.

When we reached the thirtieth floor, we stepped out into a hallway made up of huge windows, looking out over a city of enormous buildings I'd never seen before. Millions of multi-coloured lights sparkled in the darkness, stretching to the horizon.

Not Montreal. Not even Toronto.

"Where the hell are we?" I demanded.

"Singapore," the man in the suit answered, as if it should have been obvious.

"Oh, of course. How silly of me." I mimicked his calm tone. We proceeded down the hall to a set of double doors. No guards. The place seemed empty.

Our guide stopped in front of a door and turned to me, laying his palm out.

"Your beacon, please," he said.

"My *what*?"

"In your right pocket." He inclined his head toward my jacket.

I put a hand in and found Gordon's egg. A beacon? I gritted my teeth at my own stupidity. I should have known the Mab's mage would find some way to stalk me even without the sylph.

After I dropped the egg into his waiting hand, the man rapped on the door and then opened it without awaiting an answer. He ushered us inside and closed the door.

We stood in the front room of a suite done in white, blue and gold. Despite being ritzy, it was lived-in—not impeccably clean and starched. A laptop and a can of some foreign brand of soda sat on the desk, along with no doubt expensive headphones.

"That was quick." A man entered the room, clasping his hands together. "Judith. It was brought to my attention that you wanted an audience with me."

"Jude," I corrected, then added, "And let's be real, *an audience* sounds a little desperate. You're the Archduke?" Seeing him, I finally recognized Declan Raj from his picture on the Internet tabloids. Besides being Faerie, he was also brutally hot. *Down, girl. Enemy,* I warned myself.

Guitarist, a traitor voice whispered back.

The enemy guitarist appeared in his mid-thirties—definitely glamour if he had a full-grown daughter. He was taller than me, with his dark hair rolled into dreadlocks that nearly reached his shoulders. Colourful tattoos peeked from beneath his t-shirt sleeves on both arms, standing out against his bronze skin. He had a deep red bandana knotted around one wrist. Maybe not all redcaps actually wore hats.

"Have a seat." He gestured to a soft, cushy blue sofa. Two clear, matching vases of bizarre flowers flanked it. They seemed upside down in their containers—mirrored, silvery leaves shone in the water and delicate gnarled roots rose up into the air. Tiny flowers bloomed from the roots, butter-yellow.

"Saskia's favourite," the Archduke drawled, noticing me noticing. "They're difficult to cultivate here, since they won't grow in inferior earth."

"Maybe they're too weak," I shot back.

He ignored that. "You wish to speak with her, I believe?"

"Yep." I sat down and Grace lowered herself gingerly beside me.

The Archduke waited a beat to see if I'd expand on that single word. When I didn't, he offered, "I can provide a companion to entertain your pet."

The word disgusted me, but I couldn't help shooting Grace a sidelong glance. To my surprise, she gazed at the Archduke with a hazy, blank expression.

He'd done something to her.

"Stop it," I snapped, starting to get to my feet.

"I thought we could talk privately."

"You thought wrong. She stays with me. And quit thralling."

A subtle blue light flashed in his eyes, so fast I almost missed it. It made him appear less human for that instant, and it was enough to remind me that I wasn't bantering with a hot guitarist.

He snapped his gaze away and Grace gasped beside me, twitching like she'd just woken from a nightmare.

"It's okay," I told her, my words falling woefully short. Nothing was okay. We were prisoners of a Faerie rock star. I added sharply, as much to the Archduke as Grace, "He *won't* do that again."

Declan looked amused. He glanced over his shoulder into the hallway he'd emerged from, calling, "Saskia, the Mabling is here."

"The *what* now?" I started, stopping when the surly redcap appeared in the doorway. She wasn't wearing her tuque, yet she had her glamour to make her appear human. She padded into the room in red socks. Harder for me to rip off in a fight, I guess.

She and her father had the same thin, ironic mouth and predatory eyes fringed with heavy lashes. If glamour typically chose a Faerie's human form, like Gordon had said, it made sense there was a family resemblance.

"I didn't know who you were," was the first thing she said. "If I had, I wouldn't have—" Deciding better of giving away further details, she finished in a flat tone, "I'm sorry."

"That's not why I'm here," I said. "Did you do something to the guy I was with?"

"The . . . what?" She glanced to her father to make sense of the question. When that gave her nothing, her eyes flickered back to me. "There was no one with you."

"Yes, there was. Chris was with me when you jumped me."

She studied my face, lips half-parted for a good few seconds before understanding dawned on her.

"A human?" She sputtered the word, stunned. Again she threw that *are you hearing this insanity?* look to the Archduke. "I didn't touch your human. I haven't even fed since that night. I've been searching for my sword." She narrowed her eyes but didn't mention my taking it off her in front of her father.

"What were you doing in Montreal?" I asked.

The Archduke cleared his throat, indicating to his daughter that she didn't need to answer this, but she lifted her chin and told me with a hint of defiance,

"I have friends there. What were *you* doing there? Aren't you from the sticks somewhere to the west?"

"I have friends too." I hoped Grace's expression wouldn't contradict that. "Did you see anybody else after the party? Around the bus stop? Besides me and Chris?"

"No." Saskia kept her voice even. "I don't believe so, but I was . . . singularly focused."

"So, you don't remember anything else?" I wished Abe were here for this. He'd have been able to read her emotions, maybe let me know if she were lying.

Had to go off my own gut, then. Saskia seemed like the type who'd be bragging about it to me if she did know something, wanting to cut me to the bone with details about slicing the hearts out of the men I'd known.

"I have your sword," I admitted. "Safe under my bed."

Fury flared in her eyes but she controlled the rest of her expression.

"If that's all," the Archduke started to say, but I interrupted him.

"Did either of you break the Shadow Mab out of her prison and start killing men to make her corporeal?"

Grace stared at me in shock and Saskia barked a quick, startled laugh. The Archduke's initial surprise faded into a slow smile.

"No." He sounded more entertained then offended by the accusation, and took pleasure in correcting me. "We've had no such interaction with the Shadowed Mab."

That half-amused denial didn't make the Faerie guitarist trustworthy but I was on his turf, and responsible for Grace to boot. I couldn't exactly call him out or demand proof, as much as I wanted to.

Still, no reason to waste an opportunity with a guy who supposedly kept tabs on the shady magic in this world and had influence. Maybe he'd be interested in getting on my good side, as heir to the Mab's throne. It was about time for that title to benefit *me*.

"Then can you look into it for me?" I asked, in a last-ditch effort. "Poke around. Talk to people you know. Find out who's behind it."

"What will I get in return?"

"My trust."

His derisive laugh danced on my last nerve. So much for that.

"With all due respect, Mabling," he said in a tone implying that amount was zero, "I never give something for nothing. In fact, I could argue that I've allowed you to interrogate my daughter with no evidence of wrongdoing, and that constitutes a debt."

"Then I'd argue *back* that she attacked me first, which she *admitted* at the very beginning of this *interrogation*."

His smile thinned, but to my surprise, he sat back, arms resting lazily on the sides of the chair like a king on a throne.

"If you come across something of more *tangible* value to bargain with," he said, voice growing more distant and dismissive, "perhaps I can find something for you."

"If you find something, maybe I'll give a shit." I got to my feet, happy to get out while the getting was good.

Grace shot upright beside me to trail me toward the door.

The guy from the lobby opened it just as we reached the threshold like he'd been waiting for us. He took us back down in the silent, mirrored elevator.

"Your beacon," he said, offering me the small, speckled egg Gordon had given me.

"Keep it."

He returned us to the lobby and opened a door to let Grace and me back into the house. I shut it in his face and sagged against the solid wood, wondering if the deadbolt on it was just for show. My muscles went rubbery. "I feel like I just failed a quiz," I muttered, then offered, "Sorry."

"Not your fault, apparently." Grace seemed winded from the experience too. "Have I seen him somewhere before?"

"Everywhere. He's famous."

She started to shake her head, then stopped, realization dawning on her. "Oh."

"I know," I said. It still threw me that the Archduke had spoken like a politician, and not a guitarist. I guess you didn't rise to power in Faerie with a few fancy guitar tricks. Did he tour in the Faerie realm? Was the whole band Faerie? What other celebrities were—?

"How did he disrupt the door?" Grace asked.

A much better question.

"I don't know," I admitted. "This is only, like, the third time I've used it." Should have asked him how he'd managed that trick, but it would have lost me the upper hand.

Not that I'd necessarily had it, anyway—me, the uninformed, raggedy half-Faerie who'd recently rolled around in an alley and slept on a bathroom floor.

"Well," I concluded, "now you can say you've been to Singapore."

17

I MANAGED TO GET Grace and I back to Montreal on the second try. As we stepped out of a doorway that turned out to be the apartment across the hall from Daniel's, we almost walked into two people.

"Tabarnak," Zeb muttered, drawing the Quebecois expletive out in frustration as he saw us. He glanced from me to Grace and then to the door we'd emerged from, brow furrowed. "Did you just . . . is that your place?"

"No," Grace said, starting an explanation.

I barely heard it, my attention too fixed on Daniel, who leaned heavily against his friend. He didn't look right, fumbling to get his key into the lock.

"Is he okay?" I asked.

"Ça va bien, chiquita, fuck off," Zeb snapped.

The mix of languages threw me for a second but I ignored him, drawing closer. Daniel was dazed and exhausted and the air around us felt charged. He hadn't acknowledged our presence at all, which felt a little weird. I'd have understood if he was purposely ignoring me but he wouldn't pull that with his sister.

"Hey, Danny." I made my voice sharp to get his attention, then regretted it when he fixed on me, startled. Like he hadn't even seen me to begin with.

"Jude." He didn't slur my name the way he might have if he'd been drunk. He sounded distant, putting the name to my face by pure force of habit as if neither one meant anything to him.

It hurt. Beyond that, it chilled me.

"You know who I am?" I pressed

The question made Daniel sigh. His voice gained an edge of annoyance as he said, "Go away."

"Looks like he knows you," Zeb concluded, making me want to punch him.

"What happened?" Grace demanded.

"I guess we had one too many." Zeb's tone became more diplomatic than when he'd snapped at me. "Which was, uh . . . one. But he—"

"It's magic," I interrupted. "It smells like—it's not a smell. It's a . . . like the air is kind of liquid?"

As I struggled for better words, Grace extracted the keys from her brother's hand. A piece of paper fell from his fist as she did so and she swept it up. After blinking at it a moment, she asked,

"Is this a phone number?"

"Tess. Tess's number," Daniel answered, voice still distant.

A dubious expression crossed Grace's face and her lips thinned. She seemed to be suppressing an eye-roll. She crumpled the paper back into her hand with the keys and unlocked the door.

"I'll take it from here," she told Zeb, letting him transfer Daniel's weight to her shoulders. "Thanks."

The last word was directed solely at him, cutting me out. As if I hadn't gotten her to her apartment *and* safely back from Singapore.

She'd closed the door before I could argue—not that I had an argument to make, but I might have tried.

Instead, I faced Zeb's scowl.

"What are you even doing here?" he demanded.

"Helping Grace." I hated how defensive I sounded. It wasn't like I'd weaseled my way in with subterfuge or anything. *She* had called *me*. "What happened?"

He scoffed and started to push past me, but I grabbed his sleeve and hung on. Knots twisted my insides. "Zeb. Did something magic go down?"

"No." He yanked his arm away, then rubbed the back of his neck in a nervous gesture, avoiding my eyes. "I don't know. We were just having a beer and Daniel went somewhere and when he came back he was . . . like that. Pretty incoherent." His expression closed and he eyed me. "This have something to do with you? Again?"

"No!" Cringing inwardly as I shed my plausible deniability, I couldn't help adding, "But, did you see, like, anybody in a Swamp Thing costume?" Zeb's eyes widened as I continued, "Tall, green, slimy?"

"Is *that* what's after Consilium people?" he sputtered. "Some Faerie monster?"

"No. This is something . . . else." If Zeb had seen something weird and magical like the slime creature, he'd be blabbing all about it. He would have mentioned it to Grace. This was a waste of time. "Forget it."

A different concern bubbled to the surface without my permission. "Who's Tess?"

Zeb gaped at me for a moment, then to my surprise, he laughed. Not the friendly or amused kind, but a sharp, derisive one.

"I don't know," he finally said.

It didn't matter. It wasn't my business and Zeb was right to mock any shreds of jealousy trying to rear their stupid heads. Daniel had a right to all the phone numbers he wanted to collect at a bar. I had no claim on him. I shouldn't care.

"Why are you here?" Zeb drew my attention back, sounding both tired and pissed off as he repeated his initial query. "What do you get out of this? Is it some game, fucking with him every and now then?"

"No." Anger flooded my muscles but I held my ground. "Since when are you so protective, Mama Bear?"

"Since he's my friend. And since it seems like every time you show up, he ends up bleeding."

That shouldn't have made me wince, not after all this time. The words still slid through my ribs like a knife, making it hard to breathe for a moment.

"I wasn't along for this ride," I managed. "Guess Danny can get himself into trouble just fine without my help."

"Then why don't you get lost? Go back into your . . . apartment or whatever." Zeb waved a hand toward the opposite door, a hint of bewilderment breaking through his righteous anger.

It would have been funny if I hadn't been so pissed off.

"It's not my apartment," I snapped. "It's a Faerie safehouse that appears behind whatever door I want and I'm not a fucking stalker living across the hall and you can go to hell."

He stared at me for a moment, deciding whether or not to re-engage, then concluded: "Noted."

18

GRACIE HAULED HER BROTHER into his apartment and locked the door behind them. The front room was lit but empty, and the place smelled like pizza. The calm baritone of her husband's voice floated down the hall from the bedroom. He was reciting a favourite bedtime book of Riley's that both he and she knew by heart because Riley requested it at least every other night. Gracie had the physical copy in the bag on her shoulder.

She hadn't realized it was already dark outside back here in Montreal. She checked the time on her phone. Nearly eight—how had they been in Singapore that long?

Daniel moved away from her, starting to take his jacket off in a strange, automatic way. She let him go, watching with nervous anticipation and ready to jump in. He thrust his jacket in the vicinity of the hook by the door, then went straight for the sofa, kicked off his shoes and curled up there.

"Are you okay?" she asked.

"Tired," he returned with a sigh.

He sounded more or less normal. Gracie hadn't seen her brother drunk in a long time, but in the past it had tended to make him *more* conversational, not less.

"What happened?" she tried.

He murmured something she couldn't quite catch, eyes already closed.

Jude's insistence about the use of magic rang in Gracie's head like a warning bell. She grabbed the iron wrench from the kitchen bar. She passed it from one hand to the other, then made up her mind and crept over to her brother's prone form to gently press the metal against his hand.

Daniel jerked awake and blinked up at her, puzzled. He took the wrench as if she were offering it to him and studied it with a frown. Then he turned on his side to face the back of the sofa, still holding it.

Not Antagonist thrall, then. Or, probably not—Gracie didn't quite remember all of the rules about iron and magic. Maybe he *was* just drunk. Not like it'd be the first time Zeb didn't have the whole story.

Why the fuck had he gone out with Zeb, anyway? As if it were safe to just run around the city like usual.

She finally thought to put down the bulky canvas bag, leaving it on the kitchen bar before removing her own jacket. As she retrieved her brother's from the floor to hang it up, she couldn't help plunging her hand into the pocket. She didn't know what she expected to find that could explain his current state—a receipt for the bottle of whisky he'd downed before Zeb had joined him? A handful of half-smoked joints?

Her fingers brushed metal and she pulled out three dull iron nails. She turned them over in her fingers, trying and failing to suppress the unpleasant memory the uneven, hand-worked heads brought up.

When she'd been about ten years old, and Daniel eight, their mother had brought home a cache of small, hand-worked iron nails. She'd insisted on sewing them into the linings of their clothes to ward off supernatural strangers. Gracie could still feel the way the rough tips had caught her skin through the fabric, the stinging red scratches. It hadn't taken her more than an hour to get fed up. With her brother keeping a look out, she'd stolen a pair of nail scissors from the bathroom and taken them to the clumsy stitches on both her clothing and his.

Their mother hadn't gotten angry, or tried it a second time, but she had made them both hold the nails tightly in their palms for a full ten minutes to make sure they hadn't been bewitched. The weight of the nails in Gracie's palm now stirred old, painful embers in her gut. Why was her brother carrying these?

She dumped them onto the counter and dipped her hand into the left pocket of Daniel's jacket. This time, she came up with a tiny, glass vial containing something dark. She held it up to the kitchen light, feeling a strange lack of surprise when it tinged red.

"Hey." Ted appeared in the hallway. Despite the casual greeting, a strain in his calm voice gave away his relief to see her. "Where've you been?"

Gracie inclined her head toward the kitchen, inviting him through the dark living room to join her in the separate space.

"It's hard to explain," she sighed, "but Singapore."

"Jude took you to *Singapore*?"

"Not on purpose."

"An accidental trip doesn't exactly sound better."

"It was unpleasant, it's over, and the errand is finished," Gracie summed up.

"Don't do that." Ted cracked a half-smile, but there was very little mirth in it. "I want more than the Cliffs Notes."

It was something they'd struggled with. Both of them defaulted to giving the least amount of worrying information to one another—Gracie due to her childhood and Ted more as a carryover from his security job with the Consilium—but they'd been doing better the last few months.

Gracie still related an abridged version of her afternoon, mentioning the clothing and things of Riley's she'd picked up and mostly glossing over the trip to see the Faerie Archduke. She held back on the brief interlude where she'd been sitting on his sofa next to Jude then blacked out for what had seemed like only a minute. She had to process that herself first, before she could tell her husband. Nothing had happened—she was ninety-eight percent sure of that. Ninety-nine.

Ted opened the refrigerator and pulled two beers out of the back, offering one to her.

"You go ahead," she said. "One of us should stay sober, just in case."

The words chafed her, even as she said them. Her whole life right now felt like one long, cautious *just in case*. Caution hadn't kept them safely in their apartment. It hadn't kept her from being ported away to Singapore or thralled and at the mercy of some dangerous Antagonist.

"Oh, fuck it." She accepted the extra bottle and the opener from her husband and pried the top off.

He wrapped an arm around her shoulder, squeezing tightly, then used his other hand to knock his bottle gently into hers.

"Santé."

"I love you," Gracie said.

"Cheers to that," Ted agreed, planting a kiss on the top of her head before taking a swig of the beer.

As the warm weight of his arm pushed the tension from her shoulders, she was startled to realize just how much she'd been carrying. Being transported across the world without her consent, the dark and missing minutes of time, the suspense of the eerie hotel and the uncertainty of whether Jude would abandon her or they'd both be killed, the fear she'd never see Ted or Riley again . . .

It had hit her harder than she'd expected. She'd been making snap decisions and thinking on her feet to keep herself and her loved ones safe for so long that it seemed odd to realize her instincts had dulled. Her need for that high tension act, the adrenaline high, had blunted. Life had been so damn *predictable* lately. Not that raising a toddler was calm and quiet, but it was definitely a different kind of chaos.

As if reading her mind, her husband said quietly, "We can't stay here."

"I know." It was only a matter of time before somebody chased them back to this apartment, no matter what precautions her brother had taken to secure it. "Daniel's going to be a hard sell," she muttered. "He's got himself mixed up in this new Antagonist mess."

"Given your errand today, it sounds like you're both invested." Ted seemed to be picking his words carefully and it made Gracie swallow a pang of shame.

"Today was a mistake," she said. "I'm out. We're out." She took a sip of her beer. Bitter and flavourless, it left her throat dry and she set the bottle aside, regretting having opened it. "So, let's figure out where we're going."

19

"Jude!" My roommate Marie-Eve sang my name as I came through the door. Her heavily accented, melodious tone meant she was already on something. "Sort avec moi!"

After grabbing my fast food dinner, I'd been hoping for, of all things, a quiet evening at home, but Marie-Eve twirled in place to show off her tight black dress.

"We are going out dancing." She didn't specify further on the 'we,' but she had a lot of friends. "Tu veux venir?"

When I hesitated, a smile split her face.

"Ouais." A knowing twist infused her words, "You want to."

"I have to shower." It had been hard to stop off at the A&W knowing I still smelled like a dumpster and looked like I'd slept on a floor, but French fries usually won any argument. I glanced down at my jeans and long-sleeved tee, already worn out by the idea of going through my closet for something tight and sparkly to match her. "And only if you're going somewhere without a dress code."

"Jeans are fine. Maybe just change your . . ." She made vague gestures toward the rumpled top under my hoodie and coat, ". . . chandail."

I shed the coat, wadding it into a ball to throw in my laundry.

"Maybe I just stay in."

"Oh my god, non! It's been so long since we went out together. I find you something and we go. Voilà. C'est ça." She disappeared down the hall to her bedroom.

As if I could fit into her tops. Marie-Eve had a body like a ten-year-old and she liked clothes that, as my mother would have said, left nothing to the imagination. Coming from my mother, though, that was a compliment.

"I have a shirt," I told her, following her down the hall but veering into my own tiny room.

"Pas un t-shirt, la!" She appeared in my doorway, already holding three brightly coloured tops in stretchy fabric. One had sequins. Nobody'd told me sequins were back.

I moved past her into the bathroom, and into a shower that started hot and turned lukewarm before I'd rinsed the shampoo out of my hair. Even the tepid water summoned relief into my muscles. Maybe I'd just never leave the spray. Marie-Eve would get bored eventually and head out and then I could just stand in the shower all night.

Stand in the shower and brood until it ran ice cold. Rock solid Saturday night plans there. I needed a distraction from the shitty two days I'd just had, and from the numberless ones looming on the horizon.

I wrapped myself in a clean towel and contemplated the puddle of nasty clothing I'd left on the floor. I didn't want them infecting my bedroom. Marie-Eve wasn't going to spend much time in our bathroom tonight anyway, so I toed the pile to one side, almost behind the toilet, a decision to be made by tomorrow's Jude. I did remember to pull the folded papers Grace had given me from the back pocket of my jeans.

My roommate pounced as soon as I opened the bathroom door. She held up two hangers, each bearing a black dress. "Okay, je sais que tu n'aime pas les robes, mais—"

"Pants only," I told her, hugging the towel around my body and slipping into my own bedroom. "It's practically snowing out there."

I shut my door and unfolded the paper in my hands. *Chapter 12: The Extraordinary Situation of the Unfaded Mab.* It started out by glossing over what Grace had already told me about the Shadow Mab becoming a shade and being banished to some separate, fenced-off area of Faerieland. No specifics about what kept her there.

The author spent a whole page relating how they'd learned all of this information from a Faerie named Peony Leaf that they'd captured using a gold ring and a loaf of bread soaked in vinegar, left in the middle of a fresh rain puddle at midnight—pretty sus. Even more that Peony Leaf happened to have been to the Land of Shades and was happy to do an interview after being captured.

My skimming turned up nothing about breaking the curse. According to Peony Leaf, it was impossible for the shade queen to leave her realm, but corporeal, living Fae *could* go to her. It wasn't recommended as a tourist destination, on account of the Shadowed Mab turning your eyes inward and burning out your free will, but it wasn't forbidden. Every few hundred years, a daring rabble-rouser or anarchist seemed to have found their way there seeking help to overthrow the Mab, or the whole Court, or just some specific noble they had beef with, but it never worked.

History and myth. No mention of the cult. Nothing helpful to finding Chris.

"Voyons donc!" Marie-Eve whined from beyond my closed door, extending all three syllables to their breaking point and almost adding a fourth.

It felt like a betrayal to toss the papers down on my bed, so I tucked them back into the pocket of the clean, black jeans I pulled from the floor of my closet. Going out with Marie-Eve wouldn't help Chris, but neither would sequestering myself in my bedroom and staring at a few useless photocopies of Peony Leaf's Visit to ShadeLand.

I snagged a plain red halter with a plunging cowl neck-line and opened my door to give Marie-Eve a 'ta da' motion.

She wasn't impressed.

"Au moins c'est rouge, mais you are so boring," she complained. "You work dans une friperie. There's all kinds of good clothes there. Colourful, fun! Tu connais le fun?"

"Fun and I haven't been tight lately." Maybe not the best time to mention I didn't work at the thrift store anymore either.

Nor did I have a coat. I'd been getting by with variations on my fleece hoodie and the corduroy jacket and both were now officially out of commission thanks to Rogers and his partner. Despite her insistence on holding up her stretchiest dresses to share, Marie-Eve's jackets were not going to fit at all.

"Voilà!" she exclaimed, bringing something out from her own room and offering it to me. "It's Guy's. Doesn't zip, mais c'est chaud."

I had no choice but to accept her boyfriend's quilted, plaid flannel coat, undoubtedly bought in some fit of irony, given he wasn't actually a lumberjack or one of the old men from my neighbourhood sports bar. At least it was big enough that I could hold it closed by folding my arms over my chest, and the red matched my top.

We caught a bus and the métro to a club to meet her friends. Marie-Eve spent most of the trip coordinating with whoever we were meeting via messaging app, but she also gave me highlights from her workday in Frang-lish. She somehow managed to have and keep a full-time job, despite spending most of her mornings snoozing off hangovers in bed.

At our destination, she exchanged a secret handshake with the bouncer to get us in for free. She didn't have an in with coat-check though, so we both had to pay our dollar to stash those.

It was more than worth it once we'd ducked through the curtain. Along with the pulsing EDM and flashing lights, the heat of the crowd inside enveloped me like a hug.

A man sitting alone at a three-person high-top waved us over. He'd been there on his phone while other people clustered around, giving him less-than-clandestine dirty looks for holding the table by himself.

"You didn't say Guy was coming." I froze at the sight of Marie-Eve's boyfriend.

"Guy always comes," was her response. I should have known better than to think this would be a girls' night out.

I tried to take the seat furthest away from our male companion but at the round three-top, that proved impossible.

Marie-Eve kissed her boyfriend, then shouted that she knew one of the bartenders and went to get us drinks.

"Salut." Guy lifted his chin toward me, still half-playing on his phone.

"Hey." I leaned back in my chair to make it clear to any Faerie shade cultists watching that we were not together. Sylph or no sylph, I should leave. Guy wouldn't care—it would be a lot easier to slip away from him than Marie-Eve anyway.

Just as I'd opened my mouth to make some vague excuses, a group of people Guy knew flooded over to the table. They all exclaimed and exchanged air-kisses, a few of them acknowledging me with a nod.

Marie-Eve returned with some ostensibly gin-based cocktail that was too sweet to taste the booze. She made up for that by also ordering a round of vodka shots when a waitress came by.

"I forgot to tell you," she shouted. "Ton amie passed by to pick up her—" She made a wavy gesture with her hand. When I didn't get that, she looked to Guy for help translating. "C'est quoi une épée en anglais?"

"Sword." I put it together from the wreck of my day before Guy could answer. Saskia had come to my apartment? And Marie-Eve had let her in, let her into my *bedroom* to steal her damn sword back?

I didn't have the energy to marvel that Marie-Eve didn't seem bothered by the idea of my having a sword in my bedroom, but there was no use being annoyed with her. She was already deep in conversation with Guy about something else. It was my fault for telling Saskia where I'd stashed the thing.

I welcomed the pounding music that surged into my head. Let it drown out my lingering serious thoughts. Marie-Eve was right that I needed to get reacquainted with fun.

A couple of her friends arrived at our table. After we'd gone through more obligatory introductions where no one could really hear each other, I tried to pay attention to the conversation. Maybe the reason I didn't feel at home here in Montreal was that I wasn't giving it a chance, wasn't giving myself a chance at a more normal life. I'd sworn off the Faerie crown, sure, but I hadn't made an effort to do anything different.

Having a Shadow Mab gunning for me wasn't the best time to make normal friends, though. I scanned the dance floor, then the bar. It was crowded, but not too. It would be quick to grab another drink myself, then I could grind off some of this anxiety in front of the DJ and try to forget the day I'd had.

My shoulders tightened when I thought I saw Daniel walk up to the bar. Another second told me it wasn't him, just some other handsome, dark-haired guy that my fuzzy brain had imposed his features on. Danny wouldn't set foot in a place like this. Too loud, too crowded. He'd rather drink someplace quiet, where he could translate some Faerie runes in a dark corner with a glass of Scotch.

Me too, minus the busy work and swap the mouthful of ash that he called booze for a proper whisky. Still, tonight the rush of music and kinetic energy in the club made me feel easier, like I could breathe. Safely alone in a crowd.

And Daniel was safe too, at home, with Grace and Zeb there to figure out whatever magic had been worked on him. Had the Shadow Mab's cultists tried to grab him with one of those walking spells I'd encountered at Chris's place? The one I'd seen had knocked me unconscious, though, and Daniel had been awake, just not really himself.

My stomach shifted as I thought of his expression changing, his sullenly telling me to go away once he'd recognized me. Was he angry I'd put him in this situation, or still about the *other* time I'd nearly killed him? Maybe he'd just been disappointed I wasn't Tess, whoever the hell she was.

Marie-Eve nudged me with her shoulder.

"Why are you—what's the word?" She glanced to her boyfriend.

"Brooding?" Guy grinned.

"Non, ce n'est pas brooding, c'est—"

"I need to dance," I said, sliding out of my chair and away from them, bee-lining for the dance floor. I didn't want to think anymore.

The song was a pulsing remix of a Quebecois pop song I knew from the sorting room at the thrift store. It felt good to writhe the tension out of my muscles and let the anxiety, the uncertainty, and that strange, protective pique that had reared its head dissipate. I didn't know the next two songs but I kept dancing, losing myself in the heat of the strangers pressed around me.

I caught a flash of familiar electric-green eyes from the sunglasses of a club kid dancing nearby. Not from *him*—actually from the reflection in his glasses.

Startled, I spun to search the crush of dancers around me for my aunt's disapproving face. Bodies swayed against mine from both sides, knocking into me as I stood rooted to the floor.

Miranda wasn't here. When the back of my neck continued to prickle unpleasantly, I elbowed my way through the crowd and high-tailed it for the ladies room, intent on shutting myself in a stall to take a few breaths and figure out whether I was hallucinating.

I doubted I was that lucky.

As soon as I entered, the crowd of women who'd been clustered around the sink, as well as the ones in the stalls, all filed past me with a startling immediacy and disappeared out the door.

"Jude." My aunt's voice came from above the sinks.

Fuck.

Mirrors could be gateways, phones from Faerieland. Apparently I hadn't imagined it, and mirrored sunglasses lenses on a dance floor worked the same.

In what had previously been the reflective glass above the middle sink, Miranda was even more severe than the last time I'd seen her. She'd put on her human face: short, reddish hair brushed back from her face, peering down her narrow nose at me through those sharp green eyes.

"Stalking me in sunglasses is as passé as wearing them in the club at all," I said.

"I don't understand what that means," my aunt returned, "so I'll skip ahead."

"No need. Abe already filled me in on finding the Shadow Mab."

"Then you misunderstood. You're to stay away and remove yourself from everything pertaining to shades and especially the Shadowed Mab." Miranda's skin seemed to flash paler than usual. "You have responsibilities."

The word tightened the muscles in my arms, making me flex my fingers to keep from directing a fist at the mirror.

"That better not be a euphemism for popping out some royal Faerie babies."

"You and I are all that's left of the royal line. Your duty—"

"I haven't got a *duty*," I cut her off. "You're the queen, that's your deal. Just because your brother knocked up my mom doesn't mean I owe you or the Faerie Court anything."

"Yes, it does. You may not like it, but it does."

"I don't like babies. I don't want babies. The most motherly fucking thing my mom ever did was taking me to get an IUD when I was fifteen. Why don't you do it? You're the actual queen and I know Faeries don't age the same as humans." Look at the Archduke and his daughter. I had no idea how old Miranda really was.

"Because I can't." Her voice was sharp. "I haven't the ability."

"Well, sucks to be you." I refused to feel sorry for the woman trying to co-opt my womb. "Guess they'll have to switch over to a democratically elected parliamentary system when you kick it."

I flipped her the bird over my shoulder as I headed out of the bathroom. I should have left the club entirely, but I headed to the bar instead and ordered another shot, this one not on Marie-Eve's tab.

When the bartender set it down, I frowned at the rippling image of my aunt glaring at me from the surface of the vodka.

"Are you serious?" I asked her, earning me a side-eye from the bartender as he loaded a waitress's tray with shots.

Without giving Miranda a chance to ruin my last drink, I threw the glass back. Then I hit up the coat-check and headed out. I didn't bother saying goodbye to Marie-Eve and Guy. They'd figure I'd gone home with somebody.

20

Daniel came blearily awake to someone poking his spine. When he turned over, a small, back-lit face hovered in the darkness.

"Can we read about the train?" Riley whispered.

What time was it? Why was he stretched out on the sofa holding an iron wrench against his chest? He sat up slowly and his nephew took that as an impetus to crawl onto the cushion beside him, clutching a picture book with a manila envelope stuffed into it. The living room was dark but light still spilled out of the kitchen and he became aware of low voices there: Gracie and Ted.

"It's a short one," Riley added.

"What?" Daniel studied the wrench in his hand and then his nephew, who stared at him with disconcertingly serious eyes.

"Can we read the book?" Riley repeated, slower this time, pressing the thin picture book into Daniel's hands.

"Rye?" Gracie's voice made them both look up. She stood beside the bar, holding the tablet she usually gave her son to play with, which seemed have a map on the screen. "You're supposed to be asleep, kiddo."

Ted regarded them over her shoulder, volunteering, "I'll lay down with him." He kissed Gracie on the check and then slipped around her to wrangle his son. "'Night," he told Daniel, as he scooped Riley into his arms.

"Goodnight." Daniel felt like he'd woken in the middle of a dream.

"Are you drunk?" his sister asked, as soon as her husband and son had disappeared down the hall.

"No." Daniel said the word automatically, but then had to reconsider. Was he? He didn't feel drunk. He actually felt more rested than he had in weeks.

"Then why did Zeb have to drag you home like a zombie?"

"Zeb did what?" Daniel didn't remember that. He remembered seeing Zeb . . . somewhere. When he sorted back through his memory, the bar came into focus, waiting for his friend and setting up the new phone he'd bought.

Gracie turned on the lamp beside the sofa and sat down next to him.

"What is this?" She held something up between two fingers. A small, glass vial of rusty red flakes. "I found it in your jacket pocket."

Recognition flooded back in with enough force to make him double-up, elbows on knees, certain for an instant that he'd vomit. Getting a drink with Zeb, encountering Abe and the giant mage. He searched hard for the pain in his head, the dull vibration against the ward.

Silence. The buzz in his skull really was gone. He took a breath, forcing his muscles to relax, then collapsed against the back of the sofa and admitted,

"It's blood."

"Whose?"

"Mine."

Gracie stared at him, her expression unreadable. She lifted her chin like she might say something, then drew back into herself. She set the vial aside.

"What happened?" she asked. "Where were you? I thought you went to see Marianne."

His thoughts rewound to before he'd met Zeb, the flight from campus.

"Marianne Nguyen's gone," he said. "Taken."

"You're sure?"

"Per her research assistant and the two agents I ran into." He winced, thinking of the force Rogers had put into twisting his shoulder.

His shoulder that no longer throbbed. Had Abe done something about that while he'd been unconscious with the mage sifting through his memories? Daniel turned his head, pulling the collar of his shirt back to check for the familiar scars puckering his skin. Still there. He stretched his shoulder and felt his muscles extend to the reduced limit he'd come to expect in the last four months. The Antagonist healer hadn't repaired him fully, just taken away the pain of the day. Good—anything more would have meant a debt Daniel wasn't interested in repaying.

"You talked to her research assistant?" Gracie asked skeptically.

"Tess Foster." When that didn't trigger recognition, Daniel added, "She said she used to work with you at the Consilium before she left to work for Marianne."

"Wait, *Theresa* Foster?"

"She introduced herself as Tess." Daniel started to set aside the picture book his nephew had brought out, then pulled the large manila envelope from between the pages. It was the traditional, inter-office kind, with Gracie's name on it in dark marker, but no destination.

"That's mine." His sister extended a hand for the folder and he passed it over, but several papers streamed out the open bottom.

"What is it?" He retrieved one, squinting at it in the dim light. The black marks on the page were a dizzying chaos.

"Nothing. My physical inbox from when I went on maternity leave," Gracie muttered, is if that explained why she had it now.

"Written in *what*?"

"Antagonist Runes, I assume." Surprise and uncertainty tinged his sister's voice.

He snapped his eyes away from the paper, panic surging through him at the idea of Antagonist words burning back into his brain.

That wouldn't happen. He wouldn't let it happen.

So as not to upset Gracie, he forced himself to relax and skimmed the page again. It wasn't right. It was scribbles, nonsense. Not the runes he'd expected. The runes he . . . couldn't picture in his mind. When he tried to draw one up in his memory, he found only a hole with sharp edges.

"You're sure?" he asked.

"What else would it be?" Gracie frowned.

Maybe the mage's remedy had been to remove the incantation *and* the ability to read it. But, no, Daniel hadn't agreed to that. The mage couldn't have taken anything but the incantation itself.

Temporary memory loss. Remembering Abe's warning didn't make him feel any better.

"It's . . . older than what I'm used to," he said, hoping his sister didn't happen to know the actual age of the document to correct him. He handed it back to her. "Where did you get it? You went back to your apartment?"

"Yes, but I had Jude use her magic house to take me there."

The explanation was so unexpected that Daniel couldn't hold back a startled laugh.

"And *I'm* the one who had to hold iron?" He nodded to the wrench on the floor.

"She was a useful alternative to breaking back into my home in the dead of night to avoid surveillance." Gracie's voice turned huffy and defensive. "*She* thought you were under a spell, by the way."

"Jude was *here*? While I was . . .?" Daniel didn't finish the sentence. The thought of it made him self-conscious, even though Jude had seen him in any other number of vulnerable positions.

"Only for a minute, in the hallway. You told her to take a hike." Gracie hesitated. "Don't remember that either? Too bad—it was a nice moment."

Daniel ran a hand over his face, squeezing his eyes shut. The embarrassment turned to annoyance—he shouldn't have been surprised the Antagonists would just work a spell on him and let him stumble back out into the world in total disorientation: a parting 'fuck you.'

"Are you okay?" Gracie asked, voice quieter.

"Yes. Just tired."

"Me too." She gathered the last of the loose papers, shuffling them into a pile with the envelope, the book Riley had carried, and the tablet, then set the stack on the bar. She paused a moment with her hand on it. "Alan called us a liability," she said, "to our faces, the day we came back to live with him after Mom died."

Daniel heard his father's voice, rough and dismissive, growling the words at two grieving teenagers.

"A liability and a nuisance," he added, feeling raw at the memory. "Yeah, I remember."

"He wasn't wrong." Gracie hesitated. "At least, not for the world he lived in. But that's not *our* world, not anymore. We can't keep living on its periphery." When she got no response, she added, "That 'we' includes you."

Despite all of her protests to the contrary, his sister had picked up a lot of bad lessons from both of their manipulative parents. Dictating the state of the world to him as if he had no say in it was one of their more insidious exercises. It cut deeper than he'd expected.

"I'm not sure it does," he said.

Gracie didn't flinch, but something seemed to shift behind her eyes.

"Ted's got a friend who thinks he can get us on a charter flight to Halifax on Monday morning," she said, voice chillier than before. "So I guess you've got about twenty-four hours to figure it out."

21

Yellow crime scene tape flapped in the wind as Abe reached the barrier it made, undone on one end from the tree it had been looped around. Reluctantly, he opened himself up to the feeling of the space. He'd never gotten old emotions off of places before, but given Gordon's references to some magical traces at each crime scene, there was no reason not to try. Not like he had anything better to do.

The men hadn't been killed in the spots they'd been found, they knew that much. As to where their hearts had been removed, well, that was anyone's guess. Probably in this world, at least, but honestly there was no guarantee of that.

The frustration churning Abe's gut clouded his ability, keeping him from getting any read. He rubbed his hands together to warm up, wishing he'd brought gloves. He'd come out into the cold to distract himself from the events of the day—never a good way to start any empathic investigation. No use trying to rummage through somebody else's emotions if you couldn't keep a handle on your own.

He wasn't just vexed tonight, no—there was a dose of good, old-fashioned guilt along for the ride too. He'd tried days ago to contact Miranda and find out why she hadn't sent more than the single mage to help them search for their killer, and he'd tried again this morning. He hadn't caught her either time. Maybe she was avoiding him.

So he hadn't told her about Daniel Cain's new ability to build a ward, and whatever went beyond that. It shouldn't have bugged him the way it did. He and Daniel weren't friends. Abe didn't owe the man anything, but damned if he didn't respect the sheer stubbornness it took a human to face this shit on the regular, constantly outgunned. He could sympathize with it.

"Damn fool," Abe muttered to himself, grimacing at his visible breath in the cold air. No going back now, though. Maybe if he could get some break in the hunt for this killer, that'd balance the karmic scales with Miranda.

Not that he believed in karma.

He breathed a lungful of frigid air and held it to let the discomfort clear his head, then tried once more. The place remained silent and empty around him. He'd always needed a living, breathing person before him to get any use out of his power. Stupid to think an empty crime scene would produce any clues. Probably wouldn't have worked even if the poor guy's body were still here. Jude's boss. Ty, she'd said.

Maybe there'd be something at the other crime scenes to help make out a pattern. He didn't know where the other spots were. Gordon would, but Abe wanted to exhaust his own resources before he went begging to the haughty mage.

Instead, he crouched down to pluck three blades of grass from just under the taped-off area and swiped a shrivelled, brown leaf for good measure. Rubbing the lot together between his palms, he waited for a breath of chilly wind to rush through the skeletal trees. When it came, he opened his hands. He'd done this before as a kid, with sand and straw on the ranch. A little trick his grandma had used to find the calves when they hid in the brush. He'd never been good at spells, at commanding magic. It came more naturally to him to let magic dictate the terms and work through him, like with healing, so the asks he made had only ever worked about fifty percent of the time.

He didn't know if it would work here, after so long, on the trace elements of magic left behind where the body had been dumped.

The light, papery bits of leaf rushed away, caught in the breeze, and the heavier blades of grass tumbled to his feet, save one. That one remained stuck to his palm, but it had moved to lay parallel on his third finger. A breath of magic brushed his hand, distant and faint enough that he could almost dismiss it as positive thinking. It gave him a direction, though. No use ignoring the potential.

It curled away like the steamy ribbon of scent from a steak in a cartoon, drawing Abe along like the animated wolf. As he moved block by block through the dark neighbourhoods, it resonated harder, tugging him like a marionette on a string instead.

Finally, it led him to a large park, somewhere in the middle of the island of Montreal. He didn't know how far he'd walked from the other crime scene, but it couldn't have been more than ten minutes because his hands were only now starting to sting from the cold.

The neighbourhood was less dense than where he'd been—lots of single-family homes with garages on the bottom, winter snow tents already set up over driveways. He hesitated at the path that led into the park, lined with the skeletons of tall, nearly bare trees. Oughta go back for support. Maybe Gordon would be at the house and willing to come along.

But, damn his pride, he didn't want to give the mage the satisfaction of asking for help.

A woman and her Pekingese emerged from the park, heading down the sidewalk toward him. The little dog strained at its leash to growl at Abe as he passed by. He paused, opening himself up and skimming her for anything familiar. He knew right off that she was human, and another two seconds told him she wasn't of interest.

He followed the whisper of the uncanny away from her, down the paved sidewalk into the park. He hated the feeling and at the same time couldn't abandon it. A sign in French seemed to indicate that the park closed at dusk, which had come hours ago at this point of the year. High overhead lights remained on to illuminate his way, so he proceeded.

When he reached a cross-path, something stirred in his gut and he didn't want to go further. It was like the feeling he got around other Faerie folk, but deeper—a yawning dread. He'd never come across anything Faerie on this side of the portal that really scared him. Truly powerful stuff couldn't come through the portal—there was a limit to the magic that could exist in this world. Otherwise, he could usually talk his way out of a situation, skimming off the emotions of his adversary. And if not, then he had two good fists and healed quick.

This felt different, wrong. Gritting his teeth, he turned left and continued down the paved path. Under a street-lamp, a shadowy figure lay stretched on a park bench, seemingly asleep. No emotions rose from it, though, not even the slightest tinge of colour to tip him off.

Dead. When he reached the man, he didn't have to take his pulse. The corpse was sprawled over the bench: a young man with a dark, wet stain on his chest, the edges of the gaping hole in his ribs.

Abe exhaled hard to press the nausea down. He'd seen worse, healed worse, but that had been on people with a pulse. This one was long gone, both feet in the grave, but recently enough that if Abe touched him with magical purpose, he might get pulled into the psychic void.

Still, he leaned in close enough to close the man's eyes. Then he angled his phone to get a flash photo of the dead man's face. He'd have to see if Jude knew him, if it fit the pattern they had, or there was some new pattern.

He hesitated before sending it, texting her instead: *It's Abe. Got another body. Want to try and ID?*

The response came back within a minute: *Hit me.*

He sent her the photo and waited. He should call the police, alert someone. It wouldn't help the dead man now, but leaving him here in the cold, empty park seemed like a sin.

A flash of light caught his eye, and he leaned over the corpse again to pull something small and shiny from the folds of the dead man's jacket. It looked like a leaf, with a visible trace of veins in the translucent substance. Felt like one too—supple, elastic, recently alive, but it was coloured a deep, liquid silver all over.

Not flora from the human world.

Something moved nearby. Abe stuffed the leaf into his pocket. He stretched his empathic power to its limits, feeling for any hint of emotion in the darkness outside the streetlight's safe circle. It didn't have the air of a person exactly—maybe an animal or . . . something else.

A *shade*? Abe dismissed the thought. The Shadowed Mab couldn't cross through a portal until the ritual was done, and her cult hadn't collected seven men yet. At least, not that he knew of. Seemed like the total was four, counting this poor victim he'd just stumbled over.

Instinct still warned him to turn and high-tail it. *Bad shit here.*

He felt a presence behind him an instant before the blow came. The moment of precognition let him dart far enough forward that the hit glanced off his hat, spinning it from his head instead of connecting with the back of his skull. He whirled to see his attacker and received a fist to the face, knocking him to his back on the pavement.

Rolling to his feet, he made another frantic thrust with his powers to get some idea of what was coming after him. The blank wall of the creature's emotions stopped him short. It didn't have them. It didn't feel *alive.*

A soft sucking sound came from behind him and Abe spun again to meet something wet and yielding. Liquid closed over him, a gelatinous wall smothering his mouth and nose, surrounding his body so that he wasn't sure his feet were on the ground any longer.

No stirrings of emotion came off of this one either. The numbing black hole sucked him down.

22

I DELETED ABE'S MESSAGE and turned my phone over to rest its screen against the bar. I tried not to blink so I wouldn't have to see flashes of the photo he'd just sent replay behind my eyes.

Chris was dead. Abe had sent me a photo of his dead face, stiff and waxy like a mask. Outside somewhere. The cowboy had been careful to position his camera and crop out the rest of the body, so I couldn't see the inevitable red splashed across his chest.

The bulk of the folded papers felt heavy in my back pocket. They'd tried to light a fire under my ass, but I hadn't studied them well enough. I hadn't read them closely enough to find Chris and save him. No, I'd gone out to get drunk and dance, then hit up a *second* bar on the way home for a burger and a beer. Fucking typical Jude.

I pushed away the remains of the burger basket and ordered a shot of the priciest vodka they had. It helped my throat open from its sticky suffocation. I waited for the haze to set in.

When had the cult grabbed him? While I'd been fucking around at the bar reading the paper with Abe and Gordon? While I'd been in Singapore squaring off with the Archduke? While I'd been grinding away my emotions on a sweaty dance floor to make myself feel better about my ex picking up other women's phone numbers?

Bile welled in my throat but I signalled the bartender.

"Un autre."

He cocked an eyebrow. "Autre quoi?"

"Je m'en fous." That was actually one of my favourite phrases. According to Marie-Eve, 'I *don't care*' translated to something more vulgar like 'I *don't give a damn*' in French.

"Non." The sharp word came from behind me.

The bartender turned suddenly and addressed a gaggle of women to my right, like he'd forgotten I was even there.

Rage flared under my skin in tandem with the electricity that stood the hairs on my arms on end.

The man who'd spoken and denied me my drink waited behind me. He'd managed to part the crush of the crowd around the bar. People seemed to shy away from him without realizing it.

"I know you?" I snapped.

"Not formally." His English was too sharp, not the local accent. It was somehow impossible to focus on his features in the dim bar lighting. I hadn't drunk enough to create this fuzziness. Plus, I saw the strangers beside me with better clarity, so it had to be some kind of confusing glamour.

"Get lost," I said.

"Judith—"

"Nobody calls me Judith." Nobody but my aunt and her Faerie cronies. I was in no mood to chat with her again. I wasn't popping out a baby and I wasn't going to go hide in a hole. I was going to deal out some fucking vengeance for a guy I hadn't even known well enough for somebody to kill him to get my attention.

When the man didn't move, I added, "My fay-dar is oiled up and working fine. So scram."

"Your what?" He laughed.

I got to my feet and shrugged my coat back on, taut muscles wanting instead to punch him. I left some cash on the bar, even though the bartender still wasn't acknowledging my existence. Call it my good deed of the night. I'd need about a million more to balance out my inaction.

My aunt's crony didn't move as I strode past, but I thought he turned his head to watch me walk out.

The freezing air barely touched me. Chris, Trevor, JM and Ty—all innocent bystanders. In the proximity of the wrong woman at the wrong time. This Faerie ghoul had cut their lives short just because they knew me. And why *me*? I didn't know her. I hadn't fucked with her, not that I knew of. If I'd slighted her somehow while working at the Consilium, I'd have expected to at least have heard of shades before yesterday.

I kicked a clump of icy dead leaves stuck to the pavement. This heat inside my bones needed to be burned out, stoked so high that it extinguished itself, or I was going to break something. Some*one*.

I started to jog, pumping my legs as hard as they would go, stretching my muscles until they ached. I increased my speed through the brittle air, slamming my feet down on the wet concrete without using my powers and daring the universe to trip me. The further I ran, the longer it would take the flood to catch up to me.

The illuminated blue and white arrow icon of a métro station made me slow. All I wanted in that instant was to be home, where I didn't have to see anybody. Where I couldn't hurt anybody. Sit in a fucking cold shower and scream until the rage climbed up out of my throat and scuttled away somewhere it was useful.

Sleet blew in my eyes as I ducked inside. It was late enough that the ticket booth wasn't staffed so I hopped the turnstiles.

Down the escalator, I walked toward the end of the platform where the head of the train would arrive, avoiding the crowd that always gathered right by the entrance.

Even this late at night, there were plenty of people waiting.

The train pulled in, and as I'd hoped, the front of the first car was pretty empty. I sat against the window and stretched my legs over the blue plastic seats, discouraging any would-be suitors from trying to sit beside me. Doing them a favour.

Maybe I should just leave town. Why had I even come here? I could go back to Toronto, where I spoke the language. Or fucking anywhere else. Clean out my bank account, sneak across the border to the US and book a flight to Miami or San Diego. Let the Shady Mab come after me in the blinding daylight of a warm goddamn beach.

"Jude Waldron." While I'd been staring out into the blackness of the tunnels, three men had surrounded me at the front of the hurtling train car. None of them was my bar-stalker, but the hairs on my arm snapped to attention anyway, and I sat up. "The Mab has ordered that you come with us to a safe location."

"Yeah, no thanks."

The leader hesitated, as if not sure what to make of my response. Probably not the type of guy who heard 'no' very often. "What's the plan?" I asked, leaning back in the seat and folding one leg over the other. "Because I assume you're not authorized to use force here."

"A modest amount of force has been deemed acceptable." A brief smile twitched across his face.

Miranda wasn't going to pull her punches, then. As long as they didn't hit my uterus.

I risked a glance over my shoulder. The car was quiet and no one paid attention to us. Even the two people staring forward at me who should have seen a woman being confronted by three sketchy dudes seemed to look right through me.

Glamour. Miranda's goons had probably covered the cameras too. Sitting alone at the front of the first car had really made it easy for them.

I shifted gravity to push myself off the window behind me, moving up and over the heads of my groupies. Past them, I grabbed the stanchion in the front centre of the car and hoisted myself down, actually flipping upright. Using my power to spin horizontally around the vertical bar, I slammed my boots into the chest of the first Faerie who leapt at me.

The second was smart enough to pause and dodge back to avoid my second swing around the stanchion. That bought me time to leap off.

I darted over him to the ceiling, then hit the floor and dashed down the aisle of the train.

Other passengers started as I passed them, scrambling to their feet with yelps of surprise as if I'd appeared out of nowhere. Well, I had, from their view, but now I had the length of the train. *Glamour that, assholes.*

A rattle of the wheels pitched me to one side, making me slam my hip into the back of a seat as I passed. It almost spun me off balance, but I managed to swing myself into a somersault instead. The train veered again and my tuck dissolved into a sprawl against the doors. The floor slowed beneath me as I scrambled to my feet. I shot through the doors the instant they opened.

Rather than make for the stairs at the end of the platform, I grabbed the top of the car doors and swung myself up onto the roof of the train. I ran down the top of the car, heading toward the dark maw where the ceiling dipped and narrowed into the tunnel. Spinning gravity around me as I reached the head of the first car, I slid neatly onto the roof of the tunnel. The ascending tones played below to indicate that the sliding doors were closing. I pressed myself tightly to the arched cement looming over the blue metal of the train's roof.

The three Faeries had followed me off the subway car but stopped, glancing up and down the platform for me.

Beneath me, the train jerked and moved forward. It picked up speed centimetres from my ribs. The wind from the rushing cars made it momentarily hard to breathe. I squeezed my eyes shut, turning my head, and clung to the tunnel ceiling, pressing myself down to stay up.

Once the roar of the train had passed, a shout from ahead let me know that I'd been spotted. I shoved myself to my hands and knees and then gained my feet after I'd slipped back over the lip of the tunnel to the station ceiling.

I dashed down the ceiling, with the double set of tracks that divided the two nearly-empty platforms directly above—or rather below—me. A growing rumble from the tunnel behind indicated that the next train was coming from the other direction now, behind me. Good, I could use it to block the Mab's goons' view while I jumped down onto the opposite platform.

Unlike the narrow tunnel where I'd practically been pressed against the train cars, the vaulted area above the tracks had enough clearance for me to keep running as the train thundered beneath me, slowing to a stop in the station.

The rush of air it created pushed me off-balance. I lost my grip on gravity, sprawling onto the hard roof of a métro car. Pain rattled through my chin and hips as they took the hit, but I rolled off the blue metal, angling to flip upright and land on the platform with the train between me and the Mab's guys.

Beneath me, the car doors opened and another rider stepped off. I twisted, altering course at the last second to keep from slamming into her. I hit the platform tile upright on my feet but my right knee popped at a bad angle. Burning pain shot down my leg and it buckled beneath me. I collapsed, a scream stuck in my throat.

The woman who'd exited the train exclaimed in surprise, spinning to see me. Behind her, the door to the driver's compartment slid open and someone started to emerge, speaking French.

Before I could say a word, they both froze. The driver stepped back and the woman near me blinked, confused. She started to turn, hesitated as if she meant to turn back, then completed her motion and walked away like nothing had happened.

The driver returned to his booth and closed the door in the same instant three figures leapt across the roof of the train from the platform on the other side. The chimes sounded and the doors closed.

Once the train had sped off into the tunnel, the Mab's guys advanced slowly with the ease of tigers. The leader still had that smug smile on his face.

Rage flashed through me, burning brighter than the pain. I swallowed a shriek, hauling myself up to balance on my good leg in a quick, fluid movement. The surprise on their faces was almost gratifying enough, but it would be better once I'd knocked their teeth down their throats.

Something dark dropped from the ceiling behind them, making even me fall back. Putting weight on my injured knee had me on the ground again, hissing in agony through my teeth.

From beyond me came grunts and the heavy thuds of fists into bone, flesh into tile. The newcomer moved like a blur, and even in the bright station lights I had trouble keeping track of the four of them.

In another minute, it was over. All three of my aunt's goons were sprawled on the platform, not moving. Maybe not even breathing.

Through the blur of tears that had flared with the fire in my knee, I managed to fix on the man in the all-too-familiar dark wool coat.

"I tried to warn you." He came to stand over me. I could see his face a lot better under the overhead lights here than I'd been able to in the bar. He'd removed his glamour, at least the piece that had kept my brain from fixing on his features.

My breath hitched. He was older than I'd expected, with lines around his eyes and mouth. Wisps of white shot through his deep red hair, but I knew his features from an old photo. From a woman who called herself my aunt.

"Not the reunion I was anticipating either," my father said.

23

"Joshua?" I gaped at him from the platform floor, gasping half in pain and half in surprise. Trying to find words in the messy attic above my eyes, I stammered, "I thought you were dead."

He snorted a short, bitter laugh. "No."

"Not unless you're really bad at it." Fuck, had I said that out loud?

He extended both hands but I hesitated before taking them. This guy—this well-dressed, smooth-talking guy—was the man who'd knocked up my mom and split. The Faerie who'd given me the power to walk up walls. Was I supposed to thank him or punch him? Where did we even start?

Behind us, one of Miranda's henchmen groaned. That answered my question: we started away from here.

Joshua gripped my fingers tightly and supported me while I hauled myself up onto my left leg. The movement jostled my injured knee enough to make me gag at the surge of pain. Through that misery, I still flinched when Joshua slipped an arm around my waist to keep me upright. He helped me up the stairs from the platform and to the relief of an escalator.

"You look good," he said. "Aside from the injury. How old are you now?"

"Twenty-five."

That made him sigh. My mom had started giving me that sigh years ago, the disappointed *if you're getting older that means I'm getting older* sigh.

"How did you recognize me?" he asked.

"You look like Miranda."

"Then she's aged poorly." The amusement in his voice gave way to bitterness.

After helping me hobble out of the métro station, Joshua barely had to lift his hand before a white sedan with an unlit plastic topper pulled up to us at the curb. I'd expected they'd all be full already in the snow flurries.

I eased in carefully to keep from bumping my knee too much while he kept a hand on my back and one under my elbow, steadying me.

Then he slid in beside me and told the driver, in a suddenly clipped, professional voice: "Hospital, please. Emergency room."

The driver's eyes flickered to me in the rearview mirror, then shifted up to check the traffic behind us. He swung into the street and we were on our way.

As soon as the car was moving, Joshua held his hand out flat against the front seat. The seat seemed to shimmer. I hoped it wasn't my vision. "What did those idiots want?" He spoke at a regular volume, leaning back.

Noticing when my eyes snapped to the driver, he said, "He can't hear you. I've put up a barrier."

"What if he talks to us?"

"He won't. He's forgotten we're here. Only remembers the destination."

"Neat trick." The calm revelation of a spell that manipulated our driver's mind made me uneasy, but to be honest, it wasn't my primary concern. "Where'd you learn it? Same place you've been the last twenty-five years?"

"In the Bie'lelhii." He switched back to English to translate, "The Land of Shades."

"Somebody finally pull 'em?"

"That's . . ." He gazed at me a moment under the passing streetlights, as if working out the words. ". . . a joke."

"Not my best," I agreed, then hesitated at a sudden thought. "Wait, are you a shade?"

"No."

"But you were in the Bill-whatever."

"The two are not mutually exclusive." He paused, as if deciding what needed to be said, then added, "Rare, perhaps." Another hesitation I didn't like. The silence felt like he was judging me, weighing what I'd understand. Like a more polite version of Gordon, somehow.

"I was under strict orders not to cross through the portals," he explained, "and I got caught doing so. The Mab at the time had me imprisoned in the Bie'lelhii and I spent the last twenty years there. Alive. Corporeal."

"So is your real name Peony Leaf?" I refused to be drawn into sympathy without a better story.

His expression turned dubious. "What would lead you to think that?"

"No reason that's worth explaining. Why'd you go over in the first place? You need another present for my mom?"

"You found the grymoire." The assertion came out in a neutral tone, but I thought maybe I heard a note of admiration there. Maybe just a snap judgment brought on by my knee trying to burst out of my skin, but I wasn't looking for a pat on the head anyway.

"Yeah," I agreed, "just in time for an asshole to swipe it and try to merge the spheres."

"Aubrie." Contempt coloured Joshua's voice as he said the name, but rather than explain any further, he finished, "Seems like you came through it all right."

The quick, dismissive summation of what had, in my reality, been a painful, hard-won victory made me tense. I wanted to smack him for not understanding what his stupid hidden book had put me through.

"Why didn't you just give the grim-thing to Miranda?" I demanded, wanting to be furious with the person who'd, purposely or not, set all of last summer in motion. "Or just tell *someone* where it was?"

"As long as only I knew, no one could move against me. Or you, though you and Katie were already protected by the binding."

"Katie? You mean Mom?" I'd never heard anyone call her that before. She'd only ever been Katherine or Kathy to my ears. *Katie* was a name too fresh and cute for my angry, drunk mother.

Then my brain caught up and flagged a word I didn't know. "Wait, the what?"

"Binding." Joshua knew where he'd lost me. "A spell that made it impossible for a Faerie to harm you unless you harmed one first. I had to call in a few favours for that. And I've heard you broke it anyway, working for the Consilium."

"You *protected* us? You . . . *bound* us?" I worked through each weird thing in turn, as my knee made sharp, continuous burning stabs to try and take my attention. I didn't know how to feel about this man, who'd fathered me and disappeared, leaving behind a protection spell. "And you know I worked for the Consilium? Did that shade prison have a mirror where you watched the hidden camera reality show of my life?"

"I didn't break out just now."

"You *broke out* of Shade Land? When? And—for the hell of it—how?"

He hesitated again, considering his words, then said, "I honed my magic. Cultivated it, stole tiny pieces of the energy in the Bie'lelhii. Too small, too varied for the Lady to notice." His voice turned hollow but he seemed to catch himself, shifting back to a more even tone to conclude, "Eventually, I was able to break her spells and sneak out."

"Not big on details." I noted the mention of the Lady with a capital 'L'.

"Not long on time," he corrected, nodding to the window as the taxi came up on the lighted *Urgences* signs of the ER. He extended his hand toward the front seat again and twitched his fingers.

"Et voilà," the driver said, turning as he apparently remembered us with the removal of Joshua's spell.

"Thanks," I said, a little startled by his sudden inclusion.

Joshua slid out of the car and reached back in for me. I struggled out of the back seat, biting my tongue a few times so I didn't whimper when my leg shifted the wrong way. He helped me limp into the ER without stopping to pay the driver, but the driver didn't complain and I didn't have the energy to call him out on manipulating the guy again.

The ER was busy on this freezing night. Even though today was technically November, it was also the Saturday after Halloween, so the waiting room was scattered with people in costume.

Joshua set me down in a plastic chair near a girl clad in the traditionally scanty French maid outfit. She shivered and rubbed her blue knees. Beside her, a guy in a fuzzy Dalmatian suit held an exposed, bloodstained hand. A giant, plush dog head sat in the chair beside him.

I sank heavily into uncomfortable, moulded plastic, trying to move my leg into the least painful position stretched in front of me.

A few metres away, Joshua retrieved a clipboard with paperwork from the front desk and scribbled quickly across it. He returned it to reception without letting me see, then disappeared somewhere.

He was back ten minutes later with a cup of water and two round, white pills. I half-expected by that point that I'd imagined him.

"What are these?" I asked, accepting them reluctantly.

"Human pain medication." When he saw my startled expression, he added, "I told a nurse you were in a good deal of pain and she gave me those. Just take one. Save the other for six hours."

"You asked a nurse?" I studied his face. I didn't buy it. "Asked or *asked* asked?"

"English has gotten more complicated since I left." He flashed a wan smile.

"Now you're talking like a father." A note of spite slipped into my voice, matching his in an unsettling way. "You used a spell to convince the nurse to give me drugs," I clarified, clawing my way to a higher moral ground I couldn't hold. "That's illegal."

"Human legality concerns you?" He arched an eyebrow, expression somewhere between surprised and—what, disappointed?

Touché.

24

Despite taking one pill, as advised by the ensorcelled nurse, the throbbing in my knee kept demanding my attention. I tried to think of something else as we waited, but it didn't work. My fucking *father*, missing twenty plus years, was here sitting beside me and my stupid, swelling knee kept taking precedence.

"Abe would have this fixed in two minutes," I hissed, crumpling the empty plastic cup in my hand like a stress ball. How bad would it be to just take the second pill now?

Instead I pulled out my phone to fire off a text to the cowboy. The thought of the photo he'd sent made me hesitate, but then I remembered I'd deleted that message. It was safe to open my texts and send him a quick '*U up lol to fix my knee?*' message.

"Abe?" Joshua echoed the name like he thought he ought to know it. After twenty years in prison, he probably needed his memory jogged.

"He's an empathic healing cowboy," I said. If that didn't point Joshua in the right direction, nothing would, but I still heard myself add: "He said he worked with you and Miranda a long time ago, but he joined up right before you disappeared. He's a . . . friend." *Frenemy* would have been a better description, though Abe erred harder to to the 'Fr' side than Miranda and the rest of her goons.

Something told me Joshua wouldn't understand that word, anyway.

"Why were Miranda's soldiers chasing you?" he asked.

"She sent them to stash me somewhere safe so she can rent out my womb." The anger that flared took my attention off my knee. "Any chance I've got a half-sister or two running around who could take one for the team?"

"No." Joshua noticed that his certainty triggered my most skeptical expression. "There aren't many human women strong enough to bear our children." A note of admiration entered his voice as he added, "Katie was an exception."

Again with *Katie*. I'd never really considered my mom strong before. Maybe I'd been too hard on her. I couldn't help the odd surge of loyalty that made me point out, "She doesn't talk about you so lovingly."

"I'd imagine not." He sighed.

"You could have stayed." I hated myself for those words. They made me feel like the ten-year-old who'd spent nights hoping a made-up person would come through the door. I wasn't her anymore.

"Not without putting you both in harm's way." Joshua didn't meet my eyes, studying a couple dressed as two halves of a horse across the waiting room.

"That's a line," I said. When he cast me a sidelong glance, I challenged, "What harm? Give me specifics."

"To remain would have put you and Katie in the cross-hairs of the Ferryman and the Consilium."

"You're making that up." I snorted on a laugh. The painkillers were kicking in with a little bit of haze. "The *Fairyman*?"

Joshua paused, puzzled and searching for the root of my derision. It made me realize with an embarrassed start, "Wait, *ferry* like the boat? You mean a boat driver?"

"One who ferries passengers across a boundary," he agreed mildly.

The membrane between thoughts in my head and the ones coming out of my mouth had become thinner than usual.

In an effort to save face, I managed a sharp nod and concluded, "Never heard of him."

"His name was probably buried by the time you joined the Consilium."

"He was *Consilium*?"

"Martin Ames." Joshua waited a beat to see if the name would register with me. When it didn't, he finished, "Alan Cain's predecessor."

Disdain, not even remotely masked, when he spat the name of the man I'd murdered. Joshua hated Alan. Would my absent father take my side, congratulate me, the way Aubrie had?

My stomach turned. The room slanted around me and I blinked hard to make it stand still. The unwelcome memory of the letter opener in my hand, the weight of it sinking into Alan's chest, my fingers cramping around the handle—one by one, they rose to the surface of my hazy thoughts.

I tried to steer away from the subject, stammering, "Why was this Ames guy called the Ferryman?"

"He had a portal on his property and allowed our people to cross for a hefty fee. They were often fugitives from the Mab, so he would hand them to the Consilium or turn them back over to the Mab for a higher price."

"So, this high-ranking Consilium guy was bringing Faeries *into* our world? And profiting?" Why did that surprise me? It wasn't like the Consilium had been all upstanding and perfect.

I cast a glance to either side to be certain nobody in the waiting room was listening too carefully to us. "Did you take him out?"

Joshua gave me a quick, appreciative smile that reminded me too much of my own. He definitely wished he had.

The pain in my knee had finally receded, becoming a distant low roar somewhere in the back of my mind. The reprieve made me rush ahead to turn the conversation to topics more relevant to me, while I'd remember them. "If you were in Shade Land," I said, "then you must know about the Shadow Mab. She's gunning for me."

"What?" Joshua seemed surprised, frowning at me. "What do you have to do with the Shadowed Mab?"

"Her cult is killing my . . . they're killing men in my life. Taking their hearts." I masked a shudder as the memory of the photo Abe had sent flashed through my head. "There's some ritual—"

"I know the ritual." Joshua's voice turned brittle. "How many have they gathered?"

"Four, I think. The first guy died about three weeks ago." My throat felt tight, trying to keep things non-specific. If I didn't use names, I didn't have to picture them. "But it doesn't make sense. They could just snap up seven random guys in one night and be done with it. Instead, they're waiting until I shove a few in their direction."

Joshua stared at the far wall like he hadn't even heard me.

"You're sure it's four?" he finally asked. "Four men connected to you?"

"I knew them, yeah." The fury that had been brewing through my muscles since seeing Chris's photo leached in, sharpening my voice more than I meant to. "And I was betting two, *maybe* three on coincidence but at this point I'm pretty fucking sure."

Joshua got to his feet with a distracted air, not clocking my tone. He glanced over his shoulder then turned a dubious eye on the people in front of us.

Sounding reluctantly satisfied by whatever he'd determined, he told me in a low voice, "Stay here."

"That was the plan." I gestured to my knee.

He didn't seem to hear, striding away from me. He swept out of the ER waiting room, his long, wool coat billowing in the cold wind that came through the sliding doors.

Fucking dramatic.

25

GRACIE RESTED HER FOREARMS on the handle of the shopping cart, pushing it slowly down the aisle of the grocery store. She hadn't wanted to come out, but the lack of food at her brother's apartment had finally gotten the best of her, and Riley was going stir-crazy too. A quiet, early morning grocery run had seemed safe enough. She'd taken the métro a few stops to shop at a store further away, so she didn't get her face associated with their current neighbourhood. Not that it would matter for more than another day.

Ted should be confirming their seats for tomorrow's flight. He'd insisted on departing from a cargo airport, which limited their options, but there was too much chance someone would be watching for them at the Montreal airport. From Halifax, they'd be safe to go commercial to the States, or Europe. Put an international boundary between them and their pursuers.

"Mama, can we get it?" Riley asked, hauling a cereal box from the bottom shelf. It was at least the sixth time he'd asked. Grocery shopping without her son was much easier, but she couldn't just keep him cooped up in the apartment.

"No, kiddo, put it back," she said, stifling a yawn. "Come on, next aisle."

Her stomach had been twisted into knots all night. She'd thought having a settled escape plan would ease

156

her anxiety, but her brother's response—or lack of it, rather—had kept her awake again.

In the light of morning, clear-headed from *whatever* had happened last night, Daniel would have to see this was the only option. Cutting themselves to shreds picking up the jagged pieces of the Consilium wasn't a sustainable life.

Gracie turned to ask her son if he wanted a box of chocolate milk, but Riley wasn't standing beside her. She glanced up and down the aisle, then ducked back around the corner to check the last one.

No Riley.

Her heart began to pound but she took a deep breath. He'd just wandered off to look at something. The store wasn't that big. She left her cart and moved along the aisles, checking each one. At this hour of the morning, the place wasn't crowded at all, so he would be easy to spot.

As she reached the last aisle and didn't find him, she spun and nearly collided with someone directly behind her.

"Mrs. Thomson." The man from the playground two days ago. "Could you come with us, please?"

Gracie stepped back, noting another person in her peripheral vision on the left. She had to find Riley.

"I'm sorry, I've lost my son," she said abruptly, darting around the man and daring him to grab her in public.

To her surprise, he did, catching her elbow and swinging her back around.

"We have to insist." His partner had joined him, a woman. Neither seemed to be armed, but they both had long coats that could hide any number of weapons.

Gracie swung her backpack off one shoulder, slamming it into the man gripping her and knocking him back. She snatched the long umbrella she'd secured to the bungees of the backpack and opened it with the press of a button, thrusting it at the woman to ward her off as she scurried away.

She shot past the ends of the aisles, scanning at the height of her son with increasing panic. Ducking up the last one, she headed toward the cashier and the front door.

The agents were behind her, matching her brisk pace but neither breaking into a run. They seemed to fall even further back as soon as they were in full view of the cashier. *Not looking to cause a scene. Good.*

As soon as she emerged from the aisle, Gracie saw Riley. The three-year-old stood near the front door, beside a display of plastic Halloween toys. A Black woman bent down beside him, her hooded sweatshirt and jeans gleaming with drops of rain.

Theresa Foster's eyes shifted up to meet Gracie's as she kept the calm expression plastered on her face, saying something to Riley. She tilted her head almost imperceptibly toward the exit.

With an unpleasantly familiar instinct, Gracie let her own chin twitch in agreement, holding the rest of her muscles in check until the instant that Theresa wrapped an arm around Riley's chest. The other woman hoisted her son into the air and ran for the exit.

Gracie followed, knocking over a store display into the path of the agents who'd probably broken their cover to run after her. She burst through the automatic doors into the November chill, in quick pursuit of the woman carrying her child.

A city bus was just pulling to the stop at the far end of the grocery store parking lot. Theresa, holding tight to Riley, tossed herself through the doors before they closed. She must have alerted the driver because those doors stayed open for the time it took Gracie to jog across the frosty asphalt and haul herself up the step to the card reader.

Theresa thanked the driver, struggling to hold onto Riley as he almost knocked her off-balance shouting and reaching for his mother.

Gracie touched his forehead briefly, then went through her purse for her wallet, fishing for her fare card and telling the driver like an automaton to charge two fares.

Finally, the card reader light flashed green and Gracie held the overhead straps to follow her former assistant and Riley to the back of the bus.

As soon as they collapsed into the seats, Riley flung himself into Gracie's arms. She squeezed him hard enough to knock the breath from his little lungs. When he sniffled, eyes red and nose running, a fierce certainty sang through her muscles: *Never again. This will never happen again.*

Cradling her son as he snuggled into her shoulder, Gracie lifted her head to the woman in the seat beside her.

"Hey, boss," Theresa said, flashing a tired but gallant smile.

"I'm not your boss," Gracie said.

"Are you going to be petty?" The younger woman sighed heavily. "Because, *come on*, you were on maternity leave. I was going to sit in your office collecting dust for a year. Marianne offered me the position and, be real, Grace. *You'd* have taken it."

Theresa's voice stirred such affection that Gracie wanted to hug her old friend, but Riley's arms were still tight around her neck, his bulk pressed to her chest.

"I don't like that," Riley declared, breath hot as he spat into her collarbone. "No more shopping."

"It's fine. We're done," Gracie assured him, rubbing his back.

"We didn't got food."

"We'll get it later."

"Wanna go home." Riley retreated into his coat like a turtle.

"I know. We just can't right now." Gracie fought to relax her shoulders, still bunched up tight. "How'd you find me?" she asked Theresa.

The other woman deflated against the upholstered plastic, and then stiffened as the bus slowed to another stop to let passengers board. Once she'd determined them non-threatening, she answered,

"I followed them. I don't know how they found you."

Too vague. But Gracie couldn't let herself jump to the conclusion that Theresa was compromised or lying. They'd all survived something traumatic—they'd all changed. Her brother was different—sharper, more secretive, more prone to risk. She even felt at a distance from her own younger self, like someone who'd branched off of her, stepped through a mirror and down a road she hadn't even really known existed.

She had to be more prudent. She owed it to her old friend to hear her out, extend some trust. It didn't come naturally.

They rode the bus for another twenty minutes to the terminus at a métro station. Gracie left her cell phone on the seat as she and Riley disembarked. She didn't think the agents could have found her with that—it was a burner and she'd only been using it since this morning—but she didn't want to take the chance.

"Can we get a coffee?" Theresa—Tess—asked.

With no intention of letting the other woman follow her back to Daniel's, Gracie agreed. Riley refused to slide down and walk by himself, so she carried him to the nearest chain coffee shop, Tess striding along beside her.

"You got the bus, I got this," Tess said, as they ordered drinks and a chocolate chip cookie for Riley.

He picked the cookie apart at the table they chose, back near the bathrooms, and Gracie studied her former assistant.

"How did you get here?" she asked.

"After . . ." Tess seemed to struggle to come up with the right words for the Consilium's implosion, so she skipped ahead, "Marianne got me set up as a research assistant in her program."

"That was generous of her." Gracie didn't buy it. Tess was a good assistant, but she wasn't *that* good. Unless Marianne Nguyen had grown a heart in the last year. Scooping up Consilium strays didn't fit into her repertoire.

"Well, she owed me." A smile touched Tess's face but she didn't elaborate. "And she's been a decent boss."

"I guess this isn't the first time you've run into these guys?" Gracie let that refer to the agents in the supermarket. She wasn't aware that there had been any other human organizations fighting against the Faerie Court, but even if there had been, how would she have known? Alan might have known, but he'd never shared information freely.

When Tess shook her head, she added, "Do you know what they're after? Why they're scooping up the remnants of the Consilium?"

"I have a pretty good idea, actually." A cautious, resigned note in the other woman's voice sent adrenaline through Gracie's veins.

She stared at her former assistant, stunned by the expectant look on Tess's face. She should have trusted her gut, should have listened when it asked her how someone like Theresa, with no field training and no secretive family paranoia to drive her, had so easily evaded the agents that had picked off the rest of the surviving Consilium.

"You're part of it?" she managed.

"It wasn't a hard choice, actually," Tess said.

"Then why lie about it? Why help me run from your friends just now?" Gracie glanced around the coffee shop for the lurking spectres of more agents, maybe even the two they'd outrun at the supermarket. She wrapped her fingers around the warm paper cup of coffee on the table in front of her. Not hot enough to scald, but that hadn't mattered with the agent in Laval two days ago.

"They're not my friends," Tess corrected. "No more than anybody in the Consilium was really *your* friend. Apart from your family, I guess. And even then." She made what seemed like a mocking grimace in reference to Gracie's strained relationship with her father.

She sounded so casual now, almost calculating. She'd lost all traces of the timid, deferential Theresa Foster Gracie had known.

"I lied—and *rescued* your brother, by the way, yesterday—because I wanted to talk to you alone, like this," she added.

"You're recruiting." Gracie's voice came out flat.

"It's not some Evil Empire, Grace. They want what *we* want. What we were always working for. A world that doesn't *need* the Consilium or anything like it."

"That's why they're kidnapping survivors?" Gracie kept her voice low, risking another glance for familiar faces or anyone paying too close attention to them.

"It's not—"

Before Tess could quibble with her wording, Gracie fired back, "Do I get a *choice* in whether to work with you or not?"

Tess sat back, frowning.

"What do you want?" Gracie cut to the chase. She didn't need a speech about goals and glory, the triumph of humanity against all magical adversity. She'd had enough of those for a lifetime. She glanced to Riley as he sucked on his chocolate-stained fingers, watching people pass by the window outside.

"You remember I sent you a package—your inbox from the Consilium?" Tess asked.

"You dropped it off." The discrepancy struck Gracie. Theresa had shown up on her doorstep in London, handing her the envelope, giving her a last hug with her pregnant belly between them. The last time they'd seen each other.

"Right. It's been a while." Tess shrugged. "Well, there was a map in there that—"

"There wasn't a map in those files." It had been about three years since Gracie had really looked at the papers in the folder—she'd done a quick overview when Tess had dropped them off, but she didn't remember a map. She would have remembered a map.

"I don't actually know what was in there. Literally, I just swept everything off your desk into a folder and brought it over. I didn't go through it. But my handlers told me there's a map there."

Beside them, Riley reached for the plastic cup of water she'd gotten him along with the cookie. His fingers were greasy from the various cookie ingredients and the cup was too large for his little, grasping hands. Normally Gracie would have reached over to either wipe them or to hold the cup for him to sip, but she didn't move.

"What map?" she asked.

"A way into the Shade Realm."

The plastic cup slipped through Riley's small fingers, splashing across the table and sending a wash of icy water onto both Gracie's and Tess's laps.

Tess leapt up with a yelp and Gracie seized the moment to haul Riley into her arms, pulling her purse back over her shoulder in the same motion. She darted past her traitorous ex-assistant and made for the front door.

A group of people had just shuffled into the cafe, rubbing their hands from the outside cold. She barrelled through them as Riley began to wail in her arms.

26

Daniel sorted through the stack of papers from Gracie's manila folder. With her out, he couldn't help digging into the new information that had come into the apartment. Maybe puzzling over the runes on the pages that had fallen out last night—if runes were even what they were—could push his memory back into shape.

He stopped on a high-res scan of what appeared to be a stone tablet, tracing a fingernail over the curves of the characters to see if muscle memory might trigger the rest of the knowledge.

Not for the first time, he wondered if Abe's mage friend had broken his word last night, lifted something more than the incantation. He didn't remember their entire conversation anymore—maybe they'd tricked him somehow.

It might not even have been outright deceit, just a mistake. A lack of precision. Intent mattered with magic. Daniel's own days spent making the ward on his door had made that abundantly clear to him.

Thinking of Abe and the mage brought him back to marvelling at the silence in his head. He'd slept better than he had in months, even on the uncomfortable sofa, and the absence of tension in his head, in his body, made him feel like a different person.

On the page in his hand, the writing still refused to resolve into anything he could read, but by holding it under the lamp beside the sofa, he picked out faded marks between the runes. Though fairly certain he didn't own a magnifying glass, he searched the kitchen drawers for one anyway. Foiled, he angled the lamp to avoid shadows and held his phone over the page to take several pictures with the flash until he got a clean image. Then he could zoom in and see . . .

Nothing. Nothing helpful, anyway. The new phone had a better camera than his old one, and he could see that there *were* extra marks between the runes, at odd, random intervals. They weren't artifacts from the scan, but whether they were actually relevant or just chips and scrapes in the rock, he couldn't tell.

There was no use studying any of this. On top of the fact that he couldn't force his knowledge to return before whatever the giant mage at the bar had done to him healed—*if* it did—Gracie was right. The Consilium had died with their father and well it should have.

But there was something inhuman here in Montreal, killing people and taking their hearts for an arcane ritual. However questionable his ability to actually help now, it wasn't an investigation Daniel could just sit out. Or one he could run from, the way his sister wanted to.

Frustration forced his attention to something he could understand, so he moved on to the sheaf of photocopies also included in the folder: the *Treatise on the Fayrie Dead* that Lacey had mentioned. The first several chapters outlined vague speculations about the Antagonist meaning of death and their varied beliefs about the afterlife. Successive short chapters covered funereal customs, a hierarchy of honourable deaths in the Antagonist world, and descriptions of the more inglorious ends one could come to.

> *The most ignominious of these must be the*
> *curse that is called The Fade. While relevant*

*enough to the topic at hand, the reader will
find a more thorough discussion of this curse
and its outcome in chapter twelve.*

Daniel went through the rest of the stack. No chapter twelve. It wasn't in the handful of remaining papers from the manila envelope either. The rest of the *Treatise* seemed complete, but it skipped from chapter eleven to thirteen.

The name of the curse struck him again. Without Gracie present, he could go to the messiest box at the bottom of the bookshelf, a heap of loose papers and half-charred book pages. A sheaf of handwritten papers clipped together in one corner lay at the bottom, where he'd stuffed it two days ago. He'd done more than toddler-proof the apartment for Riley when Gracie had called to say they were coming—he'd also stashed a few things his sister wouldn't be pleased to know existed.

She didn't need to know that he'd copied most of the Antagonist grymoire five months ago before helping her destroy the actual book. Gracie wanted the whole spellbook gone, thinking its very existence hazardous in case it fell into the wrong hands.

While Daniel didn't disagree, he'd still wanted to know the details of what they could be dealing with in the future. He had copied it hastily and spent weeks translating as best he could to figure out if there was any important information, or just Antagonist spells. He'd kept a list of the name of every spell written in the book, along with any pertinent details about them. He'd meant to burn the copies of the actual spells, but hadn't done it yet.

The list of carefully written foreign characters on each page in his own handwriting still didn't register as familiar, but he focused on the loose English translations. A linguistics major in college hadn't quite prepared him for the nuances of an inter-dimensional language, but he could usually make out the basics with the study he'd undertaken at the Consilium.

To *disperse the ~~dimming~~ fade.* He hadn't translated the entirety of the original text word-for-word, only left notes.

- *Requires the hearts of seven human males, removed 'clean and whole' while victim is alive*

- *Uses term for 'males' not 'men'*

- *Sacrifices must be made on earth carried in hands (handfuls of earth?) from the Realm (proper noun—specific place?)*

- *Purpose???*

This had to be the spell to raise a shade from the dead. Or the Fade, as it were.

A key in the front door made him hastily stash the copy of the spellbook under the sheaf from the envelope.

It was only Ted, though, brushing some rain from his head as he hung up his coat. He glanced around the room and asked,

"Grace and Riley not back yet?"

"No." Daniel realized his sister had been gone for a while. She'd left just before seven and his phone showed 9:30 now.

"I'll call her." A note in Ted's voice made it clear he was trying not to sound worried. "Do you know which burner she took?"

Daniel consulted his left palm, near his thumb, where he'd jotted the number Gracie had told him as she'd left the apartment that morning. "Three."

Ted nodded, consulting his own phone and cross-referencing. They had some kind of system of taking different burner phones on different days, or maybe for different trips, and a list somewhere of the numbers. It sounded exhausting, but probably smarter than using the same cell phone for months at a time.

"No answer," Ted finally concluded.

"Maybe she took Rye to the playground."

"Not great weather for it." Ted eyed the window, then glanced to the papers scattered around Daniel's chair. Before he could say anything further, they both became aware of voices outside the door.

It opened and Riley bounded inside. Gracie followed. Neither were carrying grocery bags.

"Long trip," Daniel remarked, as Riley clamoured up onto his lap, dislodging the notebook and other papers. "Hey, hi, Rye, what . . .?"

"Coat off," Riley demanded, holding out his arms so his uncle could help him out of his jacket.

"Please." Gracie supplied the correction automatically as she threw the deadbolt, then dumped her empty back-pack by the door and sagged into her husband's arms as he came to the door to greet her.

"Please," the toddler repeated after his mother, then said, "Mama fell." He had a nasty, red scrape on the bottom of his elbow that Daniel uncovered when he got the toddler's coat off.

"Ouch. Took you down with her, huh?"

Gracie glared at him, pulling away from her husband.

"Do you have band-aids?" She posed the question with enough annoyed exhaustion to say the wrong answer might get Daniel disowned.

"There's a first-aid kit under the bathroom sink," he said.

"Come on, Rye, let's get your arm cleaned up," she said, inclining her head toward the hallway.

Riley climbed off Daniel's lap and followed his mother. Ted leaned back against the door, arms folded over his chest, studying his feet. He lifted his head to gaze down the hallway where his wife and son had disappeared, then caught Daniel's eye and smiled without cheer.

"They're back." Daniel tried to be reassuring despite a distinct lack of practice. "They're here, they're fine."

"Yeah." It wasn't really agreement.

27

GRACIE HAD TO WAIT until she'd gotten Riley down for a nap to give her husband and brother an account of their morning. Her son insisted on snuggling with her in bed for twenty minutes. Finally, worn out from the early morning adventure, he conked out and she could sneak out of the bedroom, leaving the door open a crack.

Ted and Daniel waited in the living room, and the tension there told Gracie they both had a good idea what had happened. She still sank onto the sofa and gave them the details about the agents, about Tess Foster and her betrayal.

She'd planned to stop at the basics, but then she went on without meaning to, "She didn't really seem . . . like Theresa."

Her husband lifted his eyebrows, waiting for more information, but Gracie didn't quite know how to give words to her feelings. "I don't know," she said. "It's probably nothing. Theresa—Tess—just seemed so . . . adept."

"And she wasn't that when you knew her?"

"She was skilled in her job. In research and artifacts. Not in dodging or stalking enemy agents. She'd never felt like the type to, well, to play me." The memory of Tess lying, leading her on, trying to convince her she was still a friend irked her all over again.

"She was pretty cocky when I met her too," Daniel agreed.

"That's it." Something shifted in the pit of Gracie's stomach. "Cocky. Confident. Tess wasn't ever shy, but she wasn't . . . take-charge."

"People step up," Ted offered. "In emergencies. For power."

"I know." Gracie fought to keep from glancing at her brother. "I did get her to mention that her new bosses—whoever they are—are looking for a map. One to the Shade Realm."

"Realm?" Daniel echoed, starting to shuffle through papers he'd stuffed on the side of his chair cushion.

"Of *Shades*," Gracie repeated, a little puzzled that he hadn't caught on to the key word.

"So, it's all connected," he agreed, flipping through several sheets to read something. He handed her a sheaf of papers that turned out to be Al-Amin's *Treatise*. "Chapter twelve's missing," he said. "Do you have it somewhere?"

"Jude has it."

"Shit." He sat back, disappointed.

"How about your errand?" Gracie asked Ted, plunging forward before her brother could get further wrapped up in the useless nonsense she'd brought back from her apartment. She stooped to retrieve the manila folder from the living room floor and started to gather the papers spread around the chair, shuffling them into a pile.

"We're set," Ted said. "Wheels up at eight tomorrow morning. Four seats."

"You'll only need three." Daniel got to his feet.

"I'm not *leaving* you." Gracie balked. She and her brother were a team—a package deal. Always had been.

"Well, I'm not running away," he shot back. "This Shadowed Mab, the Host, you spent years studying them and now that it's actually relevant, now that something's *happening*, you want to cut and run?"

"I spent years digging up moldy old texts full of rumours and fairy stories and unearthing dusty artifacts that amounted to *nothing*," Gracie corrected. "Yes, part of me wants to stay and unravel the mystery," she admitted, as if that would help her case. "But another part of me, the one I have to listen to, knows that if I do, it will never end. And it has to end."

Her next words came out in a rush of bitter exasperation. "The Consilium is gone, Daniel. It's gone and it *should* be gone. Mom and Alan, they never should have pulled us into this." She raked a hand back through her hair and then rubbed her eyes to push back the furious tears starting there. "I'm not doing this to Rye again."

"Doing what? He's got a skinned elbow. He's fine."

Gracie glared at her brother, unable to find the words to describe her son's reaction on the bus, the waves of terror and self-loathing she'd felt for putting this tiny, innocent human in that situation. She shouldn't have to explain it to him.

"None of us are *fine*." Ted came to her defence.

Daniel sank back into his chair, propping an elbow on the armrest and pinching the bridge of his nose between two fingers like he did—like he and Gracie both did, when they were frustrated. "I know," he said, startling them both with his quiet agreement. "But we can't just run away and hope for the best."

"Why not?" Gracie crushed the sheaf of papers in one hand, annoyed that even now she felt guilty about mistreating documents. The stack felt thick in her hand, thicker than what had been in the envelope originally. She couldn't help flipping through them until she found a bunch stapled together, a bunch she didn't remember.

No, she remembered them, but they hadn't been in her folder.

"Is this the Antagonist grymoire?" It wasn't the right question. That came out next, in a lower voice: "Did you make a goddamn *copy* of the Antagonist grymoire before we destroyed it?"

"They have another copy, over there across the portal," Daniel started, straightening up. "We needed to know what was in it. I needed *time* to translate—"

He stopped when Gracie laughed, dropping her hand and the sheaf of papers to her side.

"I don't know why I'm still surprised when you lie to my face," she said.

"Okay." Ted came between them. "Let's just . . . not. It's already been a day and it's only ten in the morning."

As if on cue, a wail came from the bedroom, followed by Riley's plaintive cry,

"Mama!"

"I'll go," Ted said, probably jumping at the opportunity to extricate himself, and disappeared down the hallway.

"The spell to make a shade corporeal is in there," Daniel said, gesturing to the sheaf of papers Gracie held. "And Tess Foster says these agents want a way to the Shade Realm. It's *connected.*"

"I'm tired of puzzles." Gracie said the words as much for her own benefit as his. Part of her still wanted to be swayed by his argument, talked down, and she couldn't give that part an opening. "I'm tired of all of this." She frowned at the handful of papers still in her fist. "We should burn all of this crap before we go."

"Right, why stop at fleeing like cowards?" Daniel muttered.

Gracie gritted her teeth to keep from shouting at him. "I'm not going to have Riley dragging stacks of old papers around and running for his life after I'm fucking dead."

"I'm sure he'll have scanned them into a goddamn brain chip or something by then." The cynicism in Daniel's voice made Gracie flinch but he sounded more frustrated than angry. His protest was weakening. He knew she was right but he'd fight her to the last just to prove he could.

Ted appeared in the hallway, frowning.

"No dice," he relayed. "Rye wants you."

28

Daniel waited until Gracie had disappeared down the hall to take care of her son, then searched his phone for Jude's number. He got up and moved into the kitchenette for privacy from his brother-in-law, putting the call through. He felt uneasy twice over—not just for going behind his sister's back, but for using Jude to do it.

It didn't stop him, though.

The voice that answered after two rings was cheery and calm. "Heyo."

"Jude? It's Daniel."

"Hey!" Jude didn't give him a chance to say more. "Okay, look, weird question but is there *any* chance you could, like, gift me a ride?" She spoke quickly, stumbling over words as if afraid he would hang up. "I don't have any cash and the app won't take my debit card. And I can't walk very far right now."

"Are you drunk?" Daniel took in the ramble, startled.

"No, Danny, I am on drugs." Jude's voice slurred slightly, but she added in a defensive tone, "Hospital drugs, don't get judgey."

"Why are you at the hospital?"

"It's a long story. One that I don't entirely remember at this very moment. I've been here for hours, I've got crutches, and I'm *really* bored."

"Where are you?" The words were out before he could stop them. Whatever mess she'd gotten into was yet another thing he didn't need to be involved in, but she had the missing chapter from Gracie's papers. It was probably worthless, but it would only cost the price of a taxi to the hospital to find out. Unearthing something important in it could prove to Gracie that running wasn't the answer. He had to try.

Jude's voice got more distant as she seemed to lift the phone away from her ear to repeat the question to someone else, then she relayed the name of the hospital back to him.

"I'll be there in thirty minutes," he said.

"Like a pizza. Do pizzas still do that? I mean, obviously, *pizzas* don't—"

"Just stay put."

Ted had apparently retreated to the bedroom with his wife and son, so there was no one in the front room to notice Daniel gather his coat and head out to find a taxi.

He almost missed Jude when he arrived in the crowded ER. She sat in a chair in the corner, wrapped in a bright red flannel jacket, flipping through a magazine. She'd stretched her right leg out in front of her, a black brace shining over the jeans on her knee and keeping it at an angle. Her eyes flickered up as he reached her.

"Hi!" Her voice, brighter than usual, jarred him.

"What happened?" He gestured to the brace.

"Oh." She hooked a thumb in the magazine to hold her place. "Pulled my . . . something with three letters that lives in my knee." She lowered her voice, but not quite enough to mask her next words, "I told the nurse it was parkour but, *actually*, these Faerie soldiers were chasing me and—"

"Let's get out you of here," Daniel cut her off, glancing around to see who might have overheard her. "You can explain later."

"Okay." She held a hand out. "Help me up."

He hesitated, startled. She'd normally have fought her way to her feet by herself, damn the pain. This was a little unnerving.

"Maybe you should put the magazine down," he said.

"I'm in the middle of a quiz."

Dumbfounded, he stared at her long enough that she had to wave her hand again to remind him to help her up. He gripped it and put another hand under her elbow, pulling her to her feet as gently as he could, then supporting her to keep her weight off her right leg. "Ah," she breathed, her voice a little slurred again. "If I wasn't really doped, I think that'd have hurt a lot."

"I've got a taxi waiting."

"Hang on, I have crutches." She found the pair propped against the wall by her chair. "I *rented* them. Did you know they rent crutches? The nurse told me I can get some cheap at a thrift store, but like, how am I supposed to get to a *store*?"

She tucked the crutches under her arms. She was unsteady on them, but managed to hobble along through the double doors to the idling car outside at the curb. Then she wrangled herself to the middle of the taxi's back seat so that she could keep her leg angled out a little, which meant she sat pressed against Daniel.

He realized too late that he should have taken the empty front seat. Trying to ignore her closeness, he had her relay her address to the driver. He'd get her home, pick up the missing chapter and see if there was anything in it that might keep another heart from being cut out of someone's chest. Win/win, and at least more proactive than watching Gracie pack up their lives to flee.

Jude had kept the magazine. She opened it on her lap again as the car pulled away from the curb. "Would you say I'm scrappy?"

"What?" He wasn't sure he'd heard her correctly.

"Pick the adjective that best describes you," she read. "I'm definitely not 'sultry' or 'brainy.' That leaves 'scrappy.' You think it fits?"

"I . . ." Lost on how to answer, Daniel went with, "Sure?"

"Whatever." She snapped the magazine shut. "It's stupid anyway. *Which Action Heroine Are You?* I *should* write my own categories—look at this brace. Is 'kickass' an adjective?"

"*Quiet* is." Even though the driver up front was speaking to somebody on his earpiece in what sounded like an Arabic dialect, Daniel preferred Jude not be overheard in this state.

"Look!" She opened the magazine again to another page, pointing to a photo. "That's the Archduke. Do you know what he *called* me? Mabling! What the fuck even is that? Is it supposed to be offensive?"

"Jude—"

"You don't think that's my actual title, right? Because it's patronizing as hell and—"

"Stop," Daniel hissed, putting a hand over hers and squeezing to drive his point home. When she studied his hand, startled, he withdrew it.

At the risk of starting her chatter again, he couldn't help asking, "What are you on?"

"I don't know." She laid her head back against the headrest. "My father glamoured a nurse or something."

"Your . . . father?" The word in this context felt foreign on Daniel's tongue.

"Joshua himself," Jude agreed with a sigh. She shot him a crooked, bitter smile. "I recognized him from the picture you had in your oven last summer. And from Miranda. He still looks a lot like her." She yawned and continued offhandedly, "Looked okay, after being in a shade prison for twenty years. Oh—that's where he says he was: the Land of Shades. Can you believe it?"

No. Was it smarter to humour what was likely a painkiller-induced dream, or to press for the real story while Jude might be more amenable to telling it?

He decided to play it safe: "Where is he now?"

"He just miraculously appeared," she said, sarcasm tinging her voice, "and disappeared from the hospital. He vagued out his whereabouts and some daring escape from Shade Land, but nothing else."

She sounded certain, but then again, she was doped. She could have imagined anything. The part about Joshua being involved with shades—it seemed like she was mixing up waking life with whatever delusions the drugs were giving her.

"You don't believe me." Jude's accusation broke through his thoughts, more annoyed than offended. "I saw him *before* he gave me the drugs. Before Miranda's dudes attacked." She hesitated, as if thinking back. "He might have tried to warn me about them, actually."

"Then why did he disappear at the hospital?"

"Why did he disappear *at all*? Because he's a deadbeat asshole. I'm not saying otherwise, just, like, he *was* there last night."

It wasn't worth arguing with her in this state. Probably not worth asking her about the chapter either, but that was why he'd come to find her. Waiting just made him feel more uncomfortable.

"Grace gave you some papers yesterday," he said.

"Mmm." Jude remained slumped against the seat with her face turned toward the window, as if she'd started dozing. Her body had migrated slowly closer to his over the last few minutes, her hip and elbow becoming connecting points of warmth.

"Do you still have them?"

"Mmm hmm."

Daniel tensed as her head tilted sideways to rest on his shoulder. He had to brace the muscles in his arm to keep from immediately shrugging her off. *She's on something. She's not herself.*

But the familiar weight of the head was hers, and so was the coconut scent of the hair brushing against his cheek. Her drowsy voice vibrated against his arm.

"I want a do-over. You and me."

His throat tightened. For an instant, it sounded right. He wouldn't have to lie, to hide anything, like he was supposed to do in the rest of this new life, post-Consilium. No need to pretend he was fine, ordinary, with Jude. She already knew his past, and he knew hers. They knew each other probably better than either of them had ever intended. Even when she'd been using him—for his name, for his knowledge, for a safe haven—it had been hard to deny her.

And she didn't need anything from him now.

No, of course she did. She was broke, injured, alone. Manipulating somebody into saving her.

"Let's not do this." He dipped his shoulder, leaning away toward the window to force her upright. "You're not . . . yourself right now."

"Isn't that what you want?" Jude's too earnest response made him look back to her in surprise.

"Why would I—?"

"I hurt you." She grunted, sounding disgusted with her own conclusion, and backtracked, "'Hurt.' Fucking sugar-coating."

She paused, unconsciously running the fingers of one hand over the knuckles of her other, maybe remembering the feeling of smashing them into his face six months ago. She didn't go into further detail, saying instead: "The old me. I mean, I want that to be the old me. I'm trying—"

She stopped, putting her hand on his thigh so that he could feel the warmth through his jeans. His breath froze in his throat but he couldn't make himself reach down and brush her fingers away.

"I'm trying to be better," she finished.

Then she leaned in and pressed her lips against his. She kissed him hard and hungrily, like she meant to keep his mouth too busy to refuse.

It worked. He collapsed into her embrace despite himself. The force of his racing heart drove him closer, cupping a palm around the smooth curve of her cheek. No need to think, or analyze, or find the right words—with Jude it was simply instinct, always had been.

That was what had gotten him sucked into her violent orbit in the first place.

He dropped his hand and managed to turn his head, breaking contact with her soft, searching mouth. He stared down at the grey upholstery beneath his shoes, banishing a surge of desire to seek out her lips again.

Jude slowly pulled herself upright, then turned and manoeuvred her leg so that it rested between them on the floor, creating a safe emptiness in the middle seat. She rested her temple against the window, steaming the glass with the warmth of her face.

"Leave it to my dumb ass to fall for the guy *after* I try to kill him," she muttered.

Daniel's numb uncertainty gave way and an unbidden warmth fused through him. How could confirmation of his worst possible scenario be a relief? It lifted the weight, finally knowing her intentions last April for certain. He could stop wondering and questioning what exactly had happened, what he'd misunderstood. Jude hadn't cared about him. She'd wanted him dead, or at the very least, leaving him alive had been an oversight.

But she was *glad* now, relieved that she'd failed. Or at least this off-kilter, strangely nostalgic woman on painkillers was.

Reminding himself of that distinction didn't keep Daniel from wanting to kiss her again. God, he needed a drink. But a drink wasn't going to fortify his resolve.

He realized that the front seat had gone suddenly silent, and he lifted his head to make some sort of explanation.

But no, it was the red and blue lights flashing at the far end of the residential street that had distracted the driver.

29

A MORE FAMILIAR DREAD replaced the uneasiness in Daniel's stomach as he peered up through the front seats to the flashing lights.

"C'est là-bas, ouais?" The taxi driver pointed through the windshield, slowing the car to a stop.

"Fuck." Jude shoved the cab door open without further warning. She slithered into a heap on the sidewalk, then gained her feet even though she'd left the crutches tangled in the backseat. She took off in a surprisingly quick hobble toward the lights.

Daniel fumbled to pay the driver and grabbed the crutches. He rushed out of the car, hurrying after her toward the police.

She was more nimble now—maybe shifting gravity unconsciously with each step to keep herself upright in her haste.

The police hadn't set up any perimeter yet so Jude bee-lined straight through the open door of the first-floor apartment.

When Daniel reached her, she'd come to a stop over a blonde woman slumped against the wall, wrapped in a blanket.

"C'est fou, c'est . . . je ne comprends pas, c'est . . ." the woman muttered. Rusty brown streaks stained the grey polyester of the blanket where she must have been gripping it with bloodstained hands.

"It's Guy. Oh, hell, it's Guy." Jude sagged against the wall. "Goddamn it, I didn't even *like* him. Why would that cult e—"

"Okay," Daniel cut in, stopping Jude's drug-fueled rant mid-syllable. He glanced beyond her, his gaze fixing on the motionless toes of a waxy foot just visible through a door frame. Cold horror flooded him. To shake himself out of it, he forced the crutches on Jude and urged her out of the apartment.

A police officer noticed them as they left. Daniel managed to make a hasty explanation that they were just returning from the hospital to a different apartment, and the cop, seemingly distracted by the scene around him, bought it. He paid no further attention as Daniel steered Jude back out onto the sidewalk.

"It's my fault," Jude mumbled. "I should have realized that Guy—I didn't even *like* him," she repeated.

"It's not your fault." Daniel focused on guiding her down the sidewalk to the street. He tried not to picture the lifeless foot.

"She's got five now."

"Five?"

"Oh, yeah." Jude's breath hitched. "Chris is dead. Abe found him last night."

"I'm sorry." He didn't know what else to say. He didn't know who Chris was or who he'd been to Jude.

"She left Guy here," Jude said, "at my place. Not like the others. She's getting closer. She's calling me out."

"Maybe." Daniel just wanted to get her out of the vicinity of flashing lights and uniformed figures. He pulled out his phone and ordered another taxi, leading Jude slowly to the end of the street to avoid the bulk of the emergency vehicles.

She shifted her weight to pull several folded pages from the back pocket of her jeans, then tossed them at him.

"Take this if you want it," she spat. "I fucked up and Chris is dead, so it didn't even matter."

Daniel stooped to retrieve the pages as Jude limped away, making her way more awkwardly down the sidewalk now.

"Where are you going?" he called.

"Away." She didn't turn. A chilly wind blew past, ruffling the sides of the jacket that she'd left open.

He was seized by the frustrated temptation to just let her go. Let her limp off into the cold and good fucking riddance.

But he couldn't. He didn't have the capacity at the moment to delve deeper into why, exactly, but he caught up to her.

"I called another cab," he said.

"Take it. You can't be here." She came to a wavering stop as if hobbling another step forward were too much for her. She kept her head down, shoulders slumped over the crutches. "Somebody's watching. They were fucking watching at the club and they saw Guy and *voilà*!" She threw a hand back along with her bitter words, to indicate the mess at her apartment.

Daniel touched her elbow, steadying her, but she jerked away and spun to the other side, nearly colliding with a tree on the out-lawn.

"You're not safe around me," she insisted. "You never were."

He hadn't exactly expected gratitude, but her sudden anger grated. He was in no mood to revisit their history on a cold street with Jude high on self-pity and god only knew what kind of pills.

"At least zip your goddamn coat," he snapped.

"It's doesn't zip and it's not my coat," Jude shouted back, then added a, "Fuck!" aimed at the blue sky. She started to shuck off the coat, teetering dangerously on one crutch as she struggled with the sleeve.

"Stop." Daniel caught her. She'd already exposed her bare shoulders, clad only in a tight red halter top under the jacket.

"It's Guy's coat," she insisted, trying to shake him off. "I don't want to wear it."

"I don't care." He tightened his grip until she stopped fighting. Maybe he couldn't solve a single piece of the mystery tightening around them, but he could damn well keep her from freezing.

"What is *wrong* with you?" Jude hissed, letting out a desperate, exhausted sigh. She fixed him with a dull glare while he pulled the quilted flannel back up over her shoulders. "A Faerie monster is swooping off with guys I've exchanged fewer words with in my life than you in the last five minutes."

"Then it's a good thing my place is warded."

Too tired to argue further, she climbed silently but clumsily into the next cab when it arrived. This one was a minivan, but one of the two middle seats had been torn out, which allowed her to haul herself in more easily. She took the seat in the furthest back corner, propping her brace up and claiming the whole bench.

Daniel went to the single middle seat, relieved to have the space. A sense of numbing fatigue threatened to overtake him and he wanted nothing more than to let it. The ride was silent, except for the low, tinny music from the radio up front. His mention of the ward had seemed to soothe Jude's fluctuating anger, or else she'd just lost whatever fight the crime scene in her apartment had stirred in her.

It was a bad idea, taking her to his place, yet he kept doing it. He could still feel her hands on his face, the closeness of her body, her lips against his, and he was grateful for the seat-back between them.

Back in June, after the motel room they'd reluctantly shared, his self-loathing had told him that Jude had only forced herself on him because she was bored and he was nearby. Today wasn't that, but it still didn't have to be genuine. She had pills and pain fucking up her head. *His* head was supposed to be clear now. He was supposed to know better.

As if to prove that retrieving Jude from the hospital really had been about obtaining the *Treatise*'s missing chapter, he turned his attention to the four pages she'd tossed at him. Chapter twelve didn't seem more useful than any of the other chapters he'd read, being mostly about how the Shadowed Mab had become a shade and not much else. No good evidence to sway Gracie.

He still couldn't manage to regret the trip.

When they reached his building and climbed out of the van, Jude stopped at the bottom of the first flight of stairs. She stared up with a drained, hopeless expression, then sighed heavily, buckled down and started to work her way up on her crutches.

Navigating the first five steps took her an inordinate amount of time fumbling with her crutches. She'd lost whatever adrenaline had been fuelling her back at her own apartment.

Daniel had never seen her so halting and clumsy. Even drunk, she'd always had a preternatural grace to her movements—manipulating space to move herself through it with a dancer's ease. Impatience drove him to force his way onto the stair beside her as gently as he could, and slide an arm around her waist. At least, he told himself it was impatience.

Jude tensed as if she might refuse, then let one of her crutches clatter to the stairs between them as she stretched her arm across his shoulders. She sighed with relief and what might have been a sob as she let him lift her against his side and take the weight off her injured leg.

The narrow staircase made movement difficult, pressed closely together, but they made better time.

Holding her upright, Daniel couldn't retrieve the crutch she'd dropped, so they left it behind.

"I didn't ask for help," Jude mumbled, as they reached the third floor.

Painkillers must be wearing off. Daniel didn't bother to address her more characteristic utterance, and left her bracing herself against the wall to go back for her lost crutch.

When he got back upstairs, Jude was resting one shoulder against the wall, her eyes closed. She opened them when he got close enough and accepted her crutches back without another word. She seemed tired and hazy. Maybe she didn't even remember what had happened. That would be best for both of them.

The apartment was quiet as they entered, Gracie and Riley playing some kind of game on the floor and Ted reading his phone in a nearby chair. All three looked up when Daniel and Jude came through the doorway.

Whatever Gracie and Riley were doing, it had involved drawing a series of black lines on what appeared to be an entire ream of paper, then taping the sheets in a line around the floor, up the side of the sofa, down the arm, across the back and back over to the floor.

"Train tracks," Jude said, realizing more quickly what the mess was: a long, winding set of paper railroad tracks, drawn in crayon.

Riley got to his feet, staring at her uncertainly, like he might dart to hide behind his mother. He studied the brace on her leg and then held out the wooden train engine he'd been running down the paper tracks.

"Wanna drive the train?" he offered.

"Let's give her a minute," Gracie said, tugging on the back of his shirt to prompt him to sit back down.

Daniel steered Jude toward the bedroom at the back of the apartment. He had no idea what she might say in front of Gracie and Ted, not to mention Riley, so it seemed safer to sequester her for now. Plus, his sister probably had some choice words for him and he didn't mind putting off that argument.

Jude sank onto the mattress in the bedroom without waiting for his assent. She swung her leg over to prop it up with a groan, then managed to struggle out of the big, flannel coat before falling back against the headboard, exhausted.

Daniel's phone buzzed in his back pocket and he checked his messages to find one from Zeb.

Tu mort?

He grimaced, realizing that he'd forgotten to reach out that morning and let his friend know everything was all right after last night. Given the ironic text, Zeb couldn't be too worried.

Daniel texted back: *Not yet.*

Cool. This yours? A photo of the crumpled receipt from Marianne Nguyen's office accompanied that message. It must have fallen out of his pocket in the car last night.

The books that the professor had sold were probably as worthless as the *Treatise* had been. But Tess Foster and her new bosses were looking for a map to the Shade Realm, and Marianne Nguyen had studied the Host, like Gracie. Given the store *had* at one time been frequented by Consilium researchers, going in search of the books the professor had sold felt slightly less like a ridiculous gamble.

He wasn't supposed to pursue it. Gracie wanted to cut and run, and she was probably right. No, she was definitely right. But she and Ted had something else to run toward, some prosperous, new future. He didn't. *What else am I good at? What else can I even do?*

He took his attention off the screen to make an excuse to Jude and leave, but her head had fallen to one side and she appeared to be asleep. That definitely made things easier.

Gracie waiting in the hallway didn't. She stood close enough to the bedroom door that when he let himself out of the room he wondered if she'd had an ear pressed against it.

"What's she doing here?" she demanded, as he closed the door.

"Her apartment was a crime scene."

"So?"

"You'd prefer I'd left her on the street with a busted knee and rented crutches?"

"I mean, given she left *you* bleeding on the floor with two broken ribs last winter . . . ?"

"That was—" Daniel stopped himself, because he didn't know what words to choose. That was before? That wasn't Jude? That was somebody else? She was trying to be *better* now?

All of those options were wrong.

Gracie raised her eyebrows, pressing for him to finish his thought, but he could only shake his head.

"Just let her sleep," he muttered, shouldering past her.

"Our discussion isn't over," she warned.

"Right." Daniel retrieved the folded papers Jude had tossed at him outside her apartment and passed them to his sister. "The missing chapter, for your burn pile."

"Don't treat me like I'm overreacting," Gracie snapped, crumpling the papers in one fist. "We—" she gestured pointedly between him and herself, "are not the Consilium. Alan got to give orders from behind a desk. That luxury died with him. There's no structure to protect us anymore but you're still looking for trouble. You're inviting these dangerous things into your life because you want to keep fighting them."

Daniel flinched like she'd struck him.

"I haven't *invited* any of this," he argued.

When she inclined her head to the closed bedroom door to make her point, he turned for the living room.

She stopped him in his tracks before he'd gotten more than two steps. "You'll do it until it kills you," she said, "like that's the morally superior choice. Because you think you've got something to prove to a bunch of dead people."

His chest tightened. He willed her to leave it there, but she was his sister, and she didn't.

"They're *dead*," she said. "Everybody we knew, everybody we worked with. It's—" She paused and her breath caught. "There's not a word strong enough for how much that hurts. And I regret it too—I wish I'd been there with them, but I'm also . . . so, so glad I wasn't." She swallowed hard, then offered in a softer voice, "It's okay to admit that you're glad to be alive."

"I am," Daniel said, over his shoulder. "Glad. And alive." The sick twist in his midsection felt bitterly selfish, even petty. "But what's the point if we just fuck off and let the world go to hell?"

"The point is that we *can*," Gracie said.

It was easier for her. She hadn't been there at ground zero, deep in the eye of the storm when everything went bad. *She* hadn't made the wrong choices, trusted the wrong people, been wilfully blinded.

And she had Ted and Riley. She had a full life of her own beyond the directives of their parents. She had reasons to move on, to walk away. He wanted her to take that, to be happy, to quit and get everything she needed.

But he couldn't just follow along in her footsteps like he had when they were kids.

Without turning to face her, he said, "I have to pick something up from Zeb."

30

A NOISE WOKE ME from a dreamless sleep. It took a minute to remember where I was. The night came back in a trickle. The timeline got fuzzy after the painkillers kicked in.

Guy was dead. I could still see Marie-Eve wrapped in a blanket on our living room floor repeating, "C'est fou, c'est fou."

My stomach twisted. I tried to turn onto my side to suppress the nausea, but my knee protested with a burning pain, giving me a much realer desire to throw up. I hissed through my teeth, forcing myself to take shallow breaths through my nose. That brought back the distant, hazy memories of the waiting room, the curtained-off exam room, my smart-ass "parkour" response to the nurse's question about what had happened to me, and her making me limp around to see how bad my injury was, probably in retaliation.

I wasn't in the hospital now. I was at Daniel's place, in his bedroom. He'd brought me back here after we'd encountered the violation in my apartment, but I couldn't summon other details—like where *he* was. I remembered sunlight through the car window, his arm tight around me as he helped me up the stairs, Riley offering me a toy, collapsing onto the mattress, my body wanting to melt into unconsciousness.

A knock at the door made me jerk my head up, half-expecting to see some invading agent. Then I realized an earlier knock was what had woken me.

The door opened a crack and Grace peeked in.

"Hey," she said. "How are you?"

"Not great." Seemed like the most succinct way to sum up the throbbing in my knee, aches through the rest of my body and the sheer embarrassment of not knowing quite what was I was doing here in Daniel's bed.

When she eyed my knee, I explained, "Daring escape from some of my aunt's minions last night."

She considered that and decided she had no further questions.

"Ted's making some dinner. Daniel said you should keep your knee elevated but I think you should eat something."

"How did he—?" I stopped, not sure which of the questions crowding my head wanted to come out first. How the hell did Daniel know more about my injury that I did? He hadn't even been there for most of it. "How long have I been here?"

"Since this afternoon. He brought you back because your place was compromised."

Compromised. Marie-Eve's vacant eyes flashed through my mind.

"Right," I managed. "I remember." I had the odd, pressing sensation that there was something else I was supposed to remember, something afterwards. It came back in halting flashes: my hand on Daniel's thigh, the two of us pressed together in the backseat of a car. Kissing him, my fingers brushing the stubble on his cheeks. His expression, startled and angry and maybe sad. Maybe just disappointed. Shame flooded me.

"Do you need me to bring you something?" Grace asked, jarring me out of the awkward memory.

"I'm not the stay-in-bed type." I worked my way to the edge of the mattress, trying not to jostle my knee too much. The brace had gotten loose in the last few hours because the swelling had gone down. I cinched the straps tighter, getting a snippet of the instructions that the nurse in the curtained exam room had given me: Don't do it too tightly while it's swollen. Keep weight off it for six weeks. Follow-up with an orthopaedist tomorrow for an X-ray.

Six weeks. Fuck that. Frustration gnawed at me, thoughts of everything I wouldn't be able to do. Every move had the potential to bring me down now. It was too much.

When real, human goosebumps tingled across my skin, I realized I was still wearing the skimpy, red halter top I'd gone dancing in. Feeling strangely ashamed to ask, I didn't meet Grace's eyes as I said, "Do you have, like, a warmer shirt?"

"Been living in this outfit for two days already." Her voice was wry but she went to the closet and grabbed something off a hanger, handing it across to me.

A men's long-sleeved t-shirt. It smelled like Daniel, like whatever detergent he used. Like my head against his shoulder this morning in the car, breathing him in. Like safety.

"That okay?" Grace prompted. I'd been holding the shirt without moving.

"Yeah. Thanks." I slipped my halter off and tugged the t-shirt on over my bra while Grace retrieved my crutches. She handed them across to me, noticing my flinch as I leaned to grab them.

"Does it hurt?"

"Like a bitch." I shoved the too-long shirt sleeves up to my elbows and then wrestled the crutches under my arms, almost taking Grace out at the knees with a wild swing.

"I saw hydrocodone in the bathroom," she said. "Probably leftover from one of Danny's surgeries."

"His what?"

"Shoulder." She tapped her own in explanation. "Got torn up by a griffin getting to Aubrie."

"Right." I remembered the half-changed creature slamming a paw full of sharp talons into Daniel's shoulder at Niagara Falls. I'd run Danny off afterwards to keep the victorious Court Faeries from noticing him, but it hadn't occurred to me that there'd been no Abe to heal him. Not that Faerie healing was a pleasant experience for humans, or for me, either—though I'd definitely take it right now.

Grace was still waiting for my answer to her offer. I couldn't anticipate what the medication might do to me after the stupor I'd been in most of the last twelve hours, so I shook my head to decline.

Hopping upright on the crutches was easy but using them to walk decidedly less so. I followed Grace into the living room, where Riley sat on the sofa, eating veggie slices from a brightly coloured plastic plate as he watched TV. It was dusky outside the window, and snowflakes flashed in the light as they fell past the glass. Grace had left the white snake of printer paper—train tracks—on the sofa.

Before I could reach the safety of a stool at the bar between the living room and kitchenette, Riley saw me and slid off the foldout, toddling over to investigate the brace on my knee.

"Hey," I said, pausing only momentarily to make sure I wouldn't bean him with a crutch as I made my way through the room.

"Boot." He pointed.

"Kind of."

"Why?"

"I got hurt."

"Why?"

"Fell off a roof." I let out a sigh as I reached my desired stool and settled on it, taking the weight off my legs.

"I thought 'not falling' was your whole deal," an unfamiliar voice said from the other side of the bar. A tall,

Black man stood at the stove in the kitchen, stirring some kind of red sauce. He gave me a once-over.

"Bad night," I returned. "And day."

He laughed, then, noting my distrustful look, gestured to himself with the spatula.

"Ted. Gracie's husband."

"And personal chef," Grace herself supplied from beside me.

Ted emptied a pot of boiling water and pasta into a colander in the sink, then started dishing up bowls of spaghetti and tomato sauce on the counter. He glanced over his shoulder at the bar with a frown.

"Your brother needs a dining room table."

"He needs a dining room," Grace muttered.

"Where *is* Daniel?" I asked, grateful for the opening.

"Occult bookstore."

"Quelle surprise." I *had* learned some French. "Looking for what?"

"Distractions." The word was sharp as broken glass and I managed to bite my tongue before pressing further.

I accepted a bowl of spaghetti and red sauce from Ted. It tasted amazing, and the warm food made me feel better about my knee, at least until I shifted on my stool and sent a new wave of painful heat flooding through it.

"Sure you don't want the meds?" Grace eyed me as I struggled not to gag and bring up the pasta I'd just downed.

"No. I mean, yes, but drugs are . . . unpredictable with my, uh, blood." And I didn't want to black out on any more moments of Daniel kissing me, or rejecting me, or whatever embarrassing things I'd done earlier to make him so uncomfortable facing me.

"Huh." Grace frowned at her pasta. "Didn't think of that."

"Me either." I sighed, stabbing my fork down into the sauce. Had Joshua known, when he gave me those pills? Had he actually wanted to relieve my pain or just pacify me? It seemed like unnecessary trouble to go through, glamouring a nurse and stealing pills for me, if he didn't actually care about my well-being. On the other hand, he hadn't shown any hesitation about working magic on humans at the drop of a hat to get anything else he'd wanted.

Stolen magic. Some of the answers he'd given me last night floated back in. *Siphoned out of Shade Land.* He knew the Shadow Mab. He knew the spell. But he'd seemed upset, maybe even angry, when I mentioned my connections. That was why he'd left—gone after something or someone.

Maybe he was solving the whole damn mess. I definitely wasn't going to be any help now. I twirled some pasta around my fork and tipped it to the ceiling in a sort of toast to the universe before eating it.

Grace must have taken my derisive twitch for another indication of pain. "I'm getting you a pill," she said.

"It's not the pain. I mean, yeah, it hurts but I'm—I don't know what to do." My frustration spilled out in words without my permission: "I've never been broken before."

She cocked a dubious eyebrow at me. "Weren't you in a coma last winter?"

"That was falling asleep and waking up. This is being awake the whole time with *this*." I growled down at the brace on my knee. "I'm not supposed to put weight on it for six weeks. I can barely walk. I can't fight. I can't *do* anything."

"It's probably for the best." Grace paused, realizing how that had come out. "I mean, for you to take a rest." She shook her head. "That was meant to be encouraging. And not a poem."

"Maybe not a great time to try out new material."

That drew the ghost of a smile. She slid off her stool and disappeared down the hallway.

I pulled out my phone to text Abe and was surprised to discover that I'd already texted him last night: '*U up lol to fix my knee.*'

He hadn't responded. Who could blame him, given the cringey text that had probably seemed funny while I was on painkillers. It still felt odd that I hadn't heard from him.

Grace returned and passed me a folded tissue with the hard roundness of a pill capsule tucked inside.

"For later," she said. "If you need it."

"Thanks." I tucked it into my pocket. When I lingered over my phone another few seconds, I caught her attention. "Just trying to get a bead on my cowboy healer," I explained.

She didn't miss a beat, returning dryly, "Must be rough being royalty."

"It's not all tiaras and flowers. Miranda sent some goons to grab me and haul me off somewhere safe—" I couldn't help throwing air-quotes onto that word, "—Because my uterus can't be put in danger. Which, honestly, is some bullshit because Abe said *she* sent him and Gordon over here to find me in the first place. What'd she think would happen?"

"Maybe she didn't."

"Think?" I appreciated what I first took for an extension of her dry tone but Grace corrected,

"Send them."

The suggestion struck me in an unpleasant way, prickling the back of my neck. *Had* Abe actually said my aunt had sent him and Gordon to find me? Or had I just assumed, because I'd only ever known the cowboy in the context of Miranda? Gordon was a Court mage who didn't like being in the human world, though—who else *but* the Mab could have ordered him over here?

Why the hell hadn't Abe texted me back? I'd sent him my message nearly ten hours ago. The sudden memory of trying to reach Chris the same way compressed my lungs.

But the Shadow Mab needed the blood of seven *human* men to do the ritual, and Abe wasn't human, not fully. Not even mostly.

The other niggling possibility swept in. It couldn't be Abe *running* this cult horror show, could it? The cowboy seemed protective enough of this world, going off his actions back in June. He'd called it 'his' world, supposedly grown up here, like me. He wouldn't unleash some kind of Faerie evil on it.

It wouldn't be the first time I'd trusted the wrong person, though. I had a pretty solid track record at that by now.

31

Daniel made his way down a narrow aisle packed with books and antique knickknacks of all shapes and sizes, Zeb following. There was supposed to be some semblance of organization, according to the yellowing, hand-written signs on the top of each shelf.

He'd have preferred to have come alone, but Zeb hadn't given him the choice, insisting they meet at the store to deliver the receipt from his car despite Daniel's protests.

"It's an antiques store, how treacherous can it be?" had been Zeb's exact, flip words. But his friend wouldn't have wanted to tag along if he hadn't suspected there could be some dangerous element to it that was better faced in numbers.

Daniel didn't have much experience with loyal friends. He didn't want to lose this one if he could help it, so he'd let Zeb come with him.

He'd presented the professor's receipt to the cashier, asking a few general questions. The other man didn't answer any of them, jerking his head to the left as soon as he'd skimmed the receipt and instructing them in French to go to the end of the third shelf and look near the floor.

"So, the Consilium used to do business here?" Zeb asked, voice low, as they came around the end of the long shelf. "How'd they tell the legit stuff from the bullshit?"

"Training." Daniel couldn't help adding dryly, "The fact that you're assuming there's anything legit here means you're already in too deep."

"Story of my life." Zeb ran a finger over the spines of the books at eye-level. From beyond the shelves behind them, the bell over the front door jingled and the cashier began talking to another customer.

Daniel crouched to see the bottom shelf, stirring up a host of dust bunnies. This one was mostly old, musty books, some with the titles worn off the spines. He did a cursory glance for any that looked like they might have been through a fire and pulled out each book without writing on the spine. Those he checked the covers or flipped through to see if he recognized the author. It seemed to be nothing more than neo-pagan self-help books from the '70s and old horror film magazines.

Coming here had been a mistake, a stupid excuse to avoid a hard conversation with Gracie. Another dead end.

Suppressing a sigh, he moved the last stack from the front of the shelf. A sudden charcoal scent mingled with the odour of dusty paper. He reached to the back, wincing as his fingers brushed something brittle that felt like either a dead cockroach or a *very* dead mouse, then closed on a thin chapbook. The top corner was charred and the whole thing seemed ready to fall apart if somebody looked at it wrong.

The shape of the writing on it struck him as familiar but didn't resolve into letters. More of the same on the crisp pages inside. He was becoming accustomed to the frustration that washed through him, but it still made him want to tear up the fragile, unreadable book in his hand. It had been less than twenty-four hours since the mage had dipped into his memory and taken the incantation, and yet 'temporary memory loss' still felt dubious as an excuse.

What if his knowledge never came back? Would that be so bad? Without the spell humming in his head, he could try again to step back into the normal world. Maybe this was actually a push in the direction of sanity.

Gracie would probably say so.

"Hey." Zeb stood stiffly, listening to the front of the store.

Daniel became aware of the sudden quiet. The bell over the door had rung a few seconds earlier, and now the cashier and the customer up front, previously in the middle of a boisterous conversation, had fallen silent.

Zeb leaned slowly to the right to peer around the bookshelf that blocked them. He jerked back. "Shady group. Three of them. Think there's a back way out?"

"There," Daniel whispered, noticing a doorway at the end of the next aisle. "Go."

Zeb moved for the exit and footsteps scuffed from the aisle on Daniel's right, speed increasing as the agents spotted him.

Daniel stuffed the burned chapbook under one arm and grabbed the closest hardcover. He darted around the edge of the shelf, swinging the book into the face of the first person who reached him.

It was the man from Marianne Nguyen's office, the agent who wasn't Rogers. The hit made him stumble back into Rogers himself and an unfamiliar woman, the three Zeb had seen. Their confusion blocked the narrow aisle momentarily and one shelf tottered like it might collapse to the side.

Daniel spun, getting half a metre before someone tackled him from behind and wrestled him to the ground. He kicked out from beneath the other body, clawed his way free along the grimy wood floor before shoving himself up and starting to run as he gained his feet.

Something hit him between the shoulder blades, hard enough to send him back to his hands and knees. It knocked the wind out of him, giving an agent time to fall on top of him. As he struggled to suck air back into his lungs, someone shoved him to the floor on his stomach. The man on top of him grabbed his right arm and wrenched it behind his back.

A handcuff encircled his wrist, but before it could close, the bells on the front door jangled above the sound of the door slamming open hard. Something came at them at high speed, footfalls heavy on the uneven floorboards.

"Jesus Christ!" The agent holding Daniel let go, sounding stunned as he jerked upright.

Daniel seized the opportunity to lurch to his feet. He couldn't help risking a glance behind him.

A shadowy form had knocked the other agents to the floor. It moved too fast for much more than the observation that it stood on two legs and seemed to have the requisite limbs for a person.

Daniel turned to join Zeb at the back exit, but something dropped silently from the top of a shelf to the floor beside him. A new person grabbed his arm, shoving him against the wall with a hand clamped over his mouth.

"Don't shout," a smooth voice warned. "Once Revelle gets started, anyone who interrupts is liable to meet the same fate as your would-be captors."

Removing his hand after making his point, the new man rested one shoulder against the nearest shelf, blocking the view of whatever was happening in the narrow aisle. He was tall and deceptively thin for how much force he'd used. He wore a tailored wool coat and his green eyes gleamed bright and unnatural.

The air around them felt thicker than before, liquid and claustrophobic. It was a sensation Daniel had come to associate with Antagonists. Repeated exposure to magic was rumoured to leave humans less susceptible to glamour, but he'd started to wonder if it had affected him in other ways too. It had been impossible to tell until now, with the incantation rattling around in his mind.

This feeling rivalled any he'd had before, though, even with the spell in his head. His heart raced at the man's proximity, refusing to slow even though he'd stopped struggling. All of his nerves sparked, desperate to electrify his muscles and get him the hell away from whatever this Antagonist beside him was. A mage, maybe—something powerful.

From behind the other man came a soft, sickening crunch, then the crack of bones breaking.

Daniel flinched, unable to keep from turning his head further into the wall.

Someone screamed. It trailed off into a wail.

"I don't like to watch him work either," the man beside him murmured. He didn't raise his voice but the ensuing silence made it sharper. "Where've you hidden my daughter?"

Daniel stared at the older man in amazement. "Your—?"

"Judith didn't tell you." Joshua stated it rather than asking, as if concluding something from that.

"I thought she was hallucinating."

"So did she."

Soft footsteps came down the aisle behind them and the third person joined them—a frail, stooped, human-shaped . . . *creature* with wild, dark hair and papery skin that seemed to sag off his bones. Its eyes were black without a hint of colour in the irises, and meeting the dead, hollow stare knocked fight out of Daniel's equation, leaving only flight. He couldn't make his muscles work.

Joshua murmured something to the creature in the melodic foreign language Daniel still couldn't understand. It seemed to calm the thing. Then he bent down to grab the charred chapbook dropped in the struggle. He flipped through its pages before tossing it over his shoulder.

"A forgery," he concluded. "All rumours to the contrary, I see the Consilium is still alive and well. Albeit, rather diminished."

"What is that?" Daniel hadn't taken his eyes off the other creature.

"Revelle is a wraith, borrowed from the Harbinger. He's what she makes of breathing creatures that cross her borders."

The older man's patronizing tone caused Daniel to ignore his better judgment and challenge, "But she didn't make you one?"

"Judith did tell you everything." Joshua hesitated, uncanny eyes lit with a new interest as he studied Daniel. He added languidly, "No, I was apparently useful enough to 'The Undimmed' with my mind *intact*." He put a wry twist on the title he used to refer to the shade queen, then asked, "Now where is my daughter? You took her from the hospital."

When Daniel didn't answer immediately, the older man pressed in closer.

"You *took* her," he repeated, in a voice sharp enough to draw blood.

"She's at my apartment. She's safe." Daniel wasn't entirely sure that he'd responded of his own volition. He tried not to meet the older man's gaze again, but it was difficult to do while also avoiding looking at the wraith and keeping himself from zeroing in on the back hallway. Had Zeb gotten away, or was he lying in wait somewhere there?

"She shouldn't have left the hospital injured." Joshua's accusatory words brought Daniel back to his present situation.

He held back a laugh. "You don't know her."

"No." The older man sounded similarly amused by that statement. "Tell me, then, how *you* do. Granted, my knowledge is second-hand and incomplete but it seems like you should be the last person I find retrieving her from the hospital, given that she nearly killed you several months ago. Unless the story I've heard is true, and all of that was a ruse meant to distract from your involvement in patricide."

His calm words stunned Daniel. Everyone in the Consilium who'd believed he'd hired Jude to kill his father was dead.

"Where did you hear that?"

"It's true?"

"It's *not.*"

"Then I find myself suspicious of your motives."

"That makes two of us." Daniel had to fight not to look Joshua in the eye again. "You saw us at the hospital?"

"I was in and out to discover whether my sister's minions would come to retrieve her. Imagine my surprise when you showed up instead." The Antagonist continued to stand too close, studying Daniel's face at an angle that made him feel like a sample under a microscope.

After another uncomfortable few seconds, Joshua remarked, "Someone's worked a spell on you."

When Daniel tensed but didn't argue with the assessment, the older man's condescending tone tinged with interest. "You consented to this?"

Breath caught in Daniel's throat but he managed, "Yes."

"Amateur work. It left considerable residual traces. Scar tissue, if you will." Joshua continued to examine him, sharp eyes boring deeper. "I suppose you didn't have much choice, though." He paused, then concluded, "I'll clean it up and in return, you take me to my daughter."

Without waiting for agreement, he lifted a hand. A lightning bolt of pain sizzled down through Daniel's skull.

His vision dipped and blurred. A flood of words, visions, pictures and meanings surged back into his head. His body spasmed and he realized he was on the floor. The shapes he'd seen on Gracie's scan of the stone tablet became recognizable runes as if the knowledge had simply been hovering just outside of his head, waiting to be let back in.

Dread bore down on him, sickening anticipation of the ragged scrape like fingernails on bone, the excised incantation returning to his mind. He pressed his forehead to the dirty, uneven floorboards, trying to focus on the pressure, on the damp chill of the wood under his hands, and keep his stomach from turning itself inside out.

The spell didn't return. His head stayed quiet. Daniel managed to draw a breath of the dusty air. The wash of fire in his skull receded as he crawled to his hands and knees. He had to grope for the bookshelves and the nearest one rattled as he hauled himself upright. His head kept throbbing but at least he could see straight again.

Another memory resolved, the murmur Joshua had made to the wraith in his mother-tongue minutes ago. Just a word: "*Wait.*" But it had been spoken at the level of politesse, a different conjugation. A request rather than a command.

"Not so crude after all, I suppose," Joshua remarked. If it had been meant to function as an apology, the ironic sneer the old mage put on it made it miss the mark.

Beside them, the wraith remained like a statue, with its head cocked, as if listening for noises from the front door.

"Making ourselves scarce does seem the best course now," Joshua said. "Take me to my daughter."

"I didn't actually agree to that," Daniel snapped.

"Ah, I see. How rash of me. I suppose I'll replace the residue in your memories and let it heal naturally, then." Joshua arched an eyebrow. "I'm afraid I don't remember the size though. It would be a shame if I introduced further, perhaps even more *permanent* scarring that covered your other innate human abilities. Left you a slobbering, raving mess on the floor of the nearest hospital. Runs in the family, yes?"

"Fuck you," Daniel spat.

"Or perhaps catatonia would suit you better," the Antagonist mused.

Daniel stepped back but the wraith brushed up against him, blocking his escape.

"I won't hurt her," Joshua said. "And I have no interest in your family. I'll harm neither you nor anyone in your home. I give you my word."

He gestured to the back exit, giving Daniel no choice but to lead them.

Zeb greeted them at the door, wielding a metal snow shovel he must have found nearby.

Daniel dodged to the other side of the room, giving his friend room to swing. The aluminum shovel hit Joshua's shoulder hard enough to make him grunt, and a second hit to the side of his head knocked him to the floor.

As Zeb swung a third time, grazing the wraith behind them, Daniel shoved the door to the alley open to facilitate their flight.

Zeb followed without aiming another hit at the wraith. He slammed the door behind them and jammed the shovel through the door handle. It wouldn't hold the creature for long, but long enough to gain some distance.

"Got it," he huffed. "Antique stores *are* dangerous."

32

"What are you looking for?" Grace asked, hovering in the bedroom doorway.

I'd seized on her distraction cleaning the spaghetti sauce off her son, and Ted doing the dishes, to limp my way back to the bedroom and haul the nearest box of Consilium refuse close to the bed. An echoing reminder in my head had switched from the voice of last night's nurse to Daniel and back, making me prop my knee with a pillow. Keep it elevated. Not like that would heal it today.

"I don't know," I muttered. "Something helpful."

"Well, look fast." She cast a glower at the boxes around me. "I'm getting rid of all of this."

"What? Why?" I wished I could bite the words back when her mouth settled into a thin line. Why *would* she and Danny want to keep any of this shit? It wasn't their problem anymore. No, it was mine now, for some stupid fucking reason only a dead Mab knew.

I thought again of the sylph, the new Faerie tech that could beam back magical video of me in real-time. Who had access to that feed? Who'd been watching me? Who had the resources to identify Chris from it and find his address in the two hours we'd been at the party?

There were better suspects than Abe, but none of them had any more reason to want to raise the Shadow Mab. From what I understood, the Host would try to depose Miranda and take over if they got free, so *she* wouldn't want to help the Harbinger out. Gordon was a royal mage, meaning he wanted what Miranda wanted.

Saskia knew where I lived. She'd been there, last night. And she'd been at the party a few nights ago. But she and her father *had* seemed genuinely surprised when I'd accused them and I didn't know what they'd gain from the Host decimating the Court either. Seemed like they'd lose power like Miranda.

Then there was Joshua. He knew the Shadow Mab. But he hated her. I wasn't empathic like Abe but the loathing in Joshua's voice when he'd spoken about the Land of Shades and his captivity there hadn't felt like an act. Why would he want to give his jailer more power, given he'd already had to siphon it off her to escape?

Stockholm Syndrome was a thing, right? Seemed like twenty years spent locked up with the Faerie ghosts at the edge of the world could warp somebody's mind.

Assuming he'd been telling me the truth, which honestly was a big 'if.'

"Jude." Riley came into the room, leading with a piece of paper that flapped in his hand as he thrust it at me.

It had a blue squiggle that might have been a person with something purple extending from its back, and a smaller squiggle to one side. A set of wavy train tracks ran across the bottom, same as the ones he'd drawn all over the papers in the living room.

"What's this?" I asked.

"You and me. Playing trains."

Icy shame flooded my body. I couldn't take the drawing from him. Why was this happening? Was I in some kind of hell? I was the monster who'd blown up the Consilium last year, murdered Alan and nearly done the same to Daniel, but instead of some excruciating punishment or a proper fucking prison, I'd been taken in, protected, and now was supposed to play trains with this innocent kid? This kid who had no clue what I'd done to his family.

It wasn't right. Something had to give.

"Rye, Jude's not feeling well," Grace said. "You and I can play."

"It's okay." I swallowed, lifting myself upright on my crutches despite the weight in my stomach. I'd take whatever penance the universe wanted to dish out. "As long as I can sit down, I can play trains."

I waited for her to make another excuse, even tell me point blank to keep away from her son while we were at it, but she only shrugged.

"Yes!" Riley pumped his little fist in the air as if he'd just won an Olympic medal, and trotted back toward the living room.

I relocated slowly to the living room, setting myself up on the sofa and stuffing a cushion back under my knee. The acrid odour of burned paper seemed stronger out here, somehow, even though all of the boxes I'd been rifling through were in the bedroom.

"What's on fire?" I asked Grace, as she settled on the chair behind us.

"Consilium files." She pulled her legs up under herself and flipped open the tablet beside her.

"Oh." Her sharp, forced calm made it seem even more like a sacrilege for a member of the Consilium to destroy this arcane information that had no doubt come to them at a high cost.

"In the oven," Riley told me. "Like a fireplace. We can't touch it. We can look. You want to look?"

"Nope, I'm good." I wasn't about to open a Consilium library, so why shouldn't they get rid of it and keep it from falling into more dangerous hands? "So, what do we do with these trains?"

Riley started a long, meandering backstory he'd conceived for whatever this game was. He contradicted himself on the rules several times—we had to take the train around the track three times to get the people home, but then he decided it was five times, except when he started the first run it took too long and he declared that we could start dropping the imagined passengers off right away.

The sound of a key in the front door lock made me tense. Grace set her tablet aside and Ted came around the kitchen bar. They both visibly relaxed when it was just Daniel and Zeb coming through the door.

Those two didn't look relaxed, though, both jumpy and out of breath, like they'd been running.

"More agents?" Ted asked.

"Yeah," Zeb muttered, then looked in askance to Daniel and changed his story: "No?"

With a sigh Daniel met my eyes and admitted, "Ran into your father."

I froze, mind going immediately to the bitter, angry tone in Joshua's voice when he'd mentioned Alan. At least Danny was in one piece, despite looking like he'd taken an unexpected jog, but the anxiety in his movements told me it hadn't been a *great* introduction.

I hauled myself to my feet with some difficulty, huffing when the brace pinched my knee, which had started swelling again.

"What happened?" Zeb noticed it and my crutches for the first time.

"Accident." I thumbed over my shoulder to the door. "Actually, I was just leaving."

"Absolutely not," Daniel said.

The command started a simmer in the frustrated rage that had been collecting in my chest since waking in this apartment with the pulsing background pain of my knee.

"Absolutely yeah," I snapped back. "With the Harbinger chick around and now Joshua, I can't be here."

"Well, I'm not carrying you back down those stairs."

Oh, that patronizing tone. He only wanted to hold all of this over my head. Remind me that he was a goddamn saint and he had every right to look down on me, reject my sad, pathetic attempts at reconciling and still control what I did.

"I never asked you to!" I spat. "I'm the one with the magic fucking powers anyway, so just bite me!"

My brain had not approved that response. It resulted in silence.

Then, quietly, the three-year-old behind me repeated, "Bite me."

I looked back to see Riley thoughtfully turning the words over in his mind. He got to his feet, eyes fixed on me with a wild, feverish delight. Then he looked to his uncle and shouted with more glee than I'd used, "Bite me!"

Zeb stifled a laugh, turning away from us to keep from losing it.

"Sorry," I stammered, face flushing hot as I glanced to Grace and Ted. "I just . . ."

We all jumped when a short, polite knock came at the front door. The fury, frustration and humiliation gnawing at my bones vanished, sucked into the mire of dread that filled me when a light tingle started in my skin.

Daniel seemed to know who was outside too. He remained still, maybe taking stock of whatever iron weapons he had in the apartment.

The knock came again, just as short but a little harder.

Grace moved back, reading her brother's stance and retreating to guard her son. Her husband remained at the entrance to the kitchen, within reach of at least one iron pan that could be swung as a weapon. Zeb pushed his shoulders back, mirth forgotten, and awaited an order.

"I'll get it," I said, hauling myself to the front door.

When I opened it, Joshua was in the midst of studying the door frame.

"Fancy meeting you here," I said.

He cast me a brief smile, then his attention returned to the ward. He moved forward, paused, and then put a hand to the space in the doorway, pressing against it like he met some kind of resistance.

I vaguely remembered that feeling of having the sylph ripped from the back of my neck.

"It's impressive," Joshua remarked, aiming that comment over my shoulder to Daniel. "Your work?" When he got no answer, he added in a mild tone, "More like Maggie than I realized."

I glanced back to see what that meant but only got a muscle twitch in Daniel's jaw and a sharp, startled intake of breath from Grace.

Joshua pretended not to notice. "You'll need to allow me entrance," he said. "It responds to your will."

"The deal *you* made was that I take you to your daughter," Daniel replied. "Here she is."

Joshua smiled, pushing against the invisible barrier again as if testing for weakness.

"Perhaps you misunderstood me. The ward is impressive for a human attempt. I, however, can tear it apart like smoke. If you make me do that, then the rest of our deal will be void."

"What deal?" Grace demanded, before I could.

"Not to harm any member of your vexing family while on these premises," Joshua answered her.

"Anyone *in my home*," Daniel added sharply. "Those were your words."

"Yes, yes, the imbecile who hit me with a shovel is also off-limits for now," Joshua agreed, voice thin as his eyes roved to Zeb.

"We can talk outside," I announced, starting push past Joshua to join him in the hallway.

"No." He didn't move.

I drew back, scowling at him. It wasn't worth asking why not. This was obviously a power move.

"Just come in," Daniel said, not masking the fury in his voice. "You. Not the wraith."

"Very well." Joshua cast a brief sidelong glance down the hall and nodded in agreement, then moved inside, letting me peek out the door as I started,

"What's a—"

I saw it, standing at the end of the hall like a robot switched off. A skeleton covered in bad papier mâché with a few clothes chucked on for modesty's sake. It made my skin crawl.

I jerked back inside, trying to slow my breathing as I shut the door. It helped to put even that thin barrier between me and the thing outside. No wonder Daniel and Zeb had been so shaken when they got back.

"What do you want?" I demanded, making the words sharp to let Joshua know I wasn't impressed with his bullying.

"You disappeared," he said, fixing his full attention on me.

"Hey, *you* left *me* at the hospital."

"I told you to stay there."

"Guess I didn't realize you meant *forever*."

"I didn't expect you to vanish completely from my cognizance." He cast another glance at the nails pounded into the door frame. "Now I see why."

Rather than comment further on that, he said, "I found your friend."

"My friend?" I echoed, exchanging a glance with Daniel and Zeb to see if this made any more sense to them.

"Your healer."

"Abe?" My heart jumped into my throat. "Where? How?"

"He's nearby. In the city, at least. In a cavern of some sort."

"A *cavern*?" I waited for that word to make more sense.

"Damp, chilly, rock walls," Joshua listed, as if recalling from whatever magic or vision he'd performed to get this information. "And iron."

"In the walls?"

"Close by."

I turned to Daniel and Grace, and cast Zeb a glance for good measure. "Are there any *caverns* in Montreal?"

I expected to get my disbelief mirrored back at me, and I did, from two of the three faces.

"There's one," Zeb offered. "Caverne St-Leonard."

"Nearby?" I eyed the dark window. How was there a *cavern* hidden among the dense apartment buildings and car-parked streets of Montreal?

"Kilometre or two." He shrugged uncomfortably.

"I'll map it." I turned to Joshua. "Let's go."

"How?" Daniel asked, making me spin back. His eyes were fixed on my father. "*How* did you find Abe?"

"The same way I'd have found my daughter were it not for your ward." Joshua sounded amused, as if Daniel's distrust pleased him. "A spell. One a bit more *complex* than you'd be familiar with, but fairly commonplace to someone of my level. I traced the healer's vibrations through the particular magic in his blood."

"You have Abe's blood?" I swung back around to face Joshua, startled.

"Didn't need it." Joshua answered me but kept his gaze on Daniel. He hesitated a moment, then added reluctantly, "Given the proximity of the iron I sensed, we may require human assistance. You're welcome to accompany us."

"Fine." Daniel's immediate agreement made me flinch in surprise. The wordless noise of protest Grace made indicated she was right there with me. "I'll be back before morning," he told her quietly.

She cast him a warning glower but didn't object further.

"I'm in too," Zeb volunteered.

"I don't think such a large party is advisable," Joshua started.

"I know where the place is," Zeb said, cutting off what was probably a similar admonition from Daniel. "More or less."

"So does a map," I muttered. Arguing with Zeb would be a waste of time. I didn't like him, but he always had

Daniel's back and I couldn't fault him for that. I had no interest in prolonging the awkward tension in the apartment, or giving Joshua more opportunity to dictate the terms.

"Large party it is," I concluded. "Zeb can go into the cave first and check for iron. If he gets eaten by monsters, then the rest of us can find Abe."

33

THE COLD HAD ALREADY numbed my knee as I limped down the sidewalk of the park. Zeb had offered to drive but since his car wasn't nearby, Daniel'd sprung for a taxi. Definitely the safer option, though not a group ride I ever wanted to take again. At least the wraith had been MIA when we'd left Daniel's apartment.

When asked, Joshua had only said, "He's gone ahead," which didn't make any of us feel easier.

So I half-expected a wraith to leap out from the shadows as we headed down a walkway with a dark, fenced-off baseball field to one side and an empty swimming pool, surrounded by a higher fence, on the other. I couldn't see how far the park stretched in the dark. Was there really a cave here, in the middle of this city neighbourhood? It wasn't as dense as where I lived—mostly houses and driveways out here rather than packed apartment buildings—but it still seemed unlikely we could go spelunking in the middle of this park.

I trusted Zeb, at least, and he said it was here. More than I trusted Joshua, who'd set off ahead to lead us down a paved path with intermittent lights. Apparently following some mystical Faerie sense he had, Abe's *vibrations*.

The four of us seemed alone in the dark. Most nights you'd still find people lingering in a city park after sunset with beers and cigarettes until it snowed. Too cold tonight.

We turned, wound through some trees, and came to another fenced off section of concrete stairs that led down to a shadowy bunker door. An official city sign announced that this was the entrance to the urban cavern and listed opening hours, a phone number and a website. The real deal, then. Thanks, Zeb.

"This isn't iron." I rapped a knuckle on the black metal gate. Steel, or maybe aluminum. I reminded Joshua, "You said iron."

"Maybe it's inside." Zeb studied the gate and the fence. His eyes went to the corners and I realized he was checking for cameras.

"You don't feel it?" Joshua replied to me, head slightly cocked. Without waiting for me to answer, he put his hands over the lock. After a few seconds, it clicked open.

Why would Abe be in here with the locks done from the outside? Joshua hadn't said he was incapacitated, but if there was iron in there . . . was that what he'd meant to infer?

Inside the first barrier, under a small, square pavilion and down a set of wide, stone steps, we faced a second gate, this one in front of a heavy, metal door. The light from the distant streetlight shone at a different angle on these bars. I still didn't feel iron, though, and Joshua handled both doors with the same quick efficiency as the first gate.

Zeb pulled one side open just enough to let in a crack of light. The door squealed, echoing back out into the park, and we all froze to listen for footsteps or onlookers.

Something moved inside, and I struggled past the door without waiting to see if we'd been caught. When Joshua followed, it seemed like we were in the clear for uninvited guests, but Daniel and Zeb had a brief exchange that resulted in Zeb remaining outside on the steps to keep watch.

We didn't close the door behind us because we needed the dim light. Daniel turned on his phone's flashlight to aim it at the rock walls and muddy floor of a narrow, hall-like cavern. At the far end, the light gleamed off an aluminum ladder that led down. No way was I going to manage that with my brace. As it was, my head felt light and my whole body ached from manoeuvring with the crutch. The constant, tiny shifts of my gravity I'd been using to keep myself upright had really started to take a toll. I didn't usually use my power like this, in a nonstop, drawn-out trickle.

The air inside the cave was chilly and wet, water dripping somewhere in the distance. Daniel's flashlight beam swept out, illuminating a prostrate body at the far end of the narrow cave. Back against the rock wall, the motionless form wore mud-caked jeans and a torn, diamond-checked cowboy shirt.

I gasped when the light illuminated Abe's slack face. A greenish bruise stained his left temple, creeping down over a reddish-purple swollen left eye. Cuts and dirt streaked his skin and bare scalp.

I got over to him and let my crutches fall to one side to crouch down, stretching my leg out to take the weight off my knee. My heart skipped and I had to blink tears out of my eyes to see if the cowboy was breathing. My fingers shrank from touching him, but at the same time I wanted to grab him and shake him.

"Abe?" My voice popped out, raw and louder than I'd expected it to be. It nearly made me topple backwards.

I did that when Abe's eyes opened. Pain sizzled up from my knee, but I barely felt it.

The cowboy stared at me with his good eye, the other one half-shuttered under a swollen lid. His lips moved slowly but nothing came out.

I couldn't stop myself from reaching out and touching his face. He managed with some difficulty to turn his head to meet my hand. Tears shone in his right eye. They weren't tears of joy to see me, and Daniel—kneeling near Abe's feet—voiced it too.

"Look at his throat." He angled his light to focus on the streak of darkness that ran down the front of Abe's throat, turning the skin a shadowy purple at the edges. In the centre, thick black stitches ran in a straight line. "The skin's distended." He took gentle hold of one of Abe's wrists. Under the light, it matched his throat, shadowed with black and purple and thick, ugly stitches.

He leaned back on his heels to examine the rest of Abe's body. As he got far enough back to see at the bottoms of Abe's bare feet, his expression changed again.

"There too?" I whispered. I reached down, pretty sure Abe had given me his silent consent with his good eye, and put my fingers on his throat, over the stitches.

Something long and narrow ran just under his skin. It made me queasy, a feeling I knew too well—the one I'd been anticipating since Joshua's warning.

"It's iron," I spat, choking on the words that bubbled up with hot rage. "They sewed iron under his skin."

Daniel produced a folding knife from his pocket and relegated his phone to me to provide light. It took all my willpower not to snatch the blade out of his hands and get to work on the brutal black stitches myself, but I held still at Abe's side and let Daniel cut each stitch on his throat because he could touch the iron without being burned.

He went too slowly for the rage building under my skin but took care to be certain he didn't do further damage. Blood began to seep out of the wound, dark and black in the dim light. With his free hand, Daniel parted the skin. His fingers came up stained with dark liquid but holding a long, slim piece of iron that looked like a nail file.

I swallowed bile and my muscles stiffened. The motion triggered my injured knee. I gasped when it joined the rest of my body in rage. Everything in my vision went red and black but I fought it. *Later. Come back when I need you.*

Abe's eyes had shut tight in pain. I put my hand over the wound on his throat, trying to stop the bleeding. Would it be better to press my jacket to it instead? The quilted flannel was probably good and absorbent.

Daniel moved to Abe's wrists, using the same caution. His face was pale and his hands shook like mine, but he made the cuts and dug out more long, slim pieces of iron—both of these with sharp, pointed ends.

My chest started to ache, memory coming unbidden of the time Abe had put his big hands over my throat. Or when he'd rested them on my ribs or my broken wrist—and healed me. I couldn't do the same. The blood kept dribbling out over my fingers.

Should we have left the iron in, taken him to a hospital? No, it was poisoning him. Never mind what we'd have said at a hospital. If I'd needed to kidnap a doctor and commandeer an operating room, I could have done it on the adrenaline and fury that had built inside me.

Abe's bleeding wrists weren't gushing. The Shadow Mab's accomplice didn't seem to have opened any major veins or arteries inserting the rods.

Daniel moved down to Abe's feet and I flinched along with Abe when I heard the knife snick through the stitches.

With a sudden jerk, the cowboy tried to shake my hands off of his throat.

"Stop it! You'll bleed to death!" I hissed.

"Poisoned." His voice was so soft I could barely hear it. Every word was a battle. "It's . . . poisoned. Let it . . . out."

I lifted my hands from his throat, studying the blood that stained them in the blueish light of the phone. He was right. Black blood covered my fingers, oozing from his wound, but something underneath, healthy and red, started to peek out.

Abe managed to lift his hand enough to take mine in a very weak grip. I squeezed it, shivering, and used my free hand to wipe the tears off my cheeks. The cave still seemed strangely red. An odd heat had started where my hand clenched his. My knee throbbed harder, pulsing through my body. My ribs suddenly felt battered, nearly taking my breath away.

"No!" Abe tried to yank his hand back from mine, his eyes widening as he saw my face.

A trickle of something warm and thicker than tears ran down the side of my face. I brushed it away with the back of my hand, which came away stained red.

I clenched Abe's hand tighter, another wave of pain flooding through my stomach and chest. Blue tinged the red now, turning the room purple as I blinked against the heat flooding me.

Daniel wedged himself on Abe's other side, lifting the bigger man to help him sit up. The pain ebbed out of me when he grabbed Abe, but a sudden, razor-thin line of crimson cut down the front of Daniel's throat. He blanched and lowered his head with a sharp breath.

"What's happening?" I managed.

"Projecting," Abe managed. "Instead of attracting. Let go."

Both Daniel and I complied without arguing. As soon as my fingers had released Abe's, the pain in my body dissolved, except for my knee throbbing hard enough to make me see stars. My muscles felt cold in the absence of all of the heat and extra emotion. The cave fell back to being dark and grey. I reached up to touch my temple and found blood but no wound.

With my head clearer, I thought I understood what Abe had tried to say. The iron had caused him to send his emotions out rather than absorbing others'? Where he would have drawn pain and injuries into himself and healed me, instead he'd passed his own trauma through my skin. His wounds were beginning to close, at least.

Abe groaned and managed to drag himself further upright. He only made it an inch or two before taking a breather.

"We should take him to a hospital," Daniel said.

"Don't touch me," the cowboy huffed.

"What are you going to do, walk?" I replied. "We can handle it." My pain had dulled when Daniel had taken hold of Abe. Balancing it between the two of us, we could make it out of the cavern. And with Zeb and Joshua—

As if he'd read my thoughts, Abe started, "Jude, your father—"

"I know," I cut him off. "He's alive. He's the one who found you."

Abe pulled in a deep breath and let three words hiss out: "He did this."

Outside the cave, Zeb shouted in alarm. The heavy, steel door behind us slammed shut, plunging us into almost total darkness.

34

GRACIE SPENT THE TEN minutes following her brother's departure making sure that the papers in the oven were ash, then gathering up all of the things she and Ted had brought with them—passports, papers, Riley's toys—into a pair of canvas bags and the backpack.

Ted looked up from his game with Riley as she set the heavy bags down by the door.

"We need to leave." She answered the question he hadn't asked.

He studied her face, then got to his feet and crossed the room to stand beside her. "Before your brother gets back?"

"Yes." The word was nearly lost in the rush of breath leaving her lungs. It hurt to say but she tried again, firmer the second time: "Yes." Despite the thickness in her throat, she met her husband's eyes with dry ones.

"That's cruel," he said.

As if she needed the reminder.

"He left us here," Gracie snapped, struggling to keep her voice low so her son didn't overhear. "He's not going to give this up. I honestly don't think he can." The bitter sarcasm in her brother's voice as he'd told her he'd be back before morning still grated, rubbing her insides raw. He'd made his choice, and it wasn't family. It wasn't her.

"If you leave this way," Ted said, "you're going to regret it."

"At least I know that," she returned. "If we wait, I don't know *what* I'll be made to regret."

Her husband was silent for a few seconds. Finally, he nodded and looked back to Riley, raising his voice to a more cheerful tone.

"Want to jump on the train, kiddo?"

"Where?" Riley asked, leaping to his feet.

A knock at the door stopped them all in their tracks. Gracie, the closest one to it, stood on the balls of her feet to get a good look out the peephole. Her fingers tightened on the knob.

Tess Foster stood in the hall, hugging her jacket around herself, hands in her pockets. How the fuck had she found them? Gracie had been so careful getting back with Riley this morning, done all of her cursory checks for pursuers and made several feints.

"Rye, can you please clean up the train tracks?" Gracie asked over her shoulder, giving the toddler a task that would send him further from the door as she threw a glance to her husband.

Ted recognized her warning without words, and he backed into the kitchen to find a weapon.

"Hey, hi." Tess addressed the peephole as if she'd heard either Gracie's voice or another noise. "Just to let you know, there's about twenty agents downstairs, and we don't want to scare the kid, so you need to let me in."

A flash of rage sizzled through Gracie but she forced it down, stopping her instinctive bark at Riley to hide in the bedroom. She hated the calm rationale in the core of her being, but Tess and the agents had proven more likely to hesitate having her child in plain sight.

Swallowing hard to force her throat open and keep her breathing even, she unlocked the door. She practically growled at their unwelcome visitor when they came face-to-face.

"Hi, Grace." Tess flashed a weary smile.

"It's not a good time," was the most polite, normal thing that Gracie could come up with given Riley's proximity. She wished she had her long-handled battle-axe.

"Never is." Tess shrugged, waiting to be invited inside.

Gracie stepped back to allow the other woman entrance, placing herself in front of her son and blocking his view as Ted swooped in from the right to press a long, sharp knife against Tess's windpipe.

With a grunt that seemed halfway between protest and amusement, Tess reached behind her hip and closed the door slowly and quietly, her chin tilted up to avoid the blade. She didn't seem troubled enough by the weapon, and Gracie's heart fluttered.

"What do you want?" she asked.

"You know what I want." To Gracie and Ted's surprise, Tess lifted a hand and swept the blade away in the same smooth motion that she stepped to her left, putting her body fully in their son's view.

Ted dropped his hand to his side, the knife flashing in the lamplight.

Gracie wanted to vomit. Tess seemed almost entertained, playing their son's presence against them in the same way they'd tried to use it against her.

The younger woman strode another step into the apartment, glancing around as if expecting a surprise attack.

"Where's your brother?"

"Not here." Gracie gritted her teeth. "I don't have any map," she insisted, "and I burned that folder you brought me. Plus everything else we had." She paused and let the scent of charred paper back her claim.

"Mama," Riley said from the sofa.

"Give us a minute, kiddo," Gracie said over her shoulder, refusing to take her eyes off Tess as the other woman moved toward the window. She intercepted her ex-colleague before Tess could stand in front of the glass pane and make whatever signal she'd probably intended on sending to her team.

Gracie bit back the anger churning her stomach and made her tone as reasonable as she could manage. It still sounded strangled to her own ears. "I don't have anything you want, and I'm not interested in anything you're doing. Just let us *go*."

"It's not up to me," Tess answered.

The hard, set eyes that twinkled with dark amusement weren't Theresa Foster's. This was someone else, someone Gracie didn't know. Someone she couldn't predict.

"Mama!" Riley said again.

"Not now, Rye," Ted started. His sharp intake of breath made Gracie look over her shoulder toward the front door where her son had been pointing.

Something green and gelatinous oozed under the door and along both sides, bubbling in fast.

"What the hell?" Tess's stunned, wide eyes said this was not part of her entourage.

Gracie dove to the sofa and hauled Riley off, barking at him, "Bedroom! Get under the bed and stay there."

She sent him scrambling down the hall as the mess of green ooze at the front door formed into something resembling a human shape, a good half-metre taller than Gracie herself.

Ted took a defensive position, raising the knife, and Tess stepped behind him.

Gracie spun and rooted around for the iron wrench she'd had last night, but the green thing didn't seem concerned with any of them. It sent out tentacle-like arms without fingers to caress the iron nail at the top right of the door.

She stopped herself from heaving the wrench at the creature when it succeeded in pulling out one of the iron nails. The metal dinged as it hit the floor.

Then the front door swung open, revealing a blond teenager in a puffer coat. Two more of the green slime creatures flanked him.

Gracie's fingers tightened around the wrench. Maybe the green things didn't respond to iron, but she'd bet money that the smug, solid, child-like creature would.

Ted came up behind her, probably similarly armed, though Gracie didn't take her eyes off the boy and the monsters with him.

"Spells," the teenager remarked, stepping inside, "don't keep out spells."

One of the green creatures lunged at Ted and he swung the knife. The blade slammed into the thing's face, splitting it in two like liquid. The two sides surged out then merged back together as the creature's face reformed around his hand.

Ted tugged, trying to break free.

Gracie jammed the wrench into the thing's chest, but the weapon and her hand stopped in the centre, stuck as if in heavy mud, doing no harm.

The second creature lurched up behind Ted. It brushed against his back, growing to accommodate his height, then surged over him. It absorbed him in a blink, his outline blurring into the translucent green body.

Gracie left the wrench mired in the first creature's chest and dodged around it. She snatched one of the railroad spikes from the front of the backpack by the door. Armed again with iron, she turned it on the teen boy, shouting:

"Let him go!"

The teenager ignored her, saying something to the third creature in a high-pitched tone almost like bird-song.

Gracie swung the iron spike at the monster's head again, trying to break Ted free. It side-stepped her with more grace than she'd have imagined possible for a thing of its size, and she hit the wall beside the door.

She launched herself at the boy, tackling him around the knees. She brought him down with her easily but the spike slipped out of her hand, leaving a rough scrape.

Behind them, the third green creature started to lumber toward the back hallway. Gracie shoved herself up and went for it instead.

Tess reached it first, slamming her body into the gelatinous form. It didn't absorb her the way it had Ted, seeming to root itself to the floor and solidify so that she bounced off of it. It extended a hand and covered her face, pressing her against the wall with its ooze covering her eyes, nose and mouth.

Gracie started to race past the creature to the bedroom, but someone grabbed her shirt collar and tossed her back to the sofa. She hit the cushions and rolled onto the floor, the wind knocked out of her, then found herself staring up at the creature holding her husband. Was Ted alive? Could he breathe in there?

The green monster lurched away and the teenager loomed over her, his face dark and drawn—no longer the face of a child.

She rolled to one side to avoid his blow and staggered to her feet. She made once more for the hallway on shaky legs, but the child-shaped Antagonist leapt further than any human could, cutting her off.

He landed directly in front of her and grabbed her forearms with fingers like steel talons. Her feet left the ground. She was flying in his hands, then he wasn't there anymore.

She slammed down onto the coffee table in the living room. It snapped beneath her, splintering into her skin. Her vision blurred. Spots danced before her eyes. Pain came from everywhere. Something sharp stuck in her side, but she pushed herself up on shaking arms. *Riley!*

A kick to her ribs knocked her flat on her back again amidst the debris. Fresh pain shot through her body. She fought to turn onto her stomach and crawl, but the teenager snatched one of the table legs. He swung it down at her head with a snarl.

The room around her went dark and the pain seemed to ebb. Distantly, down a far tunnel, she heard more bird-song.

35

Shifting gravity to increase my mass, I used my crutches to launch myself at the heavy, metal door that had shut us into the cave. Daniel had already tried to force it several times with no luck. I couldn't budge it either, and I snapped my teeth shut to keep from screaming when my knee twisted. It came out as a squeak of pain and fury.

I blinked tears out of my eyes and pressed a hand against the rough, chilly metal. Had Joshua just locked us in or sealed the door with his magic?

"The house," Abe rasped, from behind us. "He might not know about the house."

I had to try. I didn't have the patience to close my eyes and think, instead just slapping a hand against the door and demanding, "House! Now!"

The heat surged through me with a suddenness that made me gasp. Its intensity seemed to match my frantic anger. Pushing against the door made it creak open this time. I stared into the familiar foyer, hiccuping back a hysterical laugh. I'd never expected to be so happy to see the damn place.

Panting with exertion from ramming the door, Daniel went back into the cave to get Abe up.

"I can help," I managed, despite the obvious fact that I couldn't. I could barely even move myself as I said the words, certain that if I did I'd collapse into a mass of burning limbs.

Daniel didn't bother to respond, just nodded toward the door, prompting me to push it open further with my crutch. Even that felt almost impossible.

The three of us got through and I closed the door long enough to open it again to the dim park outside the cavern. The heavy, wooden front door of the safe house let us out through the first gate that surrounded the bunker. The concrete place was empty.

"Zeb?" Daniel shouted. He helped Abe sit on the retaining wall and moved away from us, down the pathway, searching for his friend.

"Joshua has him," I said. Joshua had taken all of them, and I'd just gone along with him, let him lead me to Abe and trap me. *Faeries lie.* It had been Aubrie's motto and the Consilium's too. I of all people, the dumbass who'd been fooled into trusting both of them along with the shifty Faerie Court run by my aunt, shouldn't have forgotten that rule *again* just because the Faerie offering me what I wanted this time happened to be my father.

Ted had been right—for somebody who tagged 'not falling' as their whole brand, I kept falling for bullshit.

Ted. Joshua knew where he, Grace and Riley were. He knew about the ward. He might have even made some way around it when he'd forced Daniel to let him into the apartment earlier. Zeb's heart wouldn't be enough to raise the Shadow Mab—they still needed a seventh man.

Daniel seemed to realize it at the same moment, because he turned back to the gate, still open to the foyer. Soft lamplight spilled out onto the sidewalk in the park.

Abe tried to get to his feet but didn't quite make it. He was healing himself, but slowly. I managed to slide my body under his shoulder, but I couldn't balance him with my crutches.

Daniel took Abe's other side and the two of us dragged him back into the house. The cowboy huffed in protest but we kept him upright between us while I changed the door to take us back to Daniel's apartment.

I'd expected to come through his neighbour's door again, across the hall, but we stepped out directly into his place.

The realization made me freeze, but Daniel looked to the door frame, searching for the ward. I followed his gaze. One of the nails had been torn out, copper wire left hanging useless on the top right corner of the door.

A small whimper came from further into the room. Daniel left me with Abe's full weight to hurry in its direction. He stopped on the other side of the sofa and crouched in a mess of broken furniture.

A smaller form wailed and launched itself up at him, clinging to his shoulders. Riley.

Abe eased his weight off of me, supporting himself against the doorjamb and nodding me away with another sigh of exertion.

When I hobbled further into the room, Grace came into view. She lay on her back in the centre of a smashed coffee table. One side of her face was bloody. She was covered in splinters from the table.

"Grace." Daniel put a hand on his sister's face, keeping one arm around his sobbing nephew. His voice was quiet and held a note of hope in it, like the sound of her name might bring her around.

She didn't move, though.

I spun back to Abe. "Can you . . .?"

"No." He shook his head. The word came out painfully but his voice was beginning to return. "I'd hurt her the way I hurt you. Worse."

Grace wheezed suddenly, making me whip my head back. She struggled to sit up, but Daniel held her shoulders, hissing something at her in a voice too low for me to hear. It seemed to work, for the most part. She fell still and stared up at him, blinking in confusion.

"Ted," she rasped. "Riley."

"Mama," Riley sobbed.

"Rye's here," Daniel said, as his nephew clawed out of his arm to cling to his mother.

"Oh, baby." Grace kissed her son's head, hugging him to her. "Where's Ted?"

"We'll find him," Daniel said.

That made her relax only a fraction, gathering her strength to sit up slowly with her brother's help. Blood stained her forehead and she still seemed dazed, but she blinked hard and took in the scene around us.

"She's concussed," Abe warned. Whether that was some hint of his empathic power talking or just a guess, he was probably right.

Grace didn't seem to care, trying to force her way to her feet with her son in her arms, even though Daniel stopped her, insisting on checking for broken bones.

"Where is he?" she demanded, voice taking on strength as she shoved her brother away and got upright. She collapsed almost immediately, holding Riley tight to her chest to keep from dropping him as she fell forward to retch.

"I'll look," I said, too loudly. Ted wasn't here. She had to know that too, but I didn't want her trying to drag herself upright again.

I staggered to the mouth of the hallway and stopped short. A woman I didn't recognize lay in a heap against the wall, eyes closed. Her chest rose and fell in a steady rhythm.

"Tess?" Daniel stood behind me. He eased around me to crouch beside her.

She twitched when he touched her wrist to feel for a pulse. Her breathing turned more uneven. She was awake.

"Danny," I warned, but he saw it too. He caught her fist when she tried to swing it up at him.

Her eyes snapped open. Her glare fixed on Daniel first, then moved to me and back again.

"Twenty agents outside," she hissed, baring her teeth. Her expression sent a ridiculous wave of relief through me. Tess was from whatever organization was hunting the remains of the Consilium. Despite being the absolute last thing we needed at this moment, that realization eased an annoying weight in my gut.

"Didn't do *you* much good," Daniel returned, earning him another glare.

Tess attacked with her free hand, aiming for his eyes. She missed, scraping her fingernails down his cheek, but that was enough to make him jerk back. She tried to rush to her feet but Daniel grabbed her again and she knocked them both into the other wall.

I loosened my grip on my crutch, prepared to jump into their struggle. Tess shrieked before I could. She rolled back across the hallway to the spot where we'd found her, clutching her bleeding hand.

My chest seized when I recognized one of the sharp iron pieces Daniel had pulled out of Abe's body protruding from the back of her hand.

He'd kept one, slipped it into his pocket after cutting it out of Abe's skin. The pointy end must have found Tess's hand when they'd been grappling. It made me uneasy but I couldn't blame him for arming up with iron whenever he found it.

And at least this piece had turned out to be useful against humans too.

Tess hissed through her teeth, but Daniel yanked the iron out of her hand before she could extract it herself, denying her the weapon. She let out another angry screech and clasped her good hand around the injured one, snarling at him.

"You're not gonna kill me," she spat, then inclined her head toward me. "Might let her do it, though. That's your M.O., right, hands clean?"

"Get out," Daniel snapped, sitting back on his heels. "Tell your twenty friends outside to fuck off."

"They're not much for orders."

"I'm not either." I jabbed the tip of my crutch against her throat, making her twitch in surprise. The fact that I had to lean against the wall to stay upright with my crutch off the floor made the threat a little hollow, but with a stone face the prone woman finally held her hands up. One still bled freely.

Someone pounded on the apartment door. Tess flashed me a malicious smile of relief.

"Back to the house," Abe said, checking the locks before pushing himself off the wall with some effort. He seemed to be gaining energy—more slowly than I'd have liked, but it was something, anyway. "Get your sister to the hospital."

I kept my crutch aimed at Tess's throat while Daniel returned to the living room to retrieve Grace and Riley.

"Where's your ID?" he asked his sister.

"I'm not going to the—"

"Grace. ID." His tone brooked no argument as more heavy pounding came at the door.

"The lining of my purse."

From the corner of my eye, I saw Daniel dig through the coats piled on the hooks by the doorway until he found the purse. Fabric tore and he removed something, then as the banging continued on the front door, he passed out of my line of vision, back to Grace and Riley.

Abe went to the nearest door and opened it to the house. He stood against the door, holding it open while Tess gaped at it from her spot on the floor.

"What the hell. . . ?" she started.

I kept my crutch on her as a commotion came from the living room. Riley's voice lifted into a wail again. After some scuffling, Daniel appeared, supporting Grace on one shoulder and pinning a struggling toddler to his chest with his other arm. Riley fought to reach his mother, squirming and shrieking.

"It's okay, kiddo," Grace heaved, soothing, but still distant and robotic. "It's okay."

I let them go first into the house, then after Abe had slipped around the door too, I released Tess and all but fell into the foyer myself.

Abe closed the door on Daniel's apartment as the sound of splintering wood came from the front room.

Daniel let Riley fight his way to the ground. The three-year-old tried to climb up his mother's leg, but Grace clutched his hand tightly and shook it to warn him off.

"Hold my hand," she said. "It's okay. Hold my hand." She swayed on her feet, trying to take her son's hand while still balancing on her brother's shoulder.

"Here." I passed her one of my crutches, leaning heavily on the other.

She nodded an exhausted thanks and propped herself up on it, then got her son's attention with a sharp voice that didn't match her broken form.

"Rye! It's okay. We're okay."

"I want up. I want up," he insisted.

"Can't right now, kiddo. Mama's hurt." Grace seemed reluctant to say the words aloud, but it worked. Riley calmed, staring at her as if he hadn't noticed the blood and the crutch. He sniffled, eyes wide and wet.

I caught myself on the banister and lowered to a stair, stretching my leg out in front of me. I dug into the pocket of my jeans and found the pill Grace had given me earlier, wrapped in a piece of tissue. I swallowed it dry.

"Which hospital?" Abe asked Daniel and Grace.

"Toronto," Daniel answered, telling his sister when she balked, "Tess knows you're injured. They could be looking for you in Montreal."

"I am *not* going—"

"Yes, you are." The firm, measured stare and deadly serious tone Daniel used reminded me of the one Grace had just given her son. He fished three cards out of his pocket, which must have been what he'd torn out of Grace's purse. They looked like a driver's license and two health insurance cards. Fake IDs.

"I'll find Ted," he said, as Grace accepted the cards.

Abe opened the door to a sterile hospital corridor.

"Rye, you take care of her and help her find a doctor," Daniel told his nephew.

Riley's little fingers twitched in Grace's, but he screwed up his mouth and whispered, "Okay."

They passed through the door out into the hospital. Daniel shut it behind them, but kept a hand on the knob as if thinking better of letting them go alone.

"You should go with her," I said. Grace had been so unsteady on her feet with only one crutch and the toddler for assistance.

"I have to find Ted and Zeb," he returned, then rested his forehead against the door with a muttered, "Fuck. They might already be dead."

"Not yet, I'd wager," Abe said. "Gordon and Joshua will have to take them to wherever they're doing the sacrifice."

Rituals have rules. Grace had said the same, eons ago—two days, probably. *A sacred location for sacrifice.*

"Where?" I demanded. "What do they need?" As if I could somehow narrow down the entire human world to a single spot in the next minute.

"I found this on your friend's body." Abe reached slowly into his pocket and withdrew something silvery. He held it out in his palm. "It's not from here."

I picked up the leaf and studied it. I knew this leaf, waving in water like the scales of a fish. Saskia's favourite weak-ass Faerie plant, *difficult to cultivate* in the human world.

"Declan Raj has a ton of plants like this in his hotel in Singapore." That couldn't be a coincidence. Just like Saskia showing up at the Halloween party and then last night at my place couldn't be either.

My fury smouldered. That asshole Archduke had played me, delighted to lie to my face. Had Chris, Guy, Ty, Trevor and JM all been somewhere in that hotel at some point, having their hearts removed? Could that be where Ted and Zeb were now?

"Wait," Abe said, stopping me before I could hobble to the door and call up the fancy hotel. "We have to be careful here. If the Archduke is involved . . ."

"Are you seriously being a diplomat right now?" I snapped. "You sound like Ilse."

"We don't know that he's involved," Abe insisted.

"I do," I promised him, picturing the amusement on the Archduke's face when I'd outright accused him. He was trying to raise this Shade Queen for some nefarious reason. Maybe she'd promised she'd get rid of Miranda and put Saskia on the throne.

I forced myself upright, clinging to my single crutch like a lifeline. I felt like a weighted balloon, teetering one direction and another before I managed to get my bearings.

"We need help." Abe eyed me dubiously. "The Mab could—"

"The Mab could waffle about it and waste time taking a poll," I interrupted. "I'm going."

"I've never *once* taken a poll." The familiar voice nearly made me jump out of my skin. I spun to see the Queen Mab eyeing me in displeasure from a small, decorative mirror on the wall.

"Huh," was all I managed on the first try, and then settled on, "I don't have time for this."

"Jude!" Miranda made my name a command. When I reluctantly turned back, she fixed me with a freezing stare. "You'll wait. You'll explain."

"Then I'll lose!" I snapped. "We'll lose and the Shade Queen will rise and Ted and Zeb will *die!*"

Miranda's gaze flickered over my shoulder to Abe. His expression must have backed me up because she returned her eyes to me.

"I'm sending reinforcements. The army is prepared to come through the portals on the next wave. Two hours."

"We don't have that kind of time!" I limped toward the mirror like that would intimidate her. "They could be cutting hearts out *right now!*" Wished I hadn't said that in front of Daniel, but he was probably thinking the same thing. "I can handle this, Miranda," I finished.

"You will not take the risk. You will *not* involve yourself." My aunt's voice lowered, her lips pressed so tightly together they'd gone white. "You will stand down," she said. "And you will wait for the army."

"Yeah, no." I slammed the handle of my crutch into the mirror, shattering it and ending the call.

36

DANIEL TRAILED JUDE AND Abe into the high-ceilinged, plush lobby of what appeared to be an upscale hotel, peopled with mostly Asians. Gold and glass glittered everywhere that there wasn't a cushy, modern sofa or an expensive drape, but it still felt airy and cold.

A crisply suited man zeroed in on them. His placid expression made Daniel tense, feeling the menace behind it.

"You remember me." Jude flashed him a dangerous smile as he reached them. "We're here to see the Archduke."

The man hesitated, then gestured for them to follow him. He led them through the lobby to a desk at the back, near a single elevator. There, he turned and surveyed them with an intensity that made Daniel certain he was somehow checking for weapons. He'd lost the iron accidentally putting it through Tess's hand as he'd tried to fight her off, but it wouldn't have done it him any good here anyway.

The three of them waited while the man made a phone call, ostensibly to warn the Archduke of their arrival. Jude's expression started to betray a hint of anxiety, but the man soon turned to them and ushered them into the mirrored elevator. He produced a special key from his breast pocket to operate it.

The elevator shot upwards, landing them quickly at the thirtieth floor. The man in the suit let them off without following.

They stepped out of the elevator and exchanged the mirrored walls for floor-to-ceiling windows. The expanse of an unfamiliar city—Singapore, apparently—stretched out far below them on the opposite side of the hallway, buildings glittering in the sunlight. Fighting a surge of vertigo as his inherent fear of heights surfaced, Daniel stayed closer to the inside wall. The phobia galled him, pathetically banal in light of their dire situation, with the lives of people he loved on the line, but it was immune to logic.

Oblivious to his hesitation, Jude limped ahead, leading the way to a door she somehow knew. She only had one crutch and she hauled herself along, half-dragging her braced leg. Either the painkiller she'd taken had started to work or she was so angry she didn't feel it anymore.

Her determination overcame Daniel's disequilibrium, stirring him to follow. He joined Abe to flank her as she hammered her fist against a set of double doors.

They waited.

Finally, a dark-haired woman opened one door. Her eyes narrowed when she recognized the primary visitor.

"Hey, Saskia," Jude said, voice like honey over steel. "Got your sword back, huh?"

The other woman's lips twitched, but instead of making a retort, she merely let them inside.

In the large front room of the suite, a man reclined in a plush chair, caught in the act of running a hand over his dark ponytail of dreadlocks. He had a rumpled air, like he hadn't been given enough time to prepare, though he was cool and collected as he gazed at them.

Daniel had heard of the Antagonist Archduke—the position, at least. He only knew this incarnation's human name because Jude had mentioned it. And hadn't she pointed him out in a magazine?

"To what do I owe the rude, unannounced visit?" The controlled, superior voice seemed affected and foreign in contrast to Declan Raj's stylishly dishevelled appearance. He studied the three of them with disdain, taking in their bloodstained, muddy clothes, courtesy of the cavern floor, and Jude's injury.

"You're working with my father," Jude said.

The Antagonist leaned back, tapping his fingers, each covered in a heavy silver ring, against his knee.

"I am financing his project," he agreed.

Jude seemed taken aback by the freely given answer. She regained her composure and challenged, "His *project* of killing men and raising the Harbinger of the Host?"

"Yes."

"And when I asked you before?"

"That's not the question you asked me."

Her fingers tightened on the handle of her crutch and Daniel felt the same frustration fuse through him at the wilfully pedantic answer.

"Tell me where to find him," Jude said.

"We've had this discussion before, Mabling. I don't take orders, I make bargains."

"I don't have time for that!" she snapped. "And neither do you if you're not in the mood to explain summoning up the Host and betraying the throne to the army the Mab's sending over right now."

Raj's returning laugh sent a shudder of surprise through all of them.

"Your father isn't aiding the mages. Quite the opposite. Our Enduring Lady—" he said the title with a healthy dose of sarcasm, "—can only be destroyed in her corporeal form. Joshua is using the mages to raise her so that he can end her."

"And the men they're killing to do it?" Jude demanded.

"Merely humans."

The dismissive response sent a flare of rage through Daniel. Before his better judgment could prevail, he'd lunged forward to grab the other man by the neck of his fashionable t-shirt, hauling him out of his chair.

"Where are they?" he demanded. "Where did Joshua take them?"

Raj didn't even deign to look at him, keeping his gaze aimed over his shoulder at Jude.

"Your other pet was much better behaved," he said.

"Don't pretend I'm invisible, you Antagonist shit!" Daniel snarled, tightening his fingers into the fabric and yanking the other man closer. He wished desperately that he still had a sharp piece of iron, aching to drive it into the creature's flesh. Make him howl in agony.

"You're keeping a *Consilium* terrier?" Raj smirked at Jude. "That's bold."

"Fucking talk to me!" Daniel shouted. It was enough to make the other man finally meet his eyes.

He regretted it instantly.

The noise of the room dimmed. All he could hear through the rushing in his ears was his own rising heartbeat. His body went cold. He lost his sense of spatial awareness. He couldn't tell if he was upright, couldn't feel the floor beneath his feet, or his hands on the fabric of the Antagonist's t-shirt. Did he still have arms and legs?

The instant nothing made sense, his panic sparked. The room came back in a rush. He became aware of a touch on his hand, something moving his fingers back from the fabric he'd clutched. He tried to tighten his fist but Raj had freed himself and taken a step back.

The Antagonist's glare held a hint of unease, as if he hadn't expected the thrall to be broken without his permission. Eyes darting again to Jude, Raj demanded, "Who is he?"

Daniel clocked him in the jaw. His punch snapped the Archduke's head back but he didn't have time to appreciate it. A sharp point pressed into the side of his neck, replacing the gratification with a rush of cold fear.

The woman who'd let them in, Saskia, had produced a narrow sword from somewhere. She held the tip at his throat with a steady intensity.

"You *dare*?" Raj recovered quickly, finally addressing Daniel in a hiss. He seemed to realize the concession and lifted his voice to Jude instead. "Surrender him to me immediately, Mabling."

"What? Hell no." She sounded startled, but Daniel couldn't turn his head to see her reaction, or Abe's.

"Then you condone this attack?" The Antagonist's lips peeled back in a sneer.

Daniel fought not to meet Raj's eyes as the other man studied his face with an intensity that made it seem like he was memorizing it for the future.

"*Attack*?" Jude repeated. "He sucker punched you, you drama queen."

Daniel winced inwardly. Insulting the Antagonist wasn't going to help any of them. Abe must have given Jude some similar warning sign, because her voice changed to become more placating.

"Look," she said, "my father has Danny's brother and his best friend and he's going to rip their hearts out."

Even done in the apparent interest of an emotional appeal, the tactless words sent a pang through Daniel sharper than the blade under his jaw. He fought not to picture Ted and Zeb, bodies bloody and inert, chests torn open.

"Yeah, okay," Jude continued, "he went off on you and I see how that wasn't *polite* or whatever, but you're being a real asshole. Plus you've been helping Joshua kill people to raise the Harbinger of the Host."

"I assure you, no one will lose sleep over a few dead humans," Raj returned, making Daniel yearn to punch him again. "Particularly when done in the service of destroying the Harbinger."

"What about when it's done behind the Mab's back?" Jude challenged. "And, come to think of it, I'm *guessing* you also forgot to pass along the little tidbit about her brother returning from the dead?"

It was apparently a good guess. Raj's expression darkened.

"I don't owe the Mab information," he said.

"Maybe not, but it seems pretty shady from where I'm standing." She added a deliberate, "Which is, you remember, at the Mab's right hand, or wherever the heir to the throne stands, I guess. Beside her ear like a little bird, maybe?"

"You haven't spoken to the Mab in months," Raj said. "Why would she listen to you?"

"Wrong, pal. I just talked to her through a mirror ten minutes ago and she's sending an army over to help me out. I guess I'll just tell them to come straight here, go through every room in this hotel, turn the place upside down, disrupt some business . . ."

Raj's jaw clenched as he weighed whether or not to call her bluff.

"No need," he finally concluded. "I granted your father use of a house in Switzerland. One built around an inter-dimensional space."

"You've been hiding the shade since the beginning," Abe snapped. "Keeping her between the worlds so nobody could find her."

Raj's eyes flickered to the cowboy with disdain. He didn't dignify the accusation with an answer. He started to turn, dismissing them with: "Paul will take you. You may direct your army there. I'll expect to be compensated for any damage."

"I'll take them," Saskia said. "I'd like a shot at that enduring bitch."

Daniel couldn't help but gasp a relieved breath when she dropped the sword back to her side.

She didn't notice, too intent on her father's approval.

"Good hunting, then," Raj said.

Saskia used her sword to salute him in a strict fashion, then returned it to a sheath on her back. She jerked her chin toward Jude and Abe to indicate they should follow her lead and headed for the door.

When Daniel started to slip around him to follow, Raj turned and caught him with a hand against his shoulder.

"Not you. You stay."

"That's not part of the deal," Jude said.

"You allowed him to make an attempt on my life. That grants me his."

"An *attempt* on your *life*?" Jude's voice dripped incredulous sarcasm. Realizing he wasn't going to back down quickly, she made a frustrated noise in the back of her throat and snapped, "What do you *want*?"

Raj considered the question.

"I will accept a favour," he said. "Something I can ask of you in the future."

"Of course you will." Jude rolled her eyes, then clarified, "*One* thing?"

"Correct."

"Jude—" Daniel started. Her putting herself in an Antagonist's debt could only lead to something worse.

She ignored him. "Do we need to shake on it?"

"Your word will suffice." Raj smirked.

"Then *my word*." Jude's sharp tone rang hollow, strained with uncharacteristic anxiety. "And let's get the fuck out of here."

Moving past Declan Raj to join her was like sidling past a lion poised to spring, but nothing stopped Daniel this time from joining the others at the door.

37

GOODBYES OBVIOUSLY WEREN'T IN the Archduke's script. Just like last time I'd visited, he shut the door behind us as soon as we'd filed out.

Saskia jerked her chin to the right to say we were to follow her. As she led us down the hallway, Daniel caught up to me.

"You shouldn't have done that," he said. Never bargain with a Faerie.

"Joke's on him," I muttered. "My word doesn't mean shit. Breaking it can't short-circuit my magic."

"You think he doesn't know that?"

"It doesn't really matter. You're assuming the Shadow Mab doesn't kill me first." I hobbled faster to put an end to that conversation, as if I could outrun him down the hallway. Of course I didn't think I'd really fooled Declan, but it had worked short-term and that was all that mattered. I didn't want to dwell on the stunned sound of Daniel's gratitude.

I caught up to Saskia, stumbling a little on my crutch and causing her to side-eye me. "Don't we get any weapons? I happen to be lacking a sword."

Zeroing in on the accusation in my tone, she quirked her eyebrows.

"You told me yesterday where to find my weapon. Was that not an invitation to retrieve it?"

"Nope."

"You should be more careful then." She cast me a little smile that I fought not to appreciate. She had me there, but I still wasn't about to walk into this place with just the Saskia Sword and Dagger Show as my defence.

"What about salt?" I asked.

"The Harbinger is not afraid of salt, and neither are mages."

"No, but it melts the gooey centre of the Sendings they're using as goons."

"Your army should be prepared enough to defend you."

I gritted my teeth. "About the army . . ."

"We should wait for them," Abe put in.

"We don't have two hours," I hissed back.

Saskia's eyes flickered from me to the cowboy and back again like we were in a tennis match.

"You intend us to go *alone* to vanquish the Shadowed Mab?" Rather than balking, the redcap's eyes gleamed. She considered it another instant, then concluded, "Yes. That's a better choice. Quiet. Stealth."

Without turning, she lifted her voice to call behind us, "Paul? Weaponized salt for the Mabling and her associate?"

She caught my eye as I turned to see the well-dressed butler guy following us.

"Don't call me that," I told her, wishing I'd had time to drive that tidbit into her father's memory too.

With a new bounce in her step, Saskia led us down another hall that seemed much longer than it had looked. She must have liked the idea of the Mab's army overrunning the place as little as I did. Or she was really spoiling for a fight.

Of course she was—she had two good legs and a sword.

And, like I'd told Abe, we didn't have two hours to wait. When we came to a door marked 36, Saskia pulled it open without fanfare and let us gaze out onto a dark, freezing gravel road underneath skeletal trees swaying in the wind. Switzerland.

"Why are you doing this?" I asked her, as we waited for Paul.

"Even my father doesn't want this world overrun with obsolete, archaic magic like the Host."

"Unless he's the one controlling it, you mean."

She cast me a warning sidelong glance and finished tersely, "It will be a great honour to vanquish the Harbinger in his name."

This girl and her speeches.

Paul re-appeared, carrying two old-school shotguns in one arm. He offered them to me, and I selected one and nodded toward Abe to have him take the other. The cowboy accepted it slowly, revealing the painful-looking bruises that still peppered his wrists and forearms as he did so.

I passed my shotgun to Daniel. When Saskia made a warning noise in the back of her throat, I gave her my best innocent face.

"Do I look like I can fire it?" I asked, nodding toward my crutch.

"You *look* like you should be sitting this out and waiting for your *army*," she shot back, scowling.

"No chance."

She apparently liked that answer. As armed as we were going to be, she herded us out the door. When she closed it, it became part of a little shed in the middle of the road—an empty guardhouse for a gated community.

I glanced at the bare trees overhead and hugged my shoulders closer in an effort to stave off the cold. Should have conjured up a heavier coat before we'd fled the safe house. I half-regretted that we couldn't have waited for the Mab's army. Not like I wanted them taking over and screwing all of this up, getting Ted and Zeb killed, but the four of us alone didn't make much of an offence.

The massive house up the driveway was lit brightly against the night. A row of giant, curtained picture windows glowed with warm, yellow light.

Saskia took the lead and approached the front door with the casual ease of the owner returning to her summer home. Before she got halfway up the brick walkway, a green mass slouched into view. The light from the windows gleamed off the shiny, green gel of two other Sendings that emerged from our right, practically melting together at the hip.

"Stand back," Abe said, hefting the shotgun into his hands. He aimed and fired, the blast echoing through the dark trees.

My ears rang, even standing a good two metres behind it.

"No recoil," the cowboy observed, sounding pleased.

"Salt's light," Saskia returned.

Abe lowered his head to line up his aim a second time. The furthest creature expanded like a screen to cover the entire front door.

A body slammed into me from the left, coming at high speed. I shrieked as we tumbled to the side, half from surprise and half from the searing pain that sizzled through my knee like lightning.

From the ground I got a better look at the thing straddling me: the wraith. Its face was awful—paper-thin, pale skin pulled over the skull, sunken eyes gleaming with an emotionless, dead light. Its hair hung lank around its face and it smelled like a corpse. It tilted its head, eyes boring into my face as if it recognized me.

Daniel grabbed it from behind and hauled it off of me. The wraith's skull-like face stretched into a horrible growl as it flung him forward, over its shoulder and onto the ground. It was on him almost too fast to see, knocking the gun from his hand and sending it bouncing across the gravel.

"Jude, move!" Abe shouted from behind me. He had his shotgun levelled at the creature pinning Daniel to the ground.

I scrambled back on my hands, choking back a sob as my knee pulsed another burst of agony. Black spots danced in my vision. The sound of the shotgun blast exploded through my head again.

The force of the flying salt knocked the flailing creature back. Abe hurried forward and swung the butt of the gun into the wraith's head. When it fell still, he extended a hand to help Daniel up.

Daniel winced as he put a hand to his side, fingers coming away bloody. Traces of white dust mixed with dark liquid on the side of his shirt and jacket.

"It's fine," he said, to Abe's and my concern. "Just going to sting tomorrow."

Two more teeth-rattling roars came from behind us in succession. Saskia had retrieved the shotgun Daniel had dropped and fired at the two remaining Sendings, one covering the door like a tent.

The rock salt tore holes through the creatures' green filmy skin and left a charred spot in the door above the handle. The gelatinous shield shrank back to its humanoid form. It continued to melt, bubbling a little until it became an oily puddle on the brick steps and disappeared. The second one lurched toward us but disintegrated before it got more than three steps.

Saskia glanced to both sides, as if checking for more Sendings, then advanced to the front door and shoved it open. She tossed the now-empty shotgun aside and drew the glamoured sword from her back to lead us inside.

Abe kept his shotgun as a cudgel. It made me wish I had a weapon. Two fists, ten fingernails, at least. Maybe I could get Gordon pontificating about the history of the Mab and cold-cock him.

My ears rang in the silence of the enormous house after the explosions of the shotguns. More giant, clear vases held even larger versions of the otherworldly, upside-down silver-leafed plant and its twining, towering roots. Saskia's favourite Faerie plants weren't flowering here like they had been in the hotel.

"Where's the inter-dimensional chamber?" I hissed.

"In the Great Room," Saskia answered.

Of course the Archduke had a room called the 'Great Room' in his house.

My knee throbbed, woken from its opiate nap, as we followed the redcap toward the back of the house. She stopped at each doorway but nothing ever jumped out at us.

Joshua and Gordon hadn't left much security. Maybe they didn't have much. Didn't need it, really, in this secluded mansion.

Saskia led us to a set of heavy, impressively carved double-doors, and knelt down to peer through the keyhole.

"Four mages, two humans," she whispered.

A growl reverberating from down the hall behind us upped the count for her, adding one pissed-off wraith to the tally. Shreds of clothing clung to its body from the rock salt blast. It was missing an eye and blood covered half its face, including the side of its jaw that had been knocked askew where Abe had beaten it with the butt of the shotgun.

Saskia straightened, tightening her grip on her sword. A ferocious glint shone in her eye. "I don't believe I invited you inside," she told it, bursting forward as the wraith came loping down the hall toward us.

Daniel muttered a curse and tried the doorknob, then reared back and slammed a foot into the centre of the double-doors. They both burst open and the three of us dashed in. Well, Daniel and Abe did—I stumbled, delayed by my crutch.

We fled into a large, empty room with heavy cross-hatched beams overhead like a movie ski lodge. All the furniture had been moved out, or *almost* all—Ted lay on his stomach on a fancy chaise lounge, one hand dangling to the floor. His eyes were open, blinking occasionally. Stunned or doped with the Sending's narcotic sedative—still alive.

Zeb slumped in an overstuffed chair shoved up against the end of the chaise. He was out cold, but his chest still rose and fell under his chin.

Abe swung his shotgun like a baseball bat, nearly taking off the head of the closest unfamiliar man just inside the doorway—one of Gordon's mages. Gordon himself and another man descended on Daniel.

The massive, open fireplace on the wall to the right demanded my attention. Five glass jars sat on the mantle, each one holding a pinkish-brown human heart in clear fluid. Little flaps of tissue waved in the liquid.

I blinked to be certain my eyes weren't deceiving me as I gazed to the back of the structure. The fireplace was tall enough for me to walk into if I stooped. No wood had been piled inside, but there were carefully arranged circles and markings in what looked like dirt on the brick. The back was made of glass or some other transparent substance. It shimmered a little.

The place felt wrong. It didn't trigger my Faerie sense, but something deeper in the pit of my stomach. A little like the wraith had—another thing that didn't fit into the flow of this world. Something that Didn't Belong.

The noise of the fight echoed in the empty room. I yearned to jump in, but I had to strengthen my grip on the crutch. My current graceless state was better spent where I could be most useful—hauling either of the unconscious humans out of this melee while the mages fought with Abe and Daniel.

And Saskia, who came flying through the doorway just behind us, seemingly tossed by the wraith. The creature stalked in after her, one arm hanging uselessly by its side from a huge wound she'd slashed through its neck and shoulder.

I didn't have to move to swing my crutch up to meet the injured monster as it flew past me. My hit knocked it off balance and sent it skidding to the side, tumbling into a mass of bloody, tangled limbs.

Someone yanked me off my feet, hauling me away from the wraith. Joshua spun me to face him, shoving my crutch back under my arm while keeping watch over my shoulder.

"You can't be here," he said. "She has to cross through."

"Declan said you were here to destroy her," I argued, remembering at the last second to keep my voice down because the other mages weren't in on that part of the plan.

"She has to *cross* in order for me to do that." He dragged me off-balance again, trying to pull me toward the open, now empty, double doors. "You have to leave. They're targeting you."

"Yeah, I figured that out!" I snapped, struggling to hold my ground with the rubber tip of my crutch. I hissed the million dollar question: "*Why?*"

"They mean to summon her into you, let her take your body and thereby your place as the heir."

Take your body. And I'd thought Miranda was the worst for just wanting to rent out the one room to a fetus. The Shadow Mab wanted to evict me entirely. Fuck that.

"Why didn't you tell me that last night?" I snapped.

"Because I didn't know," he returned through clenched teeth. "You *cannot* be here. Without a consecrated body to jump into when she comes through, she'll be weak. I can finish her."

"She only comes through if you take two more men's hearts and that's not happening!" I insisted, wrenching away hard enough that lighting shot up my swollen knee.

"You would have been safe in the cavern," Joshua snarled. "I delivered you your healer, I left you the human you favour—why didn't you just *stay there?*"

That cavern bullshit had been a ruse to keep me *safe?*

Another man reached us, interrupting Joshua's attempt at fatherly scolding. It was one of the mages I didn't know. He blocked the door ahead of us and barked something at Joshua in their foreign tongue, maybe wise to the fact that my father didn't really intend to help them in their goal.

Joshua made a calm, even reply in the other language but accompanied it with a vicious hit to the other man's throat. That stopped the guy from shouting, but he still raised a hand like he meant to call up a spell. Joshua shoved me away roughly, pushing me out of the fight.

Directly to my right, Saskia had escaped the wraith somehow and faced off against one of the other mages. The man started to multiply, splitting into three, then five, of himself. He surrounded the redcap, who raised her sword. Swinging it through one made it dissipate like smoke, but two more appeared.

A bundle of sticks and fabric fell into the fireplace like someone had dumped it, but there was no one nearby. It moved under its own power—the wraith—curling up on the hearth. I couldn't see it clearly under the shadow of the mantle, but it didn't seem to be out of commission, more like it had gone there to regenerate after the wounds Saskia had dealt it. The back of the giant fireplace began to glow. A ghostly figure appeared behind the glass, moving like a creepy, amorphous goldfish in a bowl.

Something pressed me to move closer, make out the details, but Saskia cried out and jolted my attention away. One of the circle of identical men she'd been fighting had stabbed her in the shoulder, causing her to drop her sword with a clatter.

Abe, having beaten one of the unfamiliar mages and in the midst of hauling Ted up from the chaise, stopped as if to go to her aid.

Daniel reached me suddenly, dragging a half-conscious Zeb with him. He tried to press his friend's almost dead-weight on me.

"Go with Jude," he told him, and to me, "Get out of here. I'll get Ted."

"Abe's got Ted," I started, interrupted by a squishing noise. Something warm and gooey slid past me. I swung sideways but Daniel wasted time shoving Zeb out of the way.

The Sending absorbed him. One second he was there, and the next the green goop had closed around him from behind, showing only a dark outline of his form inside.

Swallowing a mouthful of curses from the protest my knee made, I lifted a fist to beat the green monster until it spit Daniel out. Before I could even touch it, the creature started melting. It poured in rivulets of green slime to the floor, bubbling, and disappeared between the floorboards.

Daniel gasped like a man who'd been drowning. He swayed in surprise but managed to stay on his feet. The white residue from the rock salt Abe had shot at the wraith earlier stained his jacket.

"That thing's got a narcotic in it," I warned, limping closer like I could even hope to catch him if he collapsed. Was he already feeling the effects? It had taken a couple of minutes to hit me in Chris's apartment but that Sending had only gotten a sliver of my skin, not closed itself around me. Plus, I had some Faerie blood to fight it off.

Sudden agony bloomed just below my ribs. Daniel fell against me, choking off a cry of pain at the same time. He jerked backwards just as quickly and crumpled, revealing Gordon behind him.

Teen Mage brandished Saskia's discarded sword. The metal gleamed red with blood.

It didn't register until I looked down and saw the matching stain leaching into my t-shirt from the left of my stomach. Gordon had stabbed Daniel hard enough to put the blade through him and into me.

"Damn it," I managed. Part of wanted me to leap at Gordon and another part insisted that I check on Daniel. The third part wanted me to just sink to the floor in pain. I combined the last two and dropped down between Zeb and Daniel. Zeb had passed out again and Daniel was doubled over on the floor with one hand pressed against his stomach. The bloodstain blossomed across the back of his jacket.

Arms yanked me up to one knee, pinning mine back with a grip like steel while my injured leg splayed out behind me. I panted through my teeth to keep from sobbing. The screams of the pain receptors in my brain washed over me, dulling the rest of the room around me.

"You're not needed yet, princess." Gordon was stronger than I'd imagined. With his lips at my ear, I calculated that whacking my skull back into his would probably break his nose.

He let out a gagged scream when I performed that experiment. His hands tightened on my arms as he coughed on what I hoped was blood. Then he slammed a boot into the back of my injured knee, and it was me shrieking loud enough to echo through the room.

38

ABE'S BLOOD RAN COLD when Jude screamed. The raw agony in the sound rattled him from the inside out. Frantic, weak scraps of his power struggled to twine into something that could help her, but the iron laid heavy in his veins and fizzled them out.

He lowered the unconscious man he'd been struggling to get over his shoulder in a fireman's carry, preparing instead to fight with his hands free.

Gordon had Jude crumpled on one knee, holding her arms tightly behind her. Blood gushed down the mage's chin from his nose.

Joshua reached them before Abe could stumble to his feet. He said one word in a low, warning voice. Abe knew enough of the Faerie language to recognize it. His best guess was that Joshua had just warned the mage to stop what he was doing.

"*Stand down.*" Gordon's voice was louder and his accent in the foreign tongue clearer.

Exhaustion ran through Abe's body as if the mage had commanded him, not Joshua. He managed to roll his human cargo gingerly onto the floor.

"*You won't kill my daughter to restore the Lady to her place.*" Joshua spat those words slowly enough for Abe to get all of them.

"*As if you have any choice in the matter,*" Gordon sneered. "Revelle."

The wraith moved at its name. It unfolded itself and emerged from the giant fireplace, silhouetted by the eerie glow in the glass back. It fixed its good eye on Joshua and crossed the floor to join them.

Abe tried to summon his strength while the mages were distracted, but his muscles barely responded, twitching painfully. He'd been running on adrenaline and the pause had dissipated it. He sank slowly to the floor, trying to keep attention from himself to avoid being a target.

Joshua froze as the wraith bent down and took Jude from Gordon. Half-healed tendons in the bloody wound on its shoulder stretched with a nauseating, wet grinding noise, but it still used both arms successfully to lift her.

Jude moaned, flailing only a little and slapping the wraith's good shoulder weakly with one hand. It ignored her and carried her to the fireplace, Gordon trailing.

Abe flinched again at the pain in her voice. His nerves tried to yank him to his feet, sending him toward the call of her suffering. He shut off his instincts, forcing himself to stop, gather strength and formulate a plan.

Joshua still hadn't moved. *Couldn't* move. The old mage grunted and winced, straining his muscles to act, to fight, but he seemed rooted to the floor. He struggled against his own body and shrank, crumpling to his knees. He tried to resist reaching across the floorboards for the sword Gordon had dropped, but failed. Still fruitlessly battling the motion of his own arm, he gritted his teeth as one of his hands closed around the blade rather than the hilt and lifted it.

"*You can't do this without me.*" Joshua aimed the grunt at Gordon, arms trembling as he fought the compulsion to slide the sword through his own chest.

"*We won't,*" the younger mage assured him, supervising as the wraith laid Jude inside the fireplace. "*Merely a corrective reminder of who sustains you.*"

The wraith cast a glance toward Joshua and he dropped the sword. It fell onto his knees and rolled off to the floor in front of him, but he stayed frozen. What sounded like a soft sigh of relief escaped his lips.

Joshua wasn't controlling the wraith. The wraith controlled him.

The realization almost brought Abe to pity the old mage, but the horrific memory of the dark, chilly cave prevented it. It had been the wraith who'd held him down with unnatural strength, kept him from fighting, but it was Joshua who'd handled the iron. Joshua who'd burned his own fingers sewing it under Abe's skin. Joshua whose indifference to the suffering of an old ally—of another living creature, for that matter—Abe had felt before his powers were washed away. The mage had been in control then, even if only by the wraith's consent.

On the hearth, Jude lay on her back, panting. The wraith held her flat against the tile, one hand around her throat. Her eyelids fluttered as she fought to stay awake, still spitting profanities where she could.

Abe's stomach turned when Gordon bent down and dipped a finger into the red, sticky wound under her ribs. Jude jerked in the wraith's grip, yelping in surprise more than pain. She flailed to smack the mage away, but couldn't budge the strong fingers from her throat, the unnatural weight holding her to the ground. He remembered the feeling too well.

"Hold still or I'll have him snap your spine," Gordon said, switching to English for Jude's benefit.

"Then your shadow bitch is gonna have a hard time joyriding in my carcass," she spat back.

"You should be so lucky as to have the Shadowed Mab restore your unworthy body." Gordon leaned past her, using her blood on his index finger to draw symbols on the clear wall at the back of the fireplace. "You shouldn't be in the Lineage at all. You could never be Mab as you are, practically human. No, you're the loathsome flaw, the necessary evil, that will allow The Undimmed to return to Her rightful place."

"Don't want to be Mab, ass-hat," Jude choked out.

With Gordon and the wraith focused on her, Abe glanced around the room for any hope of a coordinated attack. The unconscious man beside him who he'd been trying to roust, Daniel's brother-in-law, still hadn't come to. The other human man was sprawled on the floor near Joshua, who remained inert under the wraith's power.

Daniel had shoved himself back toward the left wall, leaving a trail of red on the floor as he went. He braced his shoulder against the firm, vertical surface and pulled his feet under his body as if meaning to push himself up. That motion required the muscles in his abdomen, though, and when he tried, the wound in his midsection seemed to prevent it. He slumped back down, strength flagging.

Abe couldn't do a damn thing about it. The hot frustration of his own helplessness crashed over him again in a wave. He could smell the blood nearby, feel the pulsing pain, fear and panic swirling from his friends and foes all over the room, but he couldn't fix it. He couldn't take any of it into himself and neutralize it. If he crossed the room and laid a hand on Daniel's wound, he'd likely still do more harm than good.

That left the redcap, Saskia, as his only ally. She'd fallen to her knees, panting, surrounded by the army of identical mages she'd been fighting. He could get up, run head-down and barrel through them. Use his body, the only weapon he had left, to help her disperse them down to the single, corporeal man.

Something else rose through the bitter miasma in Abe's head, twinging at the corner of his consciousness. A new emotion, sent out purposely, beckoning his attention. A whirlwind of fury and desperate hatred.

It drew his gaze to Joshua, still doubled over where the wraith had left him. The older man had his eyes fixed on Abe. Once he had the cowboy's attention, he looked pointedly down at the sword. His lips moved, making a barely audible sound:

"Kill. It."

Abe risked another glance toward the fireplace. The wraith was laser-focused on Jude, gazing down at her with the intensity of an obsessed lover. Gordon had his back to the room, still drawing bloody runes on the glass. The soft, filmy light behind the fireplace flickered and flitted, the shade waiting for her ritual. Her body.

Would killing the wraith release Joshua? Would it take away the shocking power he seemed to draw while being under the creature's command? Abe couldn't say he truly wanted the old mage at full strength. Joshua had been calculating and unpredictable on his best days back when Abe had first began working with Miranda. He was worse now.

But the wraith with Joshua as a puppet remained the worst option. Gritting his teeth, Abe leapt over the chaise he'd been crouching behind, swiping the sword from the floor.

39

My throat ached from the wraith's steel grip. With its sharp nails digging into my skin, I summoned the last of my energy and thrust a fist through its shattered torso. My fingers searched the sticky meat inside, desperate for some thread to tug and unravel the dead thing squatting on top of me. It was shockingly light, a bag of brittle bones, for how much force it used holding me down so Gordon could use my stomach wound like an inkwell.

A scuffle came from somewhere to my left. Hot gore splattered my face at the same moment that the wraith went still. Its fingers loosened and slipped from my throat. Those hollow, gleaming eyes still bored into mine, but they'd gone dull and cloudy.

Something new poked out from between them: the tip of Saskia's sword.

Abe stood at the other end of the weapon. Tremors ran through his body, shaking him so thoroughly that I didn't know how he'd put the sword through the thing's skull with such perfect aim, never mind avoided ramming the blade straight through into mine too.

"It seems I am once more *self*-sustaining." Joshua appeared suddenly beside Gordon, flashing a smile that showed all of his teeth.

Horror drained the blood from Teen Mage's face. He leapt back.

Joshua made a small, quick motion with one hand, but Gordon burst into a flock of birds. The rush of wings evaded whatever weaponized spell my father had cast. Undeterred, he lifted both hands, eyes moving intently among the dozens of tiny creatures that flooded in panic from their single origin.

The birds burst into flame. Each burned as they flew in a wild frenzy around the ceiling, shrieking. They began dropping one by one to the floor, scattering ash and lying still.

The commotion had drawn the attention of Gordon's remaining compatriot. The half-dozen of the mage surrounding Saskia looked to Joshua in unison. They snapped back into a single man, like a paper fan folding up, and rounded for an attack.

Joshua wheeled on him. My father was almost unrecognizable now, his eyes dark and wild like the wraith's. He made another motion with his hand and the mage began to multiply again, faster. The incarnations bumped into one another as they divided into ten, twenty. The more of them there were, the fainter they became until finally they all faded into smoke, and then vanished.

The madness seemed to fade. For a moment Joshua looked exhausted, old and gaunt, like he might collapse.

Instead, he drew a breath and straightened again. Colour returned to his face along with a stony, resolute expression. He walked to the fireplace and took the jars from the mantle, one by one, flinging them at the bloody marks Gordon had made on the shimmering back wall.

Each glass shattered with a pop and a sickening, heavy plop as it sent liquid and a limp, squishy human heart streaming down the glass to pool together on the dirty brick.

My stomach turned as the faces of the men those hearts had come from surged through my memory. Alongside, a tentative relief crept through me. My father had destroyed the mages. He was tossing the hearts.

Those men had died for nothing now, the whims of some Faerie assholes, but it was better than raising the Faerie Shade Queen.

The reprieve was short-lived when Joshua turned on Abe. The cowboy raised the sword, fingers white around the handle. He knew something I didn't, had to be reading Joshua and intuiting danger from my father's emotions.

Joshua stepped forward slowly, bringing himself to the sword's tip. He twitched a shoulder and the weapon jerked from the cowboy's hand. Without giving Abe a second to bolt, he grabbed him in one quick, vicious movement and flung him down unceremoniously beside me.

"Heal her," Joshua said, voice low and warning. "And get her out of here."

He still meant to raise the Shadow Mab.

"I can't!" Abe flashed his black and blue wrists to illustrate, snarling, "You poisoned me."

With a growl of annoyance, Joshua clamped a firm hand on the back of the cowboy's neck. He bowed Abe over me.

"Try now."

Abe choked on a gasp when Joshua touched him. He reached down slowly and put one shaking hand over the throbbing slash under my ribs.

My breath hitched too at the sudden heat that came from his touch. My skin started to knit back together under his hand. Joshua was *using* Abe to heal me, funnelling power through him? He kept his hand on the nape of Abe's neck for another few seconds, then released him, but the healer stayed fixed over me, using whatever power he'd been given to fuse the wound back together. It didn't hurt. Faerie healing had always hurt before, on account of my human blood. It went faster too.

Abe had tears in his eyes. I put my hand over his and squeezed. His expression flickered between relief at having his power back and resentment toward the man who'd restored it to him.

Across the room, Joshua lingered over Zeb's unconscious form, then he started toward Daniel, who had managed to haul himself upright against the wall. He was pale and shaking, still uselessly pressing a hand to the wound in his middle.

I shoved Abe's fingers away from my new skin, hauling myself upright with more effort than I'd have liked. My knee didn't seem to hurt as much—maybe some of that healing mojo had leached down from my stomach.

I managed to reach Joshua and put my body between him and Daniel.

"Stop," I said.

"I understand that you have affection for this one," Joshua said. "But you must realize there's no use wasting a perfectly imminent death. Take one who has a chance." He indicated Zeb, still motionless on the floor behind us.

Daniel's fingers dug weakly into my shin, making me flinch. No doubt he was ready with some stupid suggestion like that I should save myself and the others and leave him here to bleed out as a heart donor. Fuck that.

When I refused to move, Joshua eyed me like a disobedient child. *Stop being stubborn and choose a different toy before I take them all away.*

"The purpose of the Consilium," he said, voice even as if presenting me with simple facts, "was to keep this world safe. At any cost." He gestured toward Daniel, finishing, "He'd doubtless still want to be useful to that goal."

Daniel muttered something bleary and indistinct, still clutching my jeans as if he meant to pull himself up. The only words I caught were "*anything*" and "*bastard*" but it wasn't hard to construct the full meaning from his bitter tone.

"You were saying?" I challenged.

"Very well." Joshua turned. "They can all die."

He strode back to Zeb, making a quick gesture with his fingers. His spell sliced open both the front of Zeb's t-shirt and the skin on his chest in a quick, straight line.

Zeb jerked awake with a strangled moan as the gleaming white lines of his rib cage were laid bare in a mess of blood and tissue.

Dizziness hit me. I had to close my eyes to let the horror and revulsion wash through. The crack of bone rang as loudly in my ears as the explosion of the shotgun had.

Zeb gave another weak, hacking sob and Daniel's grip tightened on my leg, then his fingers went slack.

No, *no, no.*

"You're the wraith!" I shouted at my father, desperate to distract him as I blinked through tears. "Abe skewered the thing but you're still doing the shade's bidding! She's playing you! Sustaining you!"

"She thought so, once." Joshua paused over Zeb's prone, bleeding body to glare at the fireplace, where the glowing had started to pulse faster, angrier. "You think these idiot mages are the only ones who ever tried to free her? To gain what she knows? They're only the latest. It ends here."

He was right about that.

Across the room, Abe had retreated to Ted and apparently used his borrowed power to bring him around, since Grace's husband was sitting up, touching his head as if trying to get his bearings.

Saskia picked herself up too, grimacing at the wound in her shoulder and starting to hunt for her sword.

I was supposed to think about numbers, odds, how all of us could bring Joshua down and banish the Shadow Mab. All I really cared about in this moment was giving Abe the space to reach Zeb and Daniel and use that borrowed power while he still had it.

I took a running—limping—start, flinging myself onto Joshua's back and flailing to sink my fingers into his eyes.

Maybe he'd weakened himself by transferring that power into Abe, or in the death of the wraith. Maybe I had a chance.

Nope.

My father flipped me over his back as easily as brushing dust from his shoulder. I hit the floor hard, breath knocked out of my lungs. Before I could get it back, he had a hand tight around my throat, gripping me the same way the wraith had.

"Don't mistake me, Judith," he said quietly, squeezing to press his point home. "I've protected you thus far, but I *will* destroy you if I must to ensure the Host gains no foothold here."

He released me, letting me gulp air back down my throat, and finished, "You'd do well to take what I've granted you and run."

I scooted away from him as quickly as a scrambled crab-walk could take me, desperate to put as much distance between us as I could. He still looked human, like the man who'd rescued me in the métro last night, spoken reverently about my mother, enthralled a nurse to ease my pain, but he wasn't.

His glamour was slipping. Not a change to his physical body, more like the draining away of every flicker of emotion and desire, boiling him down to a bloodthirsty creature with one singular focus: destruction. Through meticulously controlled movements, he brimmed with a violence and fury that was in no way human.

Defiance bloomed out of my fear, steeling my muscles as I climbed to my feet. I could do violence and fury too. I hadn't cowered before the Archduke, or Gordon and his rotting wraith. I wasn't about to just back off and let the deadbeat monster who'd donated this rage in my blood tell me what to do.

"Can't run." The malicious sarcasm felt so good it almost blotted out the pain in my knee.

"Then allow me to assist you." Joshua swooped back to meet me, grabbing my upper arm in one hand and wrenching me toward the giant picture windows. He used enough force to give me lift, sending me flying head-first toward the glass.

In a blink of instinct, I reversed my gravity and fell up toward the ceiling. The immediate, comforting response of my power stopped my trajectory just short of the looming windows, but I slammed hard into a heavy cross-beam, tumbling over it and leaving a divot in the ceiling plaster with one shoulder.

Joshua practically floated up to join me. When I shifted my gravity, it always happened fast: one minute I was being dragged toward the floor by the pull of the earth, and the next I had the same force coming from the ceiling, or a perpendicular wall, or whatever I'd focused on.

My father was able to change it more slowly, taking time to turn himself around in midair with a hypnotic grace. It was almost like he could fly. He touched the ceiling on his feet, perfectly balanced.

I lunged, aiming for his face again, but he blocked me and knocked me back. I landed on my good leg and bounced back with a lower punch. He blocked that one too, but he didn't have time to avoid the left hook I slammed into his kidney a second later.

He was larger than me. Normally I'd have had my speed and skills, but the brace made it impossible to push myself into the spring handstands or somersaults that my body wanted to naturally bring me into when I fought.

The tip of Joshua's shoe caught me behind my left heel and hauled me off-balance enough that one more punch had me literally spinning through the air to the floor. I hit hard, tasting the copper tang of blood. My vision dipped and dimmed like it might just give out for good. At this moment, that didn't feel like the worst idea in the world.

Beyond me, Joshua's feet hit the floor. He stepped carefully toward me, preparing to clobber me to safety or just rid himself of my distraction.

Something long and hard dug into my ribs. I forced myself to arch my screaming back and pulled it up, recognizing Abe's empty shotgun from the heft and shape.

My fingers closed around the handle. I swung it out to smash Joshua in the kneecap with the barrel. That brought him down so that I could slam it into his ribs and then hit him on the side of his head.

He crumpled to the floor with a moan and I dragged myself to my hands and knees, lifting the barrel high to smash it down on his skull.

A hand grabbed my wrist and jerked me backwards. The motion of having the gun torn from my fingers spun me around to see Saskia running for the fireplace.

The redcap skidded to a stop inside the massive structure, then slammed the shotgun like a bat into the clear, shimmering back wall. She swung with both hands, giving it all of her strength as she hit. Larger and larger cracks appeared.

I could finally see the shade behind the splintering glass, looming giant as she bellowed in rage. Her body was a nebulous, undulating thing moving around her like the tattered clothing of a ghost, but the enormous teeth and lidless red eyes were plenty clear pressed up against the barrier.

The Shadowed Mab opened her mouth wide and gnashed her fangs, her shriek like a drill burrowing into my brain.

Saskia kept swinging. The dented shotgun barrel finally broke a chink in the wall and the hole sucked the shade's murky, shrieking apparition back into the darkness.

40

"You look terrible." A voice broke me out of what I realized was anxious pacing—the awkward, limping sort—in the hallway outside the hospital waiting room.

"Look who's talking," I returned.

Grace was bruising faster than me, since she was the one who'd gotten hit earlier. The red puffiness around her right eye had already started turning blue, but she was upright and walking steadily.

I wanted to be relieved to see her recovering but I could only dread what came next, now that she'd found us here at the hospital.

"Are you okay?" I asked, fighting to delay the inevitable.

"Mild concussion. Anti-nausea meds and no screens for two weeks."

"Where's Riley?"

"With Ted." She inclined her head back toward the waiting room. "He told me what happened. What he could remember, anyway." She paused to let me fill in further details.

When I couldn't make words come out, she pressed, "This is the third fucking time *this year* I've been in a hospital, waiting to hear if my brother was going to be okay."

"I'm sorry." Those were all on me. The first time I'd nearly beaten Daniel to death. The second, he'd gotten torn up by a griffin coming to my rescue. And now, well.

"I don't care," Grace said. "Tell me what happened."

"We got stabbed."

"You seem fine."

I hugged Guy's coat tighter around my middle to keep from fingering the hole in my t-shirt, stiff with dried blood, and poking the unblemished skin beneath it.

"Gordon wanted to get to me, and Daniel was in the way. Abe tried—" I looked helplessly around for the cowboy, the expert, to step in and take over this explanation with more detail and his disarming empathy.

No Abe. I was on my own. I managed to stammer out a few halting sentences about how Abe had healed me, Joshua donating power to trigger his ability. But I was part-Faerie and both Zeb and Daniel were fully human, and magical healing was harder when you didn't already have magic in your blood. Zeb had been the most critical case. After putting him back together, Abe hadn't had as much juice left. He'd done what he could until his borrowed power ran out, but Daniel had already lost so much blood.

Once Saskia had banished the Shade Queen from her inter-dimensional Great Room, she'd retrieved her sword and told us all to get the hell out. Didn't want any of us stealing her thunder for vanquishing the Harbinger. So we'd brought Daniel here to the hospital in Toronto from the Swiss guard house because the portals wouldn't open in the Archduke's house itself.

Part of me wished we'd chosen a different hospital so I wouldn't be having this conversation with Grace, but it hadn't occurred to me at the time.

"Have you heard anything?" I dared to ask.

"You think I'd be interrogating you for scraps if I had?" Grace folded her arms across her chest, studying the scuffed tile beneath her feet.

"I'm sorry."

"You said that already."

"I'll leave."

"The *fuck* you will." Her head snapped up. "You're going to stay right here and wait with me, because I need somebody to be pissed at. Somebody who's not fighting through surgery upstairs." She growled in frustration. "I need a coffee," she muttered.

"Are you supposed to have caffeine?" I thought to ask, following her to the vending machine at the end of the hall. I'd lost my crutch but Abe had healed my knee enough that I could hobble along with just the brace.

When she glowered at me, I touched my head to remind her she'd been diagnosed with a concussion.

"You're really easy to hate," she said.

"It's a gift." I waited while she punched buttons, frowning at my reflection in the vending machine glass. It was hard to tell with the grainy, yellowing photos of lattes and cappuccinos behind it, but my left cheek was swollen and there was going to be a bruise stretching from there to my left eye. One along my jaw line too, if the ache there was any indication.

My knee throbbed with a steady pulse that became clearer the more I let myself think about it, and my shoulder ached from its collision with the giant crossbeam. My whole body felt like one giant bruise—at least.

It could have been worse. It *should* have been worse. I had a vivid flash of Daniel, unable to stand, fingers clutching my shin through my jeans. I jiggled my knee to make it hurt again and banish that memory.

"Where's Zeb?" I thought to ask, as Grace straightened, blowing on her steaming coffee.

"I sent him to a hotel."

"And he *went*?"

"He was still dazed. I don't think he remembers much."

Unlikely. Being nearly vivisected didn't feel like something you'd forget easily. But Zeb *had* been fuzzy after Abe's healing, weak and dizzy but jumping right in to help us carry Daniel through to the guard house and the hospital. Loyal idiot. It seemed callous that Grace would just shunt him off now but since he was breathing and back in one piece, I could understand her focusing on her brother instead.

Like I was.

After following her back to the glassed-in surgery waiting room, I wished I'd sprung for a coffee of my own. I needed something to do with my hands. Trying to hold them still in my lap was a lost cause.

Ted sat in the corner, head tilted back in sleep, making the stiff waiting room chairs almost look comfortable. He held a conked out Riley in his arms, the toddler's head rising and falling rhythmically with his chest. We hadn't really exchanged words at the Archduke's place. I'd been trying to avoid him since then.

Grace snagged a remote off the magazine table for the TV in the corner and switched channels, turning on the closed captions. They were in French, just like the conversation, so it didn't help me much. She probably knew that.

I couldn't concentrate anyway. Joshua had vanished by the time we'd recovered from Saskia breaking the Shadow Mab's fireplace fish tank. It seemed too much to hope that he'd just disappear again, go back to playing dead. I half-expected him to appear here in the hospital, in a blazing fury, come to punish me for ruining his revenge.

The hands on the clock went around the face almost twice more before Abe showed up in the hallway outside the waiting room. He hovered on the other side of the window there like he wasn't sure he should enter.

Ted and Riley were still asleep, and Grace rested in a chair beside them, her legs curled up in a cramped-looking position and her head on her husband's shoulder. Her eyes were open, watching the TV, but they darted to me as I got to my feet. She didn't say anything when I joined Abe outside the waiting room.

All of the cowboy's visible bruises and scabs had disappeared when Joshua donated him the power to heal me, but he still looked exhausted.

"Where've you been?" I asked. I fought to keep from scowling at him, thinking, *Where were you two hours ago?* That wasn't fair, though. It had been my explanation to give to Grace, since it had been my fault.

"Upstairs."

"Pitching in with surgery?" I couldn't even allow myself the hope.

"Keeping an eye out." Abe's eyes flickered over my shoulder and I turned to follow them. Just a doctor in a white coat coming toward us. "He's stable."

I spun back to fix the cowboy with wide eyes, almost afraid to confirm: "Danny?"

Abe nodded, prompting me to add, "What does stable mean?"

"Not dead."

Behind us, the doctor entered the waiting room and Grace lifted her head. Then she got to her feet, and they spoke.

I couldn't hear through the glass, but Ted opened his eyes and Grace said something to him before following the doctor out. She cast me a quick nod. It was true, then—Daniel had come through surgery.

I pressed a hand to my ribs, thinking of the bloody hole in my t-shirt. An ache started behind my eyes. I wanted to follow Grace, limp into Danny's room, fling myself down beside the bed and stay close to him until he woke. But I couldn't. He deserved a do-over. One without me fucking up his life.

"You runnin' again?" The cowboy clearly had gotten some of his powers back, presuming he could read my emotions and therefore predict my thoughts.

Or maybe I'd just let it show on my face.

"I shouldn't be here," I said. "I should have gone further away, not . . . not back here. I brought this down on them. Daniel wouldn't be here if not for me. As usual." The sterile, white walls felt blinding.

"What d'you think he'd say to that?"

"Good riddance."

"Doubt it."

"It's better for everyone if I just take off," I said.

"It's not better for me. I'll miss you."

"That'll fade fast, trust me. I left a big mess to be cleaned up. Miranda's gotta be really pissed. You can keep your mind off missing me with that. Tell her it was all my idea. You had no choice."

"She knows me too well for that." Abe folded his arms across his chest, then winced in a strange way. "Your father's downstairs," he said reluctantly.

"How do you know?" I hissed.

"Not sure. Residual effect from him flooding me with his magic, I guess. I can feel him waiting."

My chest constricted. "For what?"

Abe shook his head to say his answer would be another variation on the theme.

"Fuck him," I muttered. This was the time to go. Grace was up with Daniel. He had his family. Miranda had this mess of her traitorous mages to sort out. No one needed me.

41

GRACIE FOLLOWED THE INSTRUCTIONS the surgeon had given her to navigate the maze of hospital corridors and find her brother's room. She'd kept most of her thoughts at bay the last few hours, forcing herself to compartmentalize while the outcome was unknown, but now the full horror of the night weighed on her.

It had been almost impossible fighting against the concussion to keep herself calm and not frighten Riley. As they'd waited, her focus had returned over and over to her missing husband and her brother headed off against terrifying odds to rescue him. To the men without hearts popping up around the city. To the green, gelatinous monster that had swallowed Ted and tried to suffocate Tess.

They should have quit months ago. After Niagara. No, after Daniel had left the hospital the *first* time, in April. The Consilium was dead. They didn't have the skills or ability to keep going like this. She should have insisted they get on a plane *immediately*, not wait for this safe charter that Ted had wanted.

She concentrated on following the yellow line on the floor to the ICU, then inquired at the nurse's station, quiet so early in the morning, to find her brother.

Voices slowed her steps as she neared the room to which the nurse had directed her. She approached the half-open door cautiously, angling herself so that she could see the flash of reflections in the small window.

Tess Foster stood inside, with another man.

Gracie crept closer to peer around the edge of the door. Daniel lay on his back in bed, hooked up to all of the tubes and machines, his eyes closed. He was almost as pale as the sheets, making cuts and bruises stand out across his face.

And he was handcuffed to the bed.

Fuck. Gracie bounced back and turned on her heel to stride in the other direction. *Fuck, fuck, fuck.* She walked purposefully, listening for footsteps behind her and forcing herself not to break into the run her legs wanted. Regret grated against her with every step.

Daniel had made sure she had her fake IDs, made sure she went to a distant hospital, so she wouldn't be found. She hadn't done any of that for him. She hadn't been there to palm his wallet, protect him, fill out his paperwork with stolen information to keep their enemies from tracking him down.

How had Tess and the agents found him so damn quickly here in Toronto?

She'd go back to the waiting room, get Jude and her friend, and . . . what? Even with their questionable supernatural powers, they couldn't spirit her brother out of the hospital, not while he was recovering from surgery. That could kill him.

So could Tess and the agents in there, Gracie reminded herself, letting some urgency into her pace as she retraced her steps. They wouldn't, though. She knew that from the cautious dance Tess had done to approach them. She and her agents wanted something. *It's not some Evil Empire, Grace. They want what we want. What we were always working for.*

Gracie kept her head turned as she passed the nurse's station again, not wanting to draw attention or have the man on duty recognize her, assume she was lost and try to help. All of her training and instinct told her to run, to get herself out safely, find her husband and son and then formulate a plan to save her brother. She'd been ready to leave him, hours ago—poised at the door with her bags. She'd hated it then and she still hated it, but despite the ache in her chest and the thickness in her throat, she put one foot in front of the other and took herself further away from him.

She slowed as she got closer to the surgery waiting room, sidling up the same way she had to Daniel's room and checking it out. Ted and Riley hadn't moved, still asleep in their chair, though Gracie doubted her husband was fully asleep. There was one newcomer, but Jude and her Court friend were gone.

The new face could easily be one of Tess's agents, not going after Ted because they were hoping Gracie would return too. She didn't have the time to analyze every scenario. If that was the case, she'd have to bank on them not wanting to cause a scene in the quiet hospital.

She strode into the room and Ted's eyes opened before she could tap him. He knew from her expression that something was wrong. He got up hastily but gently, keeping Riley tight to his chest.

The toddler made a small, irritated noise and pressed his face into Ted's shirt, but didn't wake otherwise.

The other person in the waiting room glanced over to them but looked back to the TV, uninterested.

"We have to go," Gracie said.

42

COLD AIR BIT MY skin as I left the hospital. I itched to shuck off the jacket I wore—Guy's—and the bloody t-shirt, for that matter—Daniel's. I didn't let myself follow through on it. Maybe I deserved to freeze, but I wasn't going to.

There should have been lava lubricating my muscles, rage under my skin. I should have wanted to kill, deal out pain for pain. But I just felt tired and defeated, like my insides had been shredded by sharp fingernails. It wasn't a new feeling. Nothing was new. Pain and sorrow and death.

"There's something bigger here," someone said from behind me.

I didn't have to turn my head, recognizing my father's voice. I'd meant to avoid him, slipping out of the hospital through the emergency room, which was a little more crowded than the front entrance. It didn't surprise me that he'd found me.

"Bring it on," I returned.

"Gordon and the mages didn't construct this plan on their own." Joshua growled in annoyance. "If you'd simply done as I asked, we'd have ended this before it began."

"It's *my* fault for not letting you kill my friends? Humans aren't *things*. They aren't *interchangeable*!" I realized how that sounded when the memory of Zeb's bloody, exposed ribs crept in, and I backtracked. "I wasn't going to let you kill any of them."

Joshua flashed the barest hint of a smile but I didn't relent, challenging, "What if it had been *Katie*?"

"Difficult," he agreed, "but a paltry sacrifice to save every other living thing. You're doing me an injustice." His face was emotionless in the sallow light from the parking lot. "You see individuals and I see the grand scope."

"Fuck your grand scope." The words were so useless. I drew my shoulders in, wanting to curl up like a dead leaf and fly away.

"I am sorry." He spoke quietly but without sincerity.

"Sorry for what?"

He had to think about that.

"I should have realized they were targeting you sooner. I could have steered them away, kept this from affecting you."

"Then you'd have killed seven *other* people. That doesn't actually make it better."

"It had to be done. It *should* have been done." Joshua's certainty didn't waver. "The things the Shadowed Mab knows . . . she could splinter the worlds. That knowledge needs to die." He fell silent, then added, "I didn't think you would understand the sacrifice and I was right."

"Go *away*." His patronizing words filled me with bitter bile but my response came out like a sob. I put more steel into my voice. "Stay away from here, and stay away from them." I cast a hand back toward the hospital, then turned to face the street. "Don't bother *protecting* me anymore—just keep pretending you never knocked up my mom and disappear again."

"Judith." His voice turned low, warning.

My shoulders trembled under the weight of the fury that finally bore down at me. I spun to see him, anger crackling off my skin like lightning.

"Don't call me Judith!" I snapped. "Don't call me anything! Go back to your Shade Hell prison and *rot* there!"

My father held his ground a moment, eyes flashing, as if just to prove something to me, then turned and disappeared into the shadows beyond the hospital lights.

For a second, I considered finding the nearest mirror, calling up Miranda and telling her that her brother was alive. I could probably set the Mab's army on Joshua. Evading them would at least keep him busy, keep him from fucking any further with my life or the human world.

But if I reached out to Miranda, my womb and I would be back on the hook for the Faerie crown. I couldn't do it.

I stumbled away from the hospital on wooden legs. I could have Abe finish healing my knee, mend the torn muscle or whatever it was, make me good as new. But it felt like every minute I stayed was another minute my demons could pop back up. It would never be finished.

I needed to be somebody else, somebody who didn't draw pain and death toward her like a magnet. Somebody who didn't walk up walls. Somebody whose wounds healed slowly, normally. I'd pretty much bombed at being an ordinary human up 'til now, but maybe I just hadn't been trying hard enough.

Double-checking that I still had my wallet and phone, I used the latter to search for the nearest Toronto branch of my bank. It was still early in the morning, but I'd be there when they opened to close my account and withdraw all of the cash. That would give me enough time to make a rough plan for getting out of the city. Out of the province. Out of the country, even.

Maybe I couldn't slip out of my own skin, but I could still get as far away as possible from magic and Faeries.

Jude's tried to make a clean getaway, but is it enough to get her out from under the weight of the Faerie crown? Continue the story with **GRAVITY'S DAUGHTER** Book 3, **STARK RAVING MAB.**

Indie books like this one rely on word of mouth and reviews to make their way in the world.

If you enjoyed this book, please help other readers find it by leaving a review on your favourite review site.

Acknowledgements

Thanks again to everybody I thanked in Book 1. Except that one person—you know who you are. No, not you, don't worry. That *other* person.

Just kidding. Thanks, everyone, again. Additional thank you to new readers who picked up either of my books by chance (or because of Danielle Fine's beautiful covers!) and followed me into Jude's world.

It bears reiterating that this book would not be as awesome as it is without the clever, diligent eye of my editor, Julie Kay-Wallace, or the candid critiques from my beta reader Samia Hayes. It probably wouldn't even be finished sans tireless cheerleading from my sister Ronnie. You all push and prod me to improve my craft and make the story as great as it can be. My writing is always the better for it.

And thank you again, Jonathan—my partner, my person—for your shrugs and your support of this endeavour and all my others.

Stephanie Caye lives in Montreal with her partner and two furry supernatural beings disguised as cats.

www.ingramcontent.com/pod-product-compliance
Lightning Source LLC
Chambersburg PA
CBHW030806210726
48290CB00002B/457